The Legacy

Nick Evetts

Published by New Generation Publishing in 2025

Copyright © Nick Evetts 2025

First Edition

The author asserts the moral right under the Copyright, Designs and Patents Act 1988 to be identified as the author of this work.

All Rights reserved. No part of this publication may be reproduced, stored in a retrieval system or transmitted, in any form or by any means without the prior consent of the author, nor be otherwise circulated in any form of binding or cover other than that which it is published and without a similar condition being imposed on the subsequent purchaser.

ISBN 978-1-83563-653-4

www.newgeneration-publishing.com

New Generation Publishing

For Ethan, Evie, Elliott, and Fern.

You are the light in the darkness.

Prologue

Matilda crouched on the rumpled bedsheets and hissed with pain as she gently probed at the bites on her breasts. Her eye was swollen from a blow and would over the next few hours close completely. She accepted these injuries with resigned stoicism. This had happened before and would probably happen again. In her limited philosophy, she considered this to be her lot as a woman.

Her sparsely furnished room, if one could call this loft space at the top of the three-storey half-timbered bakery in central London a room, was stuffy and claustrophobic on this September evening. The small dormer mullioned window was closed, and the fetid air reeking of sweat and the sweet-sour smell of sex needed refreshing badly but until her guest had left, she dared not move.

She was naked, and her chubby body glistened with perspiration. Following her recent exertions, the sheets which were badly in need of a wash were rucked up uncomfortably beneath her ample rump. Suddenly feeling the need for their scant protection, she lifted one corner and draped it across her shoulder. It protected most of her pale body and she felt a little less vulnerable. Squatting like a cat, she peered through the gloom of the single wavering candle flame at the tall thin figure dressing near the battered wooden slatted door.

He was a man of God, she knew that, and she ought to be grateful and perhaps even proud that he had selected her for his attentions. But he was rough and could indeed be violent if she refused the most trivial of his requests. She had bitten her tongue to avoid crying out when he sank his teeth into the soft white flesh of her breast. She dared not wake her master and his family, who were asleep on the floor below. Regular employment was hard to come by in the sprawling and noisome city of London in this year of our Lord 1666 and her aged and infirm parents relied heavily on the meagre monies that she was able to take to them when she had her single half day off per month. The bed and board that came with this position were the main reason she was here. It was certainly not for the daily hard labour of washing, cleaning, and cooking that the baker and his family demanded of her. Still, it was better than nothing. She knew this well enough, so she endured their somewhat spiteful commands without demur.

The man who had almost finished donning his dark attire had accosted her in the marketplace some weeks ago with a barely concealed offer of money for sex. She was repelled at the very thought initially, but she was not a virgin by any means, having spent her young life in the crowded dark, fetid, and filthy streets of London, where sewage ran openly in the streets, and chamber pots were emptied from upper windows into the narrow and dark roadway below. Dogs, and cats, and even the odd farm animal rooted amongst the offal on street corners, so that at a very early age she had learnt all about copulation in its many forms as she watched animals and even on occasion humans rutting unashamedly. She had been raped first when she was thirteen, and her complaints had been met with only laughter from those whom she had told. There had of course been the odd permitted fumbling with men that she knew, and a couple that she indeed felt sorry for, so when a man of God had offered her money for such a service, she had agreed almost immediately.

That was some weeks ago, and their meetings had grown progressively more violent. This man seemed to enjoy inflicting pain as he recited prayers to his God during fumbling copulation. Such anomalies were of course beyond the reasoning powers of Matilda, who bore these excesses with pained acceptance. The few coins tipped into her sweaty palms made such submissions worthwhile.

Gathering the grimy sheets around her Matilda stood and threw wide the small window, hearing as she did so the bells of the church that stood at the end of the street begin to toll for the hour of midnight. It was a sound repeated both nearby and further away as the one hundred and seven churches of the capital announced midnight. She had guessed it was very late, having heard a few moments ago the tramping feet of the watch as they trudged by looking for drunks or malefactors still abroad at this ungodly hour. The waft of cooling air was welcome and resisting the urge to put her head out of the window, she turned and perched on the edge of the bed, glancing quickly at her guest as he finished dressing and appeared ready to leave.

"You won't forget to leave me something on the bedside table there will you, my Lord?" She grinned slyly up at him as he turned to her, his shadow seeming huge against the plaster wall behind him.

"I thought not to pay any further for your groaning administrations, my child," he intoned, his deep voice pompous and loud in this cramped little room. "You are after all doing the Lord's work in assuaging the modest carnal desires of one of his servants in these years of austerity."

Matilda's voice had a whining desperate quality despite her efforts to remain calm. "My Lord, I need the money, as you well know. You are a man of God, and I am proud to serve him in any way that I can, but my penury does not allow me to offer charity."

He looked down at this slattern as if he could scarcely believe what she was saying. Had she taken leave of her wits? To whom did she think she was talking? He needed to slake his carnal desires the better to perform his duties. His new young wife hardly satisfied his ever-present need, so he had seized on this filthy sweaty whore he had found in the marketplace to assuage his appetites.

"How dare you argue with me, you insolent trollop!" He raised his hand and slapped her hard across the mouth. "That's for your cheek. That you should dare to speak to a man of God in such a manner! Be thankful that I confer on you the honour of your task."

He turned to head for the door, clearly feeling that this brief admonishment was sufficient. Matilda, realising that her strenuous and obnoxious efforts that evening were to have no reward, wailed loudly and held her hand up to her face where a welt had quickly appeared.

Realising that this small room was at the top of a baker's house and that several people were sleeping on the floors below and that indeed the window was now open, the man knew that he had to shut this slattern up and quickly. He slapped her again, knocking her to the floor and turning, strode as quickly as he could across the tiny room and flinging open the door, disappeared down the darkened, creaking stairs.

What he failed to notice in his haste was that as she fell, Matilda had knocked over the single small but brightly burning candle on the tiny, rickety bedside table. The flame guttered, and appeared about to die, but flared again as it caught the hem of the thin tattered curtains that fluttered above it. Quickly, the fire took hold, and in a few short minutes the whole tinder-dry room was burning fiercely. Matilda was not aware of this, lying semi-conscious as she did on the bare floorboards. The smoke quickly rendered her deeply unconscious.

The baker, his children, and the rest of the servants and employees that worked in this little bakery in Pudding Lane all escaped by one means or another but as the small unkempt building burnt fiercely, hungry flames licked at the adjoining buildings and before long became the conflagration that is known to history as the Great Fire of London, which consumed around a third of the overcrowded old city including eighty-seven churches during the next six days. The records of the time tell us that whilst almost everyone in the bakery where it started survived, there was one recorded death, that being the maid.

Chapter One

Jane's mother was becoming agitated, she could tell. The voice at the other end of the telephone line kept fading and returning as the old lady repeatedly moved her head to look out of the window. Jane could picture the dowdy lounge in the house in which she grew up, still with too much furniture, and with the self-same patterned wallpaper that she remembered. The bow-windowed semi-detached had been built along with many thousands of the same design in the 1930s in outer London. Her mother would be standing in front of the mullioned bay window, peering up the suburban avenue to check who was about.

"…and so in the end I think I will have to go, just to keep her quiet. I can't stand it when she feels aggrieved. You know, talks in that 'hurt but I can take it tone'. Are you listening to me Jane?"

Jane grinned despite her mild irritation. These rambling moans of her mother were more frequent since her dear old Dad had died last year, and she acknowledged and understood that they were a necessary part of her mother's coping process as she unburdened her mind to her only daughter.

Moving so far from her mother just at this time had been one of the reservations that had delayed the decision of Jane Croyland and Robert, her husband of three years, as they decided to up sticks and move from the city to this idyllic looking thatched, half-timbered cottage outside of this small village in the middle of Devon on the edge of the brooding Dartmoor. Her career as a freelance art lecturer could be run from wherever she wanted, whilst Robert, as a successful architect, viewed travel around the UK as a necessary part of his life. Nevertheless, it had still taken six full months of soul searching before they had finally made the decision to 'go for it'.

There was a crashing sound coming from the stone-flagged kitchen and a waft of plaster dust billowed into the small lounge where she sat. Masculine swearing followed it in, and she grinned with pleasure at the sound.

"Jane, what on earth is that?" The petulant voice quavered a little. "Is everything OK?"

"Mum, everything's fine. It's just Rob doing some DIY. You know what he's like on the rare occasion that he actually decides to do something. Straight into it with no thought or hesitation." She laughed aloud as another less noisy crash came.

"Well really, Jane, I do think you are jumping the gun a little. You've only been there a month. What on earth is he doing? You realise of course that the place is listed? You can't just knock it about without permission." She paused to take a breath. "It's such a lovely looking cottage as well, pure chocolate box."

"It's a bit more than a chocolate box, Mum" countered Jane, trying hard not to allow impatience to surface. "After all, we've got five bedrooms, although three will need serious work to make them usable, but we've got time, and it's in an acre of its own grounds. Rob's only knocking down a small wall in the kitchen. He thinks it will give us a lot more room, maybe even space for a small study. No need to panic." Despite her assurances to her mother, a frown crossed Jane's face. Planning permission?' Her Mother might have a point. She was sure Robert had not considered that at all in his rush to get started. It was ever thus if he got a bee in his bonnet. He would rush straight in, all enthusiasm and childish infectious impetuosity. It was one of the reasons she fell for him at the start. They had rushed into marriage only months after they met four years ago, and so far, it had been a relative success. In her late thirties she had been drifting into spinsterhood with apathy. There had been suitors of course, she was an attractive, intelligent woman and men of a certain age found her a challenge, but she hated pomposity or pretentiousness in any guise and was not backward in putting such affectations in their place. She gained a reputation for being 'spiky' which limited her social interactions as she progressed through her thirties. But Robert had arrived on the scene via a manufactured table setting at the dinner party of a mutual acquaintance and the relationship had blossomed very quickly thereafter. She countered the word 'success' for their fledgling marriage with 'relative' for good reason, but Rob's brief infatuation with a secretary at his office not long after they met was behind them, wasn't it? Neither he nor she were kids anymore. In their early forties, they were hardly on the shelf, but Jane for one had started to feel a little uncomfortable when out with friends who were all settled into married life whilst she was still, in her own mind at least, young, free, and single. Then had come the meeting with Rob at a friend's party and in a trice everything had changed.

Rob was now into the second half of his forties but still looked trim and fit, especially today, dressed in baggy tracksuit bottoms, an old sleeveless t-shirt and his baseball cap on back to front.

Not long after they moved in to this, their dream home, he had noticed that the kitchen was smaller on the inside than it looked from the outside, something to do with the differing length of wall and the window position. He suspected that sometime during the last three hundred years someone had had the idea of bricking up a large fireplace.

"You never know, old thing," he had said. "We might have a huge old stone fire grate and settle in there with a hanging bar for your cauldron if we're lucky." He had laughed and yelped as she had cuffed his ear for his cheek.

The place was still full of cardboard boxes from the move, and they really must devote a couple of days to unpacking properly, she decided. The sale of their own apartment and the signing of the documents for this place had all gone by with unnerving rapidity, and they had not really had the chance or the desire yet to organise themselves properly.

"Ow, bloody thing." A cry of pain wafted in on another cloud of brick dust. Jane decided that she must end this somewhat anodyne conversation with her mother. "Mum, it's no good, I'll have to go. I'll call you in the next couple of days, OK?"

"OK dear. Be careful now. Love to Rob." Her mother sounded a little miffed at being so easily dismissed but there was nothing for it.

"Bye, Mum."

She clicked off her phone and moved into the kitchen, waving her arms to dispel the dust.

"Rob, what the hell?"

Her kitchen, which had only in the last few days begun to look like an actual kitchen, was covered in dust. The old flagstoned floor had changed colour from grey to a dusty red. The old wooden kitchen table that had come with the property, as it was frankly too large to remove, was sporting a pile of plaster shards. She moved over to the small, mullioned windows and threw them wide open, feeling the blast of fresh air as it oozed into the carnage.

"Sorry, old girl," he said grinning, knowing this phrase would irritate her. "But look at this, I told you I was right."

The old plaster had fallen away from an area of wall about six feet square. It had laid bare the brickwork underneath. The bricks, smaller and more irregular than modern bricks, were incongruous and highlighted that they were many years old, possibly hundreds. The lines were irregular as if the bricklayer had not been quite sure of what he was doing.

"Looks a bit of a bodge job to me," he said, grinning hugely. "But I knew it," he enthused. "I just knew it. I'll bet this will increase the kitchen space by a third once I've finished." His face was covered in dust, and the black baseball cap that he wore was also covered. His teeth flashed through the grime as he grinned, and she could see in his glee the schoolboy that he had once been. She could not help but return his self-effacing grin.

"Mum says we should t have got planning permission before we started knocking the place about."

He stopped grinning and looked immediately concerned. "Shit! I hadn't thought about that".

"Well, perhaps we should check before you go any further." She hated to destroy his infectious happiness, but common sense had to prevail at some stage, didn't it?

"Hmm, perhaps you're right." He laid the old sledgehammer down, carefully leaning the long haft against the wall. "Let's have a coffee anyway, I'm parched. We can clear up in a minute."

"*We* can clear up?" she mouthed with a small laugh. "I think you can do that all on your own, husband of mine. You made the mess, you can put it right. I'll make the coffee."

He snorted good-naturedly as he sat down on one of the kitchen chairs. "OK, OK, you've got a deal." He grinned at her again through his dust mask. "Bloody shrew. I'm married to a nag."

Picking up a dusty tea towel from the kitchen side she slapped him around the head with it and laughed at his yelp of pain.

"You know, back in the old days you'd have been first in line for the ducking stool." He laughed. "They knew how to keep harpies in their place in those days, especially in places like this in the middle of nowhere." He leaned over and turned on the small portable radio, itself sporting a liberal covering of brick dust. The haunting, evocative voice of Bob Marley's *Buffalo Soldier* boomed out before he hastily lowered the volume to a reasonable level.

As she filled the kettle, Jane said, "Don't forget we've got Brian and Sue coming for dinner tomorrow night, so we'll have to tidy up the place a lot between now and then."

"Oh! Bloody hell, I'd forgotten that." Robert had pulled a hanky from his tracksuit pocket and was mopping his face. "Can't we put them off?"

"Not again, that would be three times. Sue's dying to see the place, and anyway it was you who invited them in the first place, they're your oldest friends, not mine."

Rob nodded and accepted the inevitability of it. "Hmm, I suppose you're right. Any biscuits? I'm starving."

"In the cupboard behind you, and don't forget also that you invited them to stay the night. It's a long drive from London to here."

"Oh! Crap, yes, I did. Why on earth didn't you stop me?"

"Me? Don't blame me. I think it had something to do with the three pints of local hells brew that you had drunk as we investigated the local village pub. Remember?" She laughed as she said it, recalling that she had over-indulged that night also and was very giggly when they had arrived home.

"Did you tell Sue about the vicar's visit, and that he's straight out of that naff TV detective show?" laughed Rob. He liked nothing better than chiding his beautiful wife and loved to see her colour rise unbidden as he made her feel uncomfortable. At thirty-nine she was, he knew, striking in a girlish way. Not many women of her age could get away with keeping their deep auburn hair long enough to touch their backside, he knew that and once again blessed his luck in stumbling across this woman at his time of life when he was possibly settling for the lot of a confirmed bachelor.

She turned and aimed another swipe of the dishcloth at him, but he was ready this time and ducked as it whistled overhead.

"Pig," she said, "As it happened, I did mention him to her, but only because of what he told us about the age of this place."

Rob just murmured an assent as his attention was now on selecting a biscuit from the packet in front of him.

Jane unplugged the kettle and expertly poured the boiling water into two battered mugs of coffee granules. "Only instant I'm afraid, but it will do for now."

After the coffee break, she decided she would go for a brief walk. The dust was making her throat sore and irritating her eyes. Rob, feeling masterful, had told her to disappear and he would 'tidy up' as he called it. From past experience she knew that his 'tidying up' would need further tidying up when she returned but at least the rubble of old plaster would be cleared away and she could start to rebuild her kitchen before their guests arrived tomorrow.

Donning her walking boots and Barbour jacket, she set off, leaving a further round of swearing and shouting behind her. They had made the right decision coming down here, hadn't they? Neither of them was particularly handy at that awful phrase 'DIY' but the lure of living in this lovely place in a centuries-old cottage had been too great once the idea had planted itself in their minds. The blurry picture on the estate agent's website had been alluring and phrases like 'lots of character' and 'huge potential' had elicited the inevitable long drive to visit the property. Of course, once they had set eyes on the place, overgrown and neglected as it was, the deal was done, and they had put in an offer the following day.

Now, some brief weeks after moving in, they were beginning to realise the daunting task that they had so blithely taken on. True, there was nothing structural that needed doing, but two born and bred townies would have to adjust their lifestyle somewhat to accommodate the subtle demands of country living, and the insidious but relentless requests for change that the old cottage requested.

*So far so goo*d she thought as she tramped off down the lane between the thick hedgerows and into the small wood that was between the cottage and the hamlet. Below, in a fold of the rich countryside, she could see the village and its centuries-old church squatting like some old cat in the sunshine. She knew that almost two hundred people lived thereabouts but it showed no immediate signs of life from up here on this rise of ground where her cottage was. The whole place was as her mum had called it, chocolate box. A spattering of half-beamed cottages, mixed in with later Edwardian dwellings and still at its centre your actual village green with its weed-filled pond. The state of their cottage did not worry her, as she knew that they would soon pull the old place into shape, and her mum seemed to have accepted the new arrangements with equanimity and even enthusiasm. Rob's parents, both retired teachers, lived in a small village in the south of France thanks to a huge pension payout and were keen to see the place when they next condescended to visit the UK in a few months' time.

Jane grinned as she recalled their blank incomprehension when they were told that their only son was moving away from the city and buying an old place on the edge of Dartmoor. To be fair, they had made a good fist of being keen. "Oh! That's great son," Rob's dad had said, looking anything but pleased. "Follow your dream ,that's what I always say. Life's too short for reservations. Go for it." His wife had not said anything, but merely nodded. "Hmmm" was the limit of her exuberance.

Anyway, that was all some months ago now. Jane climbed over a small style from the lane and set off along the wide earthen path that skirted the wood. It was a lovely afternoon, the sort that early spring throws up as a precursor of what is to come. The sky was an unbroken sheet of azure, and the watery sun gave off some vestige of heat that afternoon. There were still the remnants of bluebell clumps dotted here and there, crozier heads nodding in unison in the small breeze. There was also the occasional group of red campion, foxgloves, and cow parsley to add further colour to the day. She felt smug at the knowledge of what they were, the result of a book her mother had bought her as a genuflection to the move, on 'British flora and fauna'. Oh well, it was a start, she mused.

Raising her head, she could see across a dozen emerald-coloured fields to the low hills of Dartmoor brooding in the blue distance. It was a lovely part of the world. "We're going to be happy here," she murmured to herself, hardly aware that she had spoken aloud.

"I'm glad to hear it."

She started and glanced around. Paul Xavier, the young parish vicar, was leaning against the old five-barred gate admiring the same view. You would not have guessed he was a vicar in his faded and slightly scruffy jeans, topped by a battered polo neck jumper. His shock of blond hair was unkempt and clearly needed the attention of a brush. His grin was infectious.

She laughed in spite of her shock. "Sorry Paul, I didn't see you there."

He returned her laugh. "I guessed," he chortled. "Good job you didn't utter any secrets. I'm a terrible gossip."

"I somehow doubt that." She smiled. "How come no dog collar today? Isn't it requisite for the clergy?"

"Nope, not all of the time, only when I'm on official business, and this afternoon I'm not. Even God's shepherds are allowed time off, you know."

She nodded companionably. "I suppose you're right. You never think that's it's a job like any other, do you?"

He smiled gently. "Not like any other. Not by a long shot." His face became serious, and she noticed that his eyes were red-rimmed as if he had not slept.

"Are you OK, Paul?" she murmured. "You look all in."

He hesitated but then decided on honesty. "Well, it's no secret I suppose, I was up all night sitting with old Mrs Taylor down at the village shop. She left us around four this morning. Just me and her middle-aged son were with her. It was expected but it's never nice." He ran his fingers through his hair, and straightened up from the gate. "Anyway, there you go, all part of the calling I'm off home now to get some sleep."

He started to move past her, but she felt that she should say something, as he was obviously upset on closer inspection.

"Paul, Rob and I are having a small dinner party tomorrow night. Nothing at all formal, just two old friends from London. They are coming down to see the cottage. It would be really nice if you could join us."

He hesitated, clearly unsure of what to say, then reaching a decision he nodded slowly in acceptance. "Ok if you're sure, that's very nice of you. I don't get out socially much. Well, this is a lovely place but well you know, it's a bit quiet."

They both chuckled. This close she was aware of how tall and wide shouldered he was. Mid-forties, she guessed but would never dare to ask.

"Seven thirty for eight?" she said.

"Look forward to it, I'll bring a bottle." He strode off along the track and did not look back.

Jane grinned to herself. "There you go Sue," she said, feeling wicked, "That will keep you happy tomorrow night. A young good-looking vicar to keep you entertained." There was the merest hint of malice in her voice and a scornful laugh bubbled up out of her like champagne.

She decided she had walked enough and turned around to retrace her steps and see what fresh mess Rob had made of the kitchen.

Chapter Two

Robert swayed slightly as he attempted to both stand and hold his glass in the air at the same time. What had started out as a request for a toast had turned into a mini speech, and Jane wished he would get on with it before it became embarrassing. Never good at holding his drink, Robert had taken several large glasses of wine as well as the pre-meal pint of real ale which he had insisted that he, Brian, and Paul quaff before they sat down to eat. He was sporting his favourite rugby shirt of white and pink stripes, augmented by a pair of white jeans that were now too tight. He'd never played a game of rugby in his life but liked the air of rugged sturdiness that this ensemble gave him.

Before them the large kitchen table was a ruin of half-eaten food, empty glasses, and the odd wine stain on the tablecloth. The meal had gone rather well, and Jane could at least take satisfaction in the fact that her modest culinary efforts had been enthusiastically received by everyone and a feeling of replete bonhomie had spread through them all. There had been lots of laughter and loud conversation, with the occasional slightly inappropriate joke thrown in for good measure, especially as one of the guests was a man of the cloth. *Well, so what?* thought Jane. *Everyone is happy and contented and that is all a hostess can ask for. If only Robert would finish his bloody diatribe and sit down.*

The kitchen had taken a lot of work to get it looking moderately habitable following Robert's recent building work, or rather demolishing work, evidence of which was present in the large patch of open brickwork showing through the plaster on the far wall. Despite this, the numerous shaded wall lights and flowery curtains drawn across the small, mullioned windows still gave the room a cosy and welcoming air, ruined only by the grey stoneflagged floor and Jane cursed herself for not remembering to lay several rugs they had bought to soften the look. Oh well, their friends must realise they had only recently moved into the place, and everything had been a bit of a rush.

"So, I'm permanently dammed in the eyes of the old bloke as a rich towny nutter."

Brian and Sue both laughed, easily amused both by the story and Rob's obvious tipsiness.

"Oh! come on Rob," said Sue brushing her curly blonde hair away from her forehead. "Why would an elderly greengrocer in a place as remote as this know anything about TikTok? I think you're being a bit unfair on him."

"Oh! Don't get me wrong. I like the old boy, but he peers at me with mild astonishment every time I go in there. It's as if he has seen people like me on the TV but never actually met one in real life."

He laughed at his own joke and sat down rather quickly. The sturdy kitchen chair had been his salvation as a brief spasm of wine-induced giddiness brought a somewhat abrupt end to his impromptu little homily.

At last, thought Jane.

Brian, a big man in his youth, was now running to fat and boasted a waistline that forced him to move his chair back from the table to aid his breathing. His ruddy face was made ruddier, by the drink and he had discarded his chunky jumper some time ago in a vain attempt to keep cool. His red t- shirt bore the legend 'I've just laid my honey', overtopping a picture of a tipsy looking bee. Jane had seen it on many occasions when they had attended barbeques at the house of Rob's oldest friend. The two had met at university, and three years of adventures had forged a friendship that would probably last throughout their lives. He was something of a highflyer now in a city merchant bank and looked the part.

"All part of country life, old mate," he beamed his eyes twinkling with good humour. "If you will leave civilisation and move down here, what do you expect?"

He winked hugely at his wife and Paul. "I'll bet they don't even sell sun-dried tomatoes, or shiitake mushrooms either, do they?"

Rob grinned hugely. "Prat" was all he could manage. Everyone laughed.

Sue was sporting a lime-green wraparound strappy dress and kept ostentatiously moving the straps on her shoulder back and forth in what she probably thought was a provocative manner. Whenever she did this, she glanced around quickly to check if either Robert or Paul had noticed.

Rob was almost indifferent as the drink was taking hold, and Jane thought that Paul was far too urbane to fall for such antics, especially when he was a guest at someone else's table.

He had sat quietly throughout the evening, laughing when required and seemingly enjoying the company. He had refused more glasses of wine than he had accepted and been quietly courteous in his complimentary remarks about the food and company. He was wearing his dog collar tonight but the faded jeans and stylishly cut black shirt emphasised his casual fashion sense and the torso beneath.

Brian raised his own glass. "Anyway," he began. "It's my turn for a toast. Here's to our gracious and stylish host Jane, who despite no doubt being hampered by my old mate here has given us a splendid meal." He rather ruined the effect by finishing with a gentle hiccup, but his remark was greeted with a chorus of "Cheers" from everyone.

"Paul," said Jane, smiling across the table. "I hope we haven't neglected you at all tonight. We four have not been all together for some time. If we have left you out at all, please bear with us."

"Not at all," answered Paul with a grin. "I've thoroughly enjoyed the banter of you all. You are all obviously very comfortable in each other's company. It's lovely to witness, and you have not left me out at all, thank you again for asking me."

"How long have you been a vicar, mate?" queried Brian. "Hope you don't mind me asking?"

"Not at all. About twelve years now." Paul looked down at his glass. "Seems longer sometimes".

Sue turned to face him, her shoulder strap falling off her shoulder again. "You must have been very young when you, how do they say it, took the cloth."

"I was almost thirty. Two or three years at ecumenical college and away I went. I was briefly a teacher before that."

He stopped abruptly as if he had temporarily forgotten himself and said too much.

Jane interrupted not wishing to probe this relative stranger's secrets in so public a forum. "Who's for coffee?"

Sue and Brian both raised their hands, although Sue continued to gaze inquisitively at the man next to her.

There was a silence, with everyone waiting for someone to say something. "Perhaps I should not leave it hanging quite like that," said Paul. He lifted his wine glass to his mouth, took a long sip of the wine and took a deep breath as if he were about to dive into water.

"My wife and baby son were killed in a car accident when I was thirty-eight. For a while I was a complete mess, drank a lot, doubted my calling, you all must have heard similar stories, then after watching me behave like an idiot for too long, my bishop broached the subject of getting back to work and said he would 'ease me in' was the way he put it, with a small parish in the West Country." He smiled around at the faces watching him, a little embarrassed at his lack of professionalism in mentioning his own history. When would he learn? He attempted a grin, but it came out as more of a grimace. "Sorry to put a dampener on the conversation."

Sue reached over and laid a hand on his shoulder. "I'm so sorry, we shouldn't have asked."

Paul shook his head and sat up a little straighter. "Not at all, you weren't to know." He moved his shoulder a little until Sue removed her hand. "Anyway," he said his voice light and dismissive. "Shall we change the subject?"

"Yep," said Robert standing up abruptly, his chair scraping on the stone floor. "You lot go into the lounge. I will make the coffee, just as soon as I can find the bloody cafetiere."

There was a chorus of relieved laughter, and everyone moved towards the lounge. "It's in the cupboard above the range," said Jane over her shoulder as she followed Paul and Brian out of the kitchen.

"I'll help him," said Sue, laughing. "And Jane, make sure Brian doesn't put something bloody awful on the CD player."

Their footsteps disappeared down the passageway that led to the lounge, and almost immediately the sound of muted music came from that direction. It sounded like Joni Mitchell.

Robert was already filling the kettle, so Sue moved over to stand next to him at the sink.

"This is bloody awful," she said, her voice low and intimate. "I can't stand being so near to you and not able to touch you."

Robert clicked on the kettle and turned to scan the door to check the coast was clear before touching his hand to her face. "I know, old thing, I feel the same, but it's only for tonight. I'm coming up to London for two days next week. Can you get any time?"

She briefly touched his arm and moved across to take down the cafetiere from the cupboard that Jane had mentioned. "Yes, I think so, well I'll bloody make sure I will. You might have given me more warning."

"I only found out this afternoon, give me a bloody chance." Rob's voice was a little petulant and she realised she was putting pressure on him, which she knew from previous experience was a mistake. Intuitively, she reached out and ruffled the hair on the back of his head. "Just make sure that it's worth it for me." She laughed the low, husky, suggestive laugh that he loved so well.

"Oh! I will," he said. "Trust me." His grin was lascivious.

"I'll tell Bri I'm going to spend a couple of days with my sister in Brighton, that will do it." She nodded to herself, glad to have arrived at a solution.

"Won't he check?" queried Robert.

"Nah not a chance, they hate each other, always have done. It was loathing at first sight." She laughed, her voice low and husky. "Anyway, problem solved."

"This is going to be really awkward from now on, you realise," she continued, a little petulantly he thought. "What the hell made you move down here?"

"It's what Jane wanted," he said, taking mugs down from the cupboard.

"And what Jane wants Jane gets, is that it?"

He shrugged. "Well…losing her dad last year was a big thing for her, you know. It's the old thing about daughters and their dads. So, if this will make her feel a little more positive, I thought why not?"

"And my feelings didn't come into it?"

He turned to face her properly for the first time. "No, not really. Let's not get carried away here. We're not going to run away with each other, are we?"

It was a statement rather than a question. She would have answered that this was exactly what she had in mind, but a burst of laughter from the three in the lounge made them both turn to look at the door and then as if by mutual agreement they stepped apart.

Sue would have liked to say more, to tell him that yes, being together was precisely what she had been thinking and daydreaming of, and didn't he feel the same? But the moment was lost. Rob had turned back and was busy filling the cafetiere, so she briefly ran her hand lightly down his back and walked away into the lounge. They needed to have a serious chat, she decided, but that could wait util next week, and for the moment there was this gorgeous young vicar to amuse her.

As she walked into the lounge she was struck by the wonderful symmetry of the room. The black roof beams were low, but not low enough to cause one to duck. The curtains, the wall-mounted lamp shades, and coverings on the deep, comfortable suite all seemed to be of a matching flowery pattern, which perfectly complemented the highly polished wooden floorboards dotted with Indian rugs. It was a homely scene augmented by the blazing log fire in the huge stone fireplace.

My God, she thought. *Could this place be any more picture book? It's almost sickly.*

Jane and Brian were perched on opposite ends of the huge sofa whilst Paul was standing, a little self-consciously, in front of the fire, still with his all but empty wine glass in his hand.

"Coffee will be just a minute," she said and plumped down beside Brian. "What was the laughter?"

"Brian just said this reminded him of a set from Poirot, cheeky bugger," said Jane.

"Well, it does," said Brian, laughter bubbling out of him. "You could imagine everyone having a round of Baccarat and smoking from long black cigarette holders. I mean it's perfect. You can just see the little Belgian geezer pottering in, all spats and dicky bow and starting his explanation of who killed whom. Brilliant." He chortled again at his own humour.

"I love it when he presents what is largely circumstantial evidence and could not possibly be proved, but the accused murderer always either confesses or takes a swipe at someone and runs off – brilliant."

Everyone chuckled in acquiescence.

Sue laughed a little tentatively. "Perhaps we should have a séance? That's what they do in lots of those episodes isn't it? This place looks tailor-made for it." She tossed her hair out of her eyes and glanced up, Jane thought a little provocatively, at Paul. "What do you think Paul?" She slipped off her shoes and drew her legs up on to the couch. "Are you game?"

Before Paul could answer, Robert came in bearing an enormous tray full of small very trendy earthenware coffee mugs and the cafetiere. "Coffee's up," he announced to an appreciative chorus.

Later, after they had all enjoyed at least two cups of thick dark coffee, and some excellent chocolate biscuits that Jane had produced from somewhere, conversation was sporadic and desultory. Everyone it appeared was replete and somnolent after the lovely dinner and plentiful drink. Apart from which, Brian and Sue had left London early for the long drive down here, and Brian at least appeared to be flagging a little. Paul was seated on the small rocking chair right next to the fire whilst Robert was in his usual position on the floor, lounging back against Jane's legs. Paul seemed to be lost in his own thoughts as he stared into the flames.

Sue decided it was time to wake everyone up before sleep insidiously crept over them all.

"So," she began, her voice a little strident in the circumstances. "What about this séance?"

Robert looked around "Séance? What séance?"

Jane said, "It's a long story, a follow-on from a conversation whilst you were doing your barista act."

"Oh, OK".

"No come on, I mean it," said Sue, lowering her legs to the floor and elbowing the mellow Brian in the ribs. "What do you think? Shall we do it?"

No one answered. It was the last thing Jane wanted but she did not wish to appear prudish or a killjoy. Robert had known Brian and Sue for far longer than he had known her, and she was loath to appear at odds with them all.

Sue would not let it rest. "Paul! What do you think? It's not against your calling, is it?"

Paul drained his tiny mug and replaced it on the coffee table. "It is, actually," he said, a little embarrassed "Sorry to be a party pooper and all that. But we are told by the Bible to absolutely *not* try to contact the dead. Especially as a party game. There are things that it's unwise to meddle with. What is it that Hamlet calls it? The undiscovered country from whose boon no traveller returns." He held up his hand and smiled gently to take the sting out of his words. He could see by the sudden flush on Sue's face and her stiffening body language that he had offended her. *We all of us take stock of the people we encounter*, he thought, making snap judgments on first meeting. He was as guilty of it as anyone; after all, he was just a man despite being a vicar. His first impression of this woman was that he would not like to cross her.

"Anyway," he said, sitting forward in readiness to stand. "I have to be going, I'm afraid. It's been a lovely evening, but I have a service in the morning."

Jane smiled across at him. "Of course, it's Saturday night, well Sunday morning now actually," she said, glancing at the carriage clock on the mantlepiece, "and Sunday's your busy workday. I'm sorry, I had forgotten."

Paul just shook his head and grinned. "No problem. Thank you, Jane and you, Robert ,for a really nice time. The food was excellent, and the company was amusing. I am the stranger here and you have all made me most welcome. Thank you."

He stood up a little self-consciously, aware that the other four were all watching him. Sue, with a little malice in her voice at being almost peremptorily dismissed, said "Oh come on now Paul, you can't get away with that. I don't want a lengthy religious diatribe but surely a little séance between friends is not the end of the world, is it?"

She turned to Robert "What do you think, Rob?"

Jane bit her tongue, as she had been hellishly close to saying, "Oh for Christ's sake will you shut up about a fucking séance." But that would have ruined the night completely and perhaps caused friction between Rob and his oldest friend.

"Well, I…" Robert was a little startled at being questioned.

"I don't want a séance in my new house, Sue." Jane's voice was friendly but firm. "We've only just moved in, and God knows what we could summon if we engaged in such nonsense." She held up a placatory hand. "No offence. But we don't know the truth of it, do we? Is it a parlour game? Or something far more dangerous? We've all heard the stories, seen the programs. Ouija boards and the like, they make me very uneasy. We just don't know, do we, so let's leave it for tonight."

She saw that Sue, not to be denied, was about to say something more, so she hurried on. "And don't forget parts of this house go back to the sixteenth century. We're not exactly on a newbuild housing estate".

"Earlier," interposed Paul who had been uncomfortably watching the exchange between the women.

"What do you mean, Paul?" said Brian, feeling in some way that he should be part of this conversation.

Paul stood with his back to the fire and put his hands in his pockets so that he did not look like a lecturer in front of his class. "Parts of this place go back as far as the fourteenth century. It's listed, and by far the oldest property in the area. Apart from the church that is. In fact, for many years, this place actually was what we would now call the vicarage." He looked down at the lounging Robert at his feet. "Which is why, Rob, you should not have even started knocking it about without permission."

Rob nodded, grinning sheepishly. "I know," he said. "Jane's already been lectured by her mother about it. I can't believe it didn't occur to me."

"Actually," began Paul. "Probably not the right time to mention this, but there's a bit of history to this place." He peered at them all to check that he was not boring them, but in fact it was quite the opposite. Jane had leant forward with interest, and even Brian looked fully awake now.

"Oh?" said Jane. "Tell us more."

"Well!" Paul elongated the word to express his reluctance. "Maybe another time, but I will tell you, although my information is very sketchy and only based on local gossip, that it was the home at one time of a renowned bad guy and what would you say? A bounder?" He chuckled at his own humour.

"Who?" Robert was interested now.

"I don't suppose for one moment you will have heard of him but there are many rumours and tales in this part of the world about the 17th century Reverend Nehemiah something. Hell-fire preacher."

There was a stunned silence. "And he lived here?" said Jane, looking over her shoulder in a ridiculous gesture, as if she thought the Reverend might be standing behind her.

Robert, himself a little nonplussed, decided on unsure derision.

"Woo," he crooned. "Creepy. There was no mention of any such person in the pages of blurb that the estate agents sent us about the place."

Paul laughed out loud. "No, I don't suppose there would be, even if they knew. He's not someone you want to hear much about. I wouldn't know anymore but for the fact my job gives me chunks of free time and I've always been interested in history and folklore." He stepped away from the fire, which was obviously warming his backside a little to fiercely. "I know a little bit about him, and this place as it happens, but perhaps not for tonight."

He moved forward and shook Jane's hand. "Once again, Jane and Robert, thanks for a lovely evening." He held up his hand in farewell. "Sue, Brian, nice to have met you."

He moved out into the passageway leading to the front door. Jane stood and followed him, and she could be heard thanking him for coming, and to be careful walking home in the dark, before the huge old oak door clanked shut and Jane could be heard throwing the bolt.

"He's a bit of alright," said Sue. "He can convert me anytime."

"Trollop" said Brian good-naturedly and gently burped into his coffee cup. "Rob, old mate, I'm done, and I think I and the good lady wife are off to bed. Full English and coffee in the morning if you would, oh and the Sunday papers." He laughed gently as he levered himself up off the clinging sofa.

"Certainly, my good man," laughed Rob as Jane moved back into the lounge. "These two are off to bed. mine hostess, can you show them up?"

Chapter Three

With a mew of alarm, Cecily started into wakefulness and quickly sat up in the large ageing four-poster bed, aware of the cloying, repressive heaviness of the homespun blankets and sheets and the uncomfortable bolster. It had almost seemed as if she had been struggling with some heavy monster that was trying to hold her down. She heaved a sigh of relief and tried to calm her breathing.

Her body was sticky with perspiration underneath her calico nightdress, and her long black hair clung damply to her forehead and shoulders. It had happened again, another nightmare. It seemed she could hardly sleep a night through recently without a recurrence of the same horrible dreams. True, she had lived through a terrible ordeal; but she knew she was one of the lucky ones, many had not survived. She realised that the fire would go down in the history books as a momentous event in the annals of England, but that was all some months ago now, so why had the dreams only recently come to her?

She closed her eyes and tried to calm herself. The images were so real, so immediate, as if she were living through it all again. It was already being called the 'great fire of London' in the childishly simple local news sheets that she had seen, handprinted and amateurish, testament to the fact that the events were already well-known even down here in deepest Devon. Bad news travels fast, wasn't that what people said? Well, it did, here was proof.

She would never forget that time of terror and anxiety as much of her home city of London was consumed and turned to ash over six dreadful days. She could not believe that the Lord Mayor, Sir Thomas Bloodworth, had been so slow to react.

She had been woken on that September morning as usual by the ageing and arthritic old servant that her husband had grown up with, to be told that "Lawks my lady the town is afire." It had taken a few minutes' close questioning of the querulous old woman to elicit the facts that a fire had started last evening in Pudding Lane less than half a mile from her bedroom, and had blazed and spread unchecked, the hungry breeze-driven flames leaping from thatched roof to thatched roof of ageing, old, dry wooden buildings, swallowing whole streets of tinder-dry, half-beamed houses whose upper stories almost touched above the sewage-smelling streets beneath.

"Weem all doomed, my lady; you mark my words" Bridget had wailed plaintively. "Doomed." Slow tears oozed from her faded old eyes and ran down her wrinkled cheeks.

Leaning out of her windows that morning, Cecily could see that the sky was indeed dark with smoke and drifting cinders, the smell of burning was strong in the air, and she coughed uncontrollably for a few moments. Leaning further out of the casement, she saw that the narrow, dark road below was choked with people all carrying or pushing their meagre possessions as they fled the flames. Like so many refugees from an invading army, they shoved and jostled each other in their haste. Strong words and swearing vied with the crying of children and the barking of dogs in the noisome throng.

Cecily had dressed as quickly as she could whilst the clucking Bridget fussed around her trying to help her with her stays, more hindrance than help.

"Where is the master?" enquired Cecily, somewhat testily as she bound up her long hair before hiding it as best she could beneath her small calico bonnet. The old lady was doing the best she could with bent and useless fingers, and it was no use remonstrating with her.

"He be out Missus, but he said he would be back afore noon." Bridget collected the nightgown that Cecily had dropped to the floor and limped out, still talking in a strained voice to no one in particular. "Doomed, mark my words."

Cecily had been married to the Reverend Nehemiah Morton only a twelvemonth , and still acknowledged that she hardly knew the man. Tall and cadaverous with salt-and-pepper hair that was thinning and straggled to his shoulders, and with a slight stoop to the upper back, he was hardly a suitable match for the twenty-three-year-old Cecily, but her rapidly ageing father wanted his three daughters settled to the best of his ability before he entered his dotage. His trade as a respected if modest shoemaker did not allow him to pick and choose possible matches for his girls with any degree of fastidiousness. So when out of the blue the ageing Reverend had arrived at his door offering marriage to his youngest, and as yet unmarried girl Cecily, he had little choice but to accept. After all, at twenty-three she was almost a confirmed spinster, and he did not want to go to his maker to join his late wife in their rest, leaving one of his beloved girls to fend for herself in this wicked world.

Cecily was not at all sure she would not have been better off fending for herself rather than suffer the caprices of this stern and pompous martinet on whom she had been foisted. True, he had only struck her a few times in the months they had been married and knowing little of the lives of married people, she had presumed that this was the norm. Although she did acknowledge that these outbursts of violent temper were happening more often. He rarely spoke to her as an equal and was oftentimes pompous and distant, dictating to her in a loud stertorous voice as if addressing her from a pulpit. She accepted his sexual fumblings and demands without qualm, and although some of his demands seemed a trifle strange, they did not as yet cause her much physical discomfort. She was young and strong, and innocent in the ways of men, but so far, she could endure her married life with resignation, and he had given her old Bridget to look after her. She, Cecily Morton, a shoemaker's daughter had a servant! What next?

But all of that was months in the past. She had a new life now here in this remote Devonshire village.

Cecily dressed slowly in her homespun voluminous grey gown – her husband insisted she always wore grey lest she appear 'wanton and sinful' in front of his flock. She descended the stairs to the kitchen below her bedroom. The huge kitchen fire was already lit, and the large black iron kettle suspended above the flames hissed gently. The middle-aged cook Margaret curtsied briefly as the master's young wife came in and asked if she would like to break her fast.

"No thank you, Margaret," said Cecily. "I wondered where my husband was."

"He's gone down to the church, Mam" replied Margaret, "something about a burying this afternoon." She moved to open the small, mullioned window. "Would you like some cordial, Mam?"

The smells of the farmyard from the muddy quagmire outside of the window permeated into the kitchen, overriding the more domestic aromas.

"No thank you," said Cecily, turning. "I will be in the study for this morning. I have a letter to write."

She left the kitchen followed by the muted observations of the disapproving servant. Something about writing being the devil's works, and it was not fit that a young lady, especially a Reverend's wife should be able to do so, let alone indulge in it.

She felt uncomfortable that morning. Everything seemed to be conspiring against her. The thick woollen gown and layered calico petticoats felt heavy and cumbersome and seemed to rub and itch at the skin of her bare legs as she moved. The wooden clogs she knew she must wear if she ventured outside rubbed the soles of her feet painfully. Her hair, normally thick and lustrous, seemed to be heavy and greasy this morning. She must wash it soon, but Margaret always seemed loath to fetch water from the well for such 'frippery.'

She smiled to herself with self-satisfaction hearing the grumbling servant's mutterings about women and learning. It was true that very few women could read or write still in this year of our lord 1667, but Cecily thanked her God that her dear old father had insisted part of his meagre earnings be paid to a part-time down-at-heel tutor for his three daughters to be taught the rudiments. Cecily had taken to it far more adroitly than her elder sisters and took great self-righteous pleasure in demonstrating this skill by sending them occasional short missives.

Moving through the house, she decided to take the air before she did anything else and went outside to the muddy yard that backed the house and sat on the old bench which leaned against the wall under the dining room window. It was her favourite spot, especially when the weather was warm, and the sun made a welcome appearance. During the mornings the warming rays shone directly on to the rear of the house. What grass there was grew in unruly clumps there and was trimmed as best as Margaret's aged father Walter could manage when he could do it at all. Margaret had told her that her old dad suffered cruel from the rheumatism. Cecily had asked her once about her husband and in a short, sharp sentence which brooked no further enquiry, she was told that "The bloody fool had gone off to be a soldier during the late civil wars and got himself killed over at Langport fight." Cecily had not thought to ask more. Margaret's son Thomas was rarely able to spare the time to help, so busy was he at the many local farms who were only too willing to give daily work to a stocky, strapping young man of twenty-odd. The money that he earned was a great help.

At the edge of the yard, wildflowers grew among the ankle-length grasses and honeysuckle grew up the cottage walls and in these early months of the year the scent was pleasant and refreshing. The muddy path that led from the back door to the much-used well was a slippery scar across the sparse and untidy grass and footprints in the mud attested to several visits to fetch water already that morning.

Her husband had insisted they left London five days after the conflagration began, when it was clear that the authorities were ineffectual and clueless as to how to stop the flames and the panicking population began to sink into semi-barbarism and recrimination. Many Dutch and French emigres, wrongly and ludicrously blamed for starting the fire, were beaten badly and in a small number of cases killed by angry and intoxicated mobs of citizens.

The mighty Cathedral of St Pauls had caught fire and been severely damaged three days in, and even the precincts of Whitehall began to be threatened. It was at this point that Nehemiah had called enough and announced that they were going. He had a relative of sorts in the county of Devon and they would visit for a few weeks.

He engaged an elderly horse and even older cart with a driver at a hugely inflated price to carry their goods, such as could be saved. The wailing Bridget, clearly unable to make such a journey, had been left alone and destitute to fend for herself. Cecily would always remember her last sight of the old and infirm retainer standing in the doorway of their residence, wringing her hands in despair and sobbing into her apron. Her husband, who had known the old lady since childhood, marched ahead, refusing to look back, his bleak eyes pitiless under the large brim of his black hat. Glancing back for the final time, Cecily could see that the end of the narrow street behind the wailing servant was freshly aflame and clearly the whole area would be consumed during the day. Building with wood and thatch within the city walls of London had been banned for many years but few had taken any note, and the narrow cobbled streets burned gleefully in the slight breeze. Cecily had fruitlessly remonstrated with her chilly husband to take the old lady with them but to no avail. Deaf to her entreaties and seemingly uncaring about Bridget's fate, he had not even deigned to speak to the old retainer, merely stating in his sermonising strident voice that God in his infinite wisdom would provide, and not for the first time Cecily found herself wondering if her husband was in full possession of his wits. Her last sight of the street on which they had lived was of two small children, their muddy feet bare and bleeding, standing crying amidst the turmoil as they called for their parents, who, by neglect or design, had lost them in the crush. Cecily called out to her husband that she could not pass them by without helping but was literally manhandled on her way by the angry Nehemiah, who snarled again that God would provide and that it was none of their affair. The strength of his grip on her wrist had hurt her and she had cried out, but he had taken no note and with a mighty shove sent her stumbling in front of him.

After six days of dangerous and eventful travel across roads which were oftentimes little more than dusty or muddy tracks, her husband's unwitting relative, old Barnaby Scudamore, white-haired and ridden with ague, had not been at all delighted to see them, and it took some long minutes of unseemly wrangling on his doorstep before

Nehemiah could convince the old Reverend that there was indeed a family link between their houses. Grudgingly, the old man had allowed them to enter but announced that he could not give them house room for long, as he was not a rich man, and his house, which passed for the village vicarage, was only partially furnished and indeed parts were very close to falling down altogether. His live-in only servant Margaret was scathing in her comments when she had a chance to speak with her old employer.

It had always seemed strangely fortuitous to Cecily that only three weeks after their arrival, old Barnaby had fallen down the steep winding stairs of the place and broken his neck. Nehemiah, who had forcefully taken on the role of unwanted helper to the old man and shamelessly ingratiated himself with the richer members of the small local congregation, pompously announced that God must have guided him to this place, and he would fulfil the Lord's obvious purpose and take unto himself the care and guidance of this flock left untended lest the devil should take them. He would, of course, continue to live in this rambling and now ownerless house. That had been almost a year ago now and for better or worse the village had grudgingly accepted the replacement to the old and kindly man who had watched over them for many years.

Cecily closed her eyes, enjoying the feel of the spring sunshine on her face. Somewhere above her she could hear the shrill singing of a skylark. She stretched out her legs beneath the restricting weight of her homespun gown and waggled her feet, remembering that she used to do this often when she was a little girl. The memory of it brought a smile to her face, and she glanced down idly watching as two of their pigs waddled around the corner and plonked themselves down in the sunshine, luxuriating in the warmth in just the same way that she had. Scruffy chickens strutted about in their never-ending search for seeds, and the two or three scraggy geese waddled past in search of insects in the mud. The sounds and smells of this place, so alien to her when they first arrived, were now the everyday that she was becoming used to. In the kitchen at the front of the house, she could hear Margaret singing, and she decided that the troubles and indeed terrors of the last year might be behind them, and she could look forward with a little less trepidation to the life of the wife of the local spiritual leader of this little community on the edge of Dartmoor. She would take each day as it came, she decided. Maybe even some degree of happiness might be had. She would see. She sighed and closed her eyes.

A little later, deciding to rouse herself from this obvious sloth, she collected a few chicken eggs from the undergrowth and triumphantly bore them into the kitchen.

"Why thankee mistress," said Margaret up to her elbows in flour as she made bread. "Could I ask you to put them on a shelf in the buttery please? Dear of un."

The buttery was the slang name for what passed as a pantry or storage cupboard at the end of the kitchen, a tiny room which had been deliberately built for this purpose. A small door led off the kitchen and into it and as it boasted no windows, it was always cool and dark. Cheeses, bread, beer and what little wine they possessed were kept there, as were vegetables. Leeks and onions hung from the rafters and the odd plucked and gutted chicken, with even the occasional rabbit.

Cecily did as she was bid and then strolled back out to the yard again, feeling virtuous and appreciated. Perhaps it would not be so bad here after all.

****

The radio was on low when Brian entered the kitchen, and the Teskey Brothers were entreating people to not hold them down. Jane was busy over the range, and he inhaled deeply the delicious smell of grilling bacon.

"Morning Jane," he called breezily as he took a seat at the table, now cleared and wiped. "All, OK?"

Jane turned and grinned at him. "Morning Brian." She had a spatula in her hand and had clearly been turning the several rashers in the large frying pan. "Yep, fine thanks, how about you, did you both sleep well?"

"Like a top, must be the country air." He guffawed hugely. "Or the large amounts of drink taken. You'd think as we got older, we would learn to slow down a little, wouldn't you?" He rubbed his forehead lightly and squinted against the glare of the bright windows. "Got any aspirin?"

Jane laughed and reaching into one of the new wall-mounted cupboards, tossed him a container of tablets. "Coffee coming up to wash them down with."

"Fantastic. Rob not up yet?"

He's awake. He'll be down in a minute. It's an old strategy of his that he doesn't think I'm wise to. Hang about looking vague and inattentive until the wife gets up and starts breakfast, then come down and complain that you were just about to start breakfast yourself."

Brian chuckled good naturedly as he prised the lid of the pill container. "Huh nothing changes, he used to pull that one at uni. I can't remember the number of breakfasts I made for the lazy slob. Ah, talk of the devil, and he appears."

Rob sidled into the room, a grin on his face – he had obviously been listening. He had on his tracksuit bottoms again and an old black t- shirt.

"Bastards," was all he said as he sat down opposite Brian.

"Coffee's in the percolator," said Jane. "Tea in the pot, it's under the cosy."

"Bloody hell," laughed Brian again. "You are organised. You've got a good one here, Rob."

Rob just grinned and helped himself to a coffee. He held up an empty mug in enquiry to Brian, who nodded. "Please".

"It's probably the novelty of a new kitchen," said Jane, sitting down herself to sip her own coffee.

"Bit more than a new kitchen," replied Brian. "I mean, new house, new part of the country, a new life really."

Jane just nodded not committing. "Hmmm."

Adele was singing now about rolling in the deep, the sound tinny from the small transistor, which could only just be heard above the sizzling of the pan.

"Oh, fuck me!" expostulated Brian with a laugh as Sue walked into the room, still in her red silk pyjamas, her hair all tousled and uncombed, mascara blurry beneath her eyes. "Look what just appeared. Opus 24 in the museum of life, 'woman with a hangover'." He laughed again at his own humour.

"Piss off," said Sue grumpily. "Pour me a coffee Rob, there's a love."

Rob did as he was told.

"Sue, do you want a bacon sandwich?" enquired Jane, standing and leaning across the work surface to open the kitchen window.

Sue just groaned and rested her head on her hand. "Ooh no thanks. What the hell did I drink last night?"

"Everything," grinned Brian. "And then some. Serves you right."

"Oh, piss off," repeated Sue unimaginatively.

Conversation continued on this lofty plane as some of them ate their bacon sandwiches and devoured several cups of coffee. It was part of Brian and Sue's culture to insult each other, albeit playfully, in front of friends and only rarely did the insults contain a bite. Three of the four were completely at ease with each other as old friends are, and Jane did her best to fit in and not appear awkward.

Sue rallied a little after her second coffee but still studiously ignored the sandwich in front of her.

"By the way," she said into a brief silence as they all sat contentedly sipping their brews. "Did anyone hear a noise last night?"

"Like what?" enquired Rob. He had his legs crossed, his ankle resting on his knee and was massaging it to get rid of a muscle ache.

"I went to the loo in the middle of the night," said Sue. "This prat's snoring had woken me up." She waited for the returning insult but none came so she carried on. "Anyway, as I came back across the landing, I could have sworn I heard someone crying down here."

"Crying?" said Jane. "What do you mean crying?"

Sue shrugged. "Well just that, a woman crying softly, almost to herself. I called down in case it was you Jane, but it stopped abruptly, and no one answered. There was no way I was coming down those narrow dark stairs on my own to take a look, so I just got back into bed and fell asleep again. I'd forgotten until just now. I just assumed that someone had left the radio on."

She had everyone's attention now. Jane shrugged. "Strange thing," she said. "Well, it wasn't me, I was dead to the world. May have been a fox outside. They can sound remarkably eerie, let me tell you."

"Rob, old mate, sounds like you have a ghost," laughed Brian.

"It was probably the radio," said Robert nodding to himself. "Yes, that's it surely, could have just come on."

"Nah," said Brian, seeing an avenue for fun here. "It was a ghost." He gave a low mournful moan. "Who you gonna call?"

Both men sang out together, "Ghostbusters!"

Everyone laughed, even Sue, who immediately groaned as if her laughter had triggered another bout of headache.

"You two," she said. "You're incorrigible. Do you know, Jane, I remember one night before Rob met you that they came back from the pub a bit the worse for wear and had a long, involved discussion about how Noddy and Big Ears can sleep together and not be gay." She shook her head in mock despair.

Jane smiled dutifully, trying not to think that Sue had mentioned a time when she was not part of the group deliberately. A time when she had both men to herself, although not in a sexual sense. At least she thought not.

"Anyway, husband of mine," said Sue, standing, "we have to be away by twelve, and I need to shower first." She laid her hand on Rob's shoulder, and peered down at Jane. "Rob, Jane, thank you for your hospitality. I've really enjoyed it, and I know you will both be very happy here." Jane and Rob both waved dismissive hands and said there was no need for thanks, they had enjoyed their company. Sue continued. "And Jane, thank you so much for that meal last night AND…" she continued, glancing down artfully at Brian. "Thank you for inviting that dishy vicar, that was a real bonus."

Brian stood up himself and moved towards the kitchen door without a backward glance. "Trollop," he said over his shoulder.

Jane noticed without meaning to that before she turned away herself that Sue gave Rob's shoulder an extra squeeze with her long expressive fingers, topped as they were with very dark blue nail polish.

Chapter Four

'The Arnolfini portrait by Johannes Van Eyck is one of the most important paintings in early European art. Is it merely the celebration of the marriage of an Italian merchant who lived and worked in Brugge or is it something far more subtle, far more elusive? Theories abound, and we shall probably never be sure of the absolute truth....'

Jane stretched out her bare legs under the kitchen table and considered her next sentence. The bright, sharp morning sunlight streamed through the window to her right and bounced off the old battered wooden tabletop, giving it a deep honey-coloured glow. She had had to pull one of the chintz curtains across a little to shield her from the sunlight which would otherwise have made the laptop screen unreadable. It was not the ideal place to write her forthcoming lecture to be given to students at Taunton Uni but the small box bedroom that she had adopted as her study was dark and a little claustrophobic at this time of the day, so she had decided on the kitchen.

The percolator bubbled comfortingly on the range, and the muted choral sounds of the William Byrd CD spinning in the sunlight on the small player perched on the windowsill gave a calming background noise of choral voices in harmony to facilitate her efforts.

She leaned back a little and stretched her bare arms up to the ceiling beams, feeling her bones crack. She had not dressed yet and was comfortable in the lemon-coloured knee-length flannelette nightdress that she loved. She remembered so well her mum wearing exactly the same sort of nightwear when Jane was a small child. How often does life repeat itself? she thought. Continuity was so important in this ever-changing world. Anyway, she liked flannelette and there was no one else to see it, so what the hell.

Robert had left for London very early before it was fully light, and she had decided, once she could summon the energy and the will to come downstairs, that today was as good as any to make a start on writing her forthcoming lecture. She was booked to do the same lecture on three occasions next month. Taunton, Bristol, and Falmouth universities had all leapt at the chance to take up her offer, sent by email, of her availability to present the latest academic thinking about the famous Dutch painter and the so called 'northern Renaissance'. She smirked a little smugly, realising that she must have attained some degree of minor celebrity during the last three years, as her highly informative, and always entertaining talks were inevitably very well-attended.

She stood up and sauntered across to the percolator to refill her coffee mug. The flagstoned floor was cold against her bare feet, but she did not mind, rather she took pleasure in her new lifestyle, and the fact that although she was technically working, she did not need to dress if she did not want to.

Idly she glanced out of the window and briefly considered going for a walk. It was such a beautiful spring morning, the hedges were all in bud, and the lawn of the large garden at the front of the cottage had an emerald glow in the morning sunshine. The brochure advertising the property had emphasised the 'immaculate' and well-stocked gardens at front and rear, and some echo of the perfectly manicured front lawn still remained, although given the indifferent gardening skills of both her and Robert, Jane did not think this would continue for much longer. She knew by heart Rob's diatribe when mowing or trimming lawns was mentioned in conversation. His catechism was about it being a complete and utter waste of time as despite a day spent in cutting, trimming, and hedging it would all need doing again in a month or so. "What a complete waste of time," he would expostulate with feeling. She grinned now as she heard his agitated voice chanting this litany. Perhaps they could hire some old, retired chap from the village to come in once a week to take care of these tasks. She made a mental note to ask at the village shop if they knew anyone.

Now, she decided, she needed to get on, this thing would not write itself. She slouched back to her chair. Briefly she ran a hand through her tousled hair and realised what a sight she must look. But no one would see her so what did it matter?

'The Arnolfini Portrait is one of the great unsolved mysteries of the northern renaissance…' She continued where she had left off. *'Is it indeed a marriage portrait? We quite simply do not know. There are many theories. The tall almost cadaverous figure of Giovanni Arnolfini standing holding the hand of his bride is a complete enigma. The couple both have their shoes off, wooden clogs and slippers both claim a place on the floor. Oranges are on the windowsill and there are cherries on the tree glimpsed outside of the window. Both are summer fruits, but if it is summer why are the couple both wearing heavy fur-lined winter clothes? The woman looks heavily pregnant although the possibility exists that this cannot be considered of any great note as it was the fashion of the time in portraits for women of a certain class to appear thus.*

Jane leaned back again, taking another sip from her mug. Would she ever be pregnant? Did she want a baby? She was not sure. She had mused about it, of course, but she was not certain at all what Robert thought about the idea. Whenever she mentioned it, he had been gloriously elusive and non-committal. Now was not the time to think about it she thought, she had work to do. But she knew somewhere in the back of her mind that they must make a decision one way or the other soon. She had a private dread of being the oldest mum at the school gates.

'It has even been promulgated that the woman in the picture, his wife, had in fact died the previous year and this picture is some form of a memorial. Evidence the single candle that burns in the brass chandelier above the couple, the symbol of the presence of God. A letter recently discovered which is attributed to the wife's mother contains the statement that her daughter Constanza had died in childbirth the year before. So, this is a possibility. The small dog that crouches at their feet was a well-known symbol of fidelity and loyalty in paintings of the period.' Jane took a sip of her coffee and considered her next statement. *'The mirror on the wall behind them is a triumph of fifteenth century art, drawing our eyes as it inevitably does between the couple to peer into it and see the reflection of two people in the doorway where we must be standing. Closer inspection of this mirror shows tiny little rondels around its edge each one no bigger than your little fingernail and each one showing a scene from the passion of Christ which must have been painted with a single bristle brush.'.*

Jane stopped and decided she needed to look at the portrait itself again before she continued, and quickly called it up on her laptop. She knew this painting very well indeed, having gazed at it possibly too often for comfort, but it was such an important work. *'Why has the artist signed his name on the wall above the mirror?'* she typed. *'It translates roughly as Johannes Van Eyck was here. It was a very strange thing to do.'*

She gave a satisfied smirk as she realised that during previous lectures, as she mentioned this portrait there had been an audible rustle of paper as students inevitably opened their books to glance at the picture. *My God, Jane*, she thought smugly. *You're getting good at this*.

She laughed out aloud and stood once again stretching her arms in front of her. That was enough for now – Johannes could wait for a while. She needed to get dressed and maybe have a slice of toast and marmalade.

"And let's have something a little livelier," she said out aloud. "Away you go, William." She ejected the Byrd CD and replaced it with Robert's latest musical purchase, the new album by Micheal Kiwanuka.

Glancing again out of the window, she was surprised to see a tall, slender woman dressed in a very old-fashioned, floor-length voluminous grey dress standing at the front gate seeming unsure whether to come further down the path. She appeared to be wearing some sort of small white calico bonnet, which could not fully contain her long dark hair. Jane had been about to open the window to let some fresh air in, but she hesitated. The woman unnerved her a little with her immobility. She seemed to be gazing wistfully at the cottage.

Jane leant forward a hand on the latch and opening the window a few inches was about to call out if she could help, when with a loud retort the front door knocker sounded, making her jump. She stepped back hurriedly and realising she was hardly dressed for visitors, moved smartly back from the window. Feeling at once foolish, she stepped forward again and tweaked back the closed curtain, noticing with some puzzlement that the woman had gone.

Moving into the hall, Jane stood at the bottom of the stair and called out, "Who is it?"

"It's only me," Paul's voice was muted because of the thickness of the old oaken door. "Sorry if I'm intruding. If I am, please tell me to bugger off, but I was passing and thought to pop in and say thank you once again for the other night."

Jane laughed, and quickly shrugged into her Barbour coat which she took down from the rack of hooks behind the door and moving forward, opened the door.

"Sorry Paul, you took me by surprise, I was in lecture writing mode. Come on in. Excuse the nightwear, I haven't had chance to dress yet, I've been working." As he passed, she looked down the garden towards the lane. Still no sign of the woman.

She closed the door and guided him into the kitchen. "Give me two minutes and I'll be presentable. Pour yourself a coffee, it's in the perc."

He grinned, showing immensely white teeth against his tan. *Where did he got a tan at this time of year?* Jane wondered.

"Don't worry on my behalf," he chuckled. "I love having coffee with attractive women in their nightclothes."

She returned his grin, at the same time registering that he had said she was attractive. Were vicars allowed to say such a thing to female parishioners? *Of course they are, you bloody fool* she thought. *What century do you think this is?*

"Back in a jiffy," she said, moving towards the stairs. "By the way who was that woman down near the gate?"

"Woman?" said Paul "I didn't see a woman. Where?"

"Standing down near the gate, tall, good looking, dressed in grey."

Paul had moved to the percolator and was in the process of pouring himself a cup, but he seemed to freeze at her words.

"Dark-haired?" he said, his face suddenly serious.

"Yes," said Jane ."That's the one. Do you know her?"

Paul finished pouring, replaced the percolator on the range, and sat on one of the kitchen chairs. He seemed to be considering his reply.

"Don't know," he said as casually as could manage. "I didn't see her."

"Oh OK." Jane bounded up the stairs and could be heard bumping around in the main bedroom which was above the kitchen.

Paul sat deep in thought, his eyes staring at the opposite wall considering how much he should say at this stage about the little he knew of this place. He did not want to spook this good-looking newcomer, whom he liked. It was too early in their friendship to lay his musings about the many sightings of this mysterious woman on to her. *Leave it be*, he decided. *For now, anyway*.

A little later Jane, dressed in a baggy t-shirt, frayed jeans, and one of Rob's old cardigans, was sitting opposite Paul nursing a mug herself. She noticed that today he looked quite formal, black jacket and shirt, with the traditional white dog collar. Against the darkness of his clothes his hair looked very blond in the sunlight.

Paul had unashamedly read what was still displayed on the laptop screen and they enjoyed a pleasant few minutes discussing early Dutch painting. He had enjoyed a brief flirtation with old Flemish masters whilst at university and was unrepentant in his championing of Vermeer's 'Girl with a pearl earring' as superior to the Arnolfini Marriage. They had both laughed in disagreement, comfortable enough in each other's company to do so.

"You look very vicarish today, Paul," said Jane after a further sip of coffee. "Something on later?"

He nodded "Yep, couple of home visits early afternoon, and a Christening later. Strange day for such a ceremony but the dad's a sailor and must get back to his ship."

Jane nodded. "We've only been here five minutes but everyone I have spoken to seems to like you if you don't mind me saying. You're a hit with the locals it seems." She grinned as she noticed him blush.

He laughed a little ruefully. "Yes, thank the Lord. When they told me they were giving me a recently vacated post in a country parish I was wary to say the least." He took a sip from his coffee. "I've watched *Straw Dogs* too many times in my youth, I guess. Bloody film. Everyone here is very nice, and very normal, if a little staid. Not what I expected at all."

Her face suddenly became serious as she remembered something. "I meant to say by the way I'm so very sorry to hear about your wife and child, that must have been awful for you."

He was silent for so long that she thought he was not going to answer and was about to make some other inane remark to cover her gaffe, but he suddenly spoke, looking straight into her eyes.

"It's not something I mention a great deal. I was distraught when I got home the other night that I had mentioned it at all. One too many glasses of wine, and convivial company can make one say the silliest things or blurt out stuff best kept to oneself."

She was acutely embarrassed and unsure quite what to say. She covered this by taking another long sip of her coffee, which by now was only lukewarm.

He looked down at his own mug and seemed to reach a decision,

"Perhaps I shouldn't leave it like that."

Without thinking she reached across and touched his hand as it held his mug, then feeling that this was inappropriate with someone she hardly knew, withdrew it quickly. "No, really," she stuttered. "It's none of my business, I'm sorry I mentioned it."

He gave a weak smile intended to show that it was OK, but just made him look vulnerable and unsure. He cleared his throat and looked away, anywhere but at Jane.

"She'd gone shopping, my wife that is, and taken our two-year-old son with her in that bloody car seat." His hands, both wrapped around the mug, were trembling a little she noticed. "As far as the police could gather, she must have turned around to do something with him and lost control. She ploughed straight through a bridge parapet and on to the railway track below. Both were killed instantly." He blew out his cheeks and she could see emotions running rampant behind his eyes. "I was at work; I was freshly ordained and taking a carol service at the local church. It was near Christmas. I wasn't even needed there, it wasn't even my church, I was filling in as a favour to a friend who wanted to go Christmas shopping."

He stopped, unable to go on and took one or two deep breaths.

"Anyway," he managed, "that was that. It's a few years ago now, but you can understand I had to get away. I went on sabbatical for a year, but it didn't help, so cut it short after eight months and asked for something well away from the city. They sent me here."

Jane shook her head, her long auburn hair bouncing around her shoulders. "I shouldn't have asked. I'm so sorry Paul."

"Don't be." He gave her a half smile to show it was OK. "Now you know, and I'm glad. I like you and Robert a lot, and secrets don't go well with friendships. I'm not interested in being an international man of mystery."

He raised his hands in dismissal of this conversation. He wanted to dispel the maudlin mood. "I must be going soon," he said. "Any more of that coffee?"

She gave a half laugh and standing, moved over to the percolator, very aware of his eyes following her. Vicar or no, she decided she liked it. Any woman likes to feel they are being admired, don't they? *We are all fragile and needing attention in one way or another* she thought, *even me.*

Paul smiled softly as he watched her and was aware that she had liked his comment about her looks. *None of them can resist a compliment*, he thought, not unkindly. *None of them.*

She refilled his mug and sat down again.

"So," h'e said, "Roberts gone up to the smoke?"

She groaned in mock exasperation. "Yep, some work meetings that he has put off for too long. He'll be gone a couple of days. I don't mind, we're both used to it, and I have enough to be getting on with here."

Paul smiled "I liked your friends. Have you known them long?"

"Rob has, he and Brian go way back. Sue not so long, only since she married Brian but that's a good few years ago now. When we all first went out together, I felt a bit like the outsider, but they were very welcoming to me." She hesitated a little. "Well, Brian was anyway. Sue not so much. No blatant hostility and we get on fine now, but for a while it was almost as if she thought she had some obscure claim on Rob as she had known him longer. Do you know what I mean?"

Paul nodded and chuckled. "Yep, I do. There's nothing as complicated as human relationships."

They both laughed easily.

Unexpectedly, Jane said, "So who is this woman in grey? Don't tell me you don't know – I saw it in your eyes before I went upstairs, and you *must* have seen her as you came in."

Strangely, Paul hesitated and she thought for a moment that he was going to deny it. He stood up suddenly and smiled. "I do know a little about her about her as it happens, but you're wrong. I didn't see her when I arrived. Anyway, sorry but I must go now, or I'll be late. Let's leave it for another time. OK?"

Jane was slightly miffed at this dismissal but decided to let it go.

"Oh. OK," she said. "I have lots to do anyway, you can tell me next time."

"It's a date," he said, moving towards the door, at the same time considering whether he would tell her that this apparition had been seen on numerous occasions in the village for years and years. *Maybe not just at this moment*, he decided.

****

Chapter Five

It was draughty standing here on this bloody platform. For the umpteenth time Sue moved her weight from one leg to the other, grimacing as the pain in her feet spasmed again. Had it been a good idea to wear thin strappy high-heeled shoes this early in the year? Looking down, she smirked and acknowledged that yes it was. Her feet looked so bloody good sheathed in the sheer stockings, each burgundy-painted toenail gleaming in the fitful light of a Paddington Station mid-morning.

The huge girdered ceiling built by Isambard Kingdom Brunel arched above her, high and elegant even if only for the roof of a train station. She glanced up and noticed the pigeons fluttering beneath the framework and wondered like everyone else does how long such birds lived. It was the age-old question, why do you never see baby pigeons? She smiled briefly at such an absurdity, but the smallest of reasons brought glee to her this morning, so great was her excitement. She would shortly see Robert and the world would be a better place for the next two days.

Her cream trench coat-style mac, belted tightly at the waist, reached only to just above her knees and with only sheer hold-up stockings beneath it made for a distinct draught in a very personal area, but it was worth it – she knew she looked good. The workmen servicing the turnstiles as she entered the station earlier had not attempted to disguise their lascivious stares as she passed.

She lifted her arm again to check the time on her stylish gold watch. It was five minutes since she had last done so but it seemed an age ago. Irritably, she tapped her foot and reaching into her small glossy black Gucci shoulder bag, removed her hairbrush and ran it gently through her curled blonde hair. She had been looking forward to this day since Robert had mentioned he was coming up to the city during that interminable dinner party at his new cottage. As he had promised he would, he had sent her a text as soon as he boarded the GWR train in Exeter, telling her that the journey was roughly three hours and forty minutes, and he guessed at his arrival time. Her phone had pinged its signal for the message at seven this morning as she lay wide awake in the untidy double bed, staring at the ceiling.

"Who the hell is that?" Brian had mumbled from beneath the bedclothes. "And what time is it?"

Sue sat up and had hurriedly deleted the message in case he snatched the mobile from her. "It's only a circular about some clothes sale," she had said. "I thought you were asleep; you were snoring your head off five minutes ago." She lifted the t-shirt that she habitually wore in bed over her head and threw it on to the floor. She felt hot and sweaty.

His head appeared, hair tousled, eyes red-rimmed and scummy. "Piss off," he had announced wearily. "I don't snore."

She decided not to pursue the same old semi-good-natured argument yet again. "Of course you don't". She sneered and glancing across at his bleary countenance decided to make some coffee. She leapt out of bed, throwing the bedclothes back, taking perverse pleasure in his groan of annoyance as most of his own bed coverings were jerked aside. As she made her way to the bathroom, she could not help but grin. It was going to be a lovely day.

That was hours ago now, and she was getting chilly standing here on this bloody platform. How much longer?

The tannoy above her blared out its tinny message that the 7.05 from Exeter was now arriving on platform three. *At last*, she thought and hopped excitedly from one foot to the other, wobbling just a little on the high heels. Quickly, she checked the black electronic notice board with its glowing orange letters that she was indeed on platform three. Yes, she was.

The green painted GWR engine, seeming huge and almost primeval inside the station, groaned as it lumbered past her, its wheels squealing. She felt the hot fumes that blasted from it move over her like the breath of a landing dragon.

The doors of the carriages opened and what seemed like hordes of people lurched out on to the platform and surged past her, each one seeming to be in a desperate hurry and anxious to elbow anyone aside in their rush for the gates. The crowd seemed a living thing and it was all she could do to maintain her position. She craned her neck, peering intently, and suddenly there he was, grinning broadly at her, his backpack slung over one shoulder, his laptop case hanging from the other. In his scruffy black fleecy jacket, he looked like he was a student coming home from term-time.

She answered his laugh and melted into his arms for the huge hug that he always gave her at times like this. He had thought about little else but her for the last few days. Their on-off relationship had been the great secret of his recent life and he knew with a delicious pang of fear that every time they met like this, he was risking not only his marriage but the friendship of his oldest mate. It added extra spice to the mix, and he revelled in it.

"I thought you would never get here," she breathed as he kissed her hungrily. "Was the train delayed?"

"No," he laughed. "It's exactly on time. "Your anticipation must have made you impatient, you hussy".

It was a typical statement from him and once again she noticed the difference between his urbane cultured language and something far cruder that Brian would have said.

Standing back, her hands on his arms, she looked up at him and laughed herself in pure glee, and yes, she acknowledged, lust. "I've booked you in at the Excelsior, we'll have to get a taxi outside. How long have you got?"

"Three days. I've got a very important meeting tomorrow morning, but for the rest of the time I'm all yours".

She gave a mock excited groan and hugged him.

"OK, let's go." Robert smiled down at her.

She linked her arm through his and tried to imagine what it would be like to be married to him. "Yes," she breathed, "let's get a move on. I'm bloody frozen from standing here, and I haven't got any knickers on."

He stopped and looked down at her with mock amazement. "You haven't what?" he said and guffawed hugely. "You're a terrible wanton woman, and I love it".

He kissed her on the forehead and grabbing her hand, chivvied her through the crowd. "Come on," he blurted out, "lets hurry."

****

When it was a bright but blustery day like this, there was nothing more exhilarating than hanging on for dear life to a sailing dinghy that felt alive under your hands.

Rob had been sailing since he was a boy, taught by his father at an early age, and almost as soon as they began going out, Jane had been initiated into the secret society of sailors. It was a world she loved, full of light and space, and sunshine and sparkly water, well sometimes anyway. He owned a dinghy called 'Hissing Sid' which he kept in the boatyard at the local reservoir close to his flat. He told her it was a big dinghy called a Wayfarer, which looked very small to Jane when she first climbed into its sixteen-feet length, although he had told her that the chap who had designed the prototype had actually sailed one to Iceland. She had never checked out this breezily stated fact so had no way of knowing if it was the truth or not.

Sometimes when the breeze was fitful and light, 'HS', as Rob shortened the name to, could feel bulky and unresponsive, but on days like today with a stiff breeze approaching a mild gale, and the sunshine sparking myriad reflexions off the choppy water, the little craft seemed to come alive and try to run away with them. She could feel every gust of wind through the rope that controlled the jib sail at the front of the boat. It reminded her of when she was a little girl, and her dad would take her up to the park to fly her kite. The pull of the rope in her hands brought back so many memories, but this tugging was much more ferocious, and sometimes it took all of her strength to hold it.

Rob was perched on the side of the boat near the stern, the tiller in one hand and the rope controlling the larger main sail in his other hand. His backside was only just in the boat as he leaned way out over the water which rushed past his head and shoulders only inches below. He was held in this position by the kicking straps which ran the length of the dinghy fastened to the floor and under which his feet were braced. He let out a huge whoop of joy and exhilaration as a particularly strong gust almost ripped the rope from his hands and HS seemed to bound forward, moving even faster.

Jane was soaked to the skin, her wet t-shirt clinging to her body beneath the bright orange buoyancy aid that she wore, her bare legs that poked out from her cut-off jeans running with the water that splashed regularly over the prow of the little craft and sluiced them both with its icy touch. She had forced her own feet under the kicking straps and was able to lean far out herself at the front of the boat, her weight adding to Rob's and together they managed to keep HS upright as it surged on towards the far shore of the lake. She let out a howl of pure joy herself and acknowledged that at this moment she loved life, loved Rob, loved this boat, loved sailing. She laughed out loud again with pure happiness.

Lying up to her chin in the hot bath in the cottage surrounded by the suds from the bubble bath that she had poured into the hot water, Jane grinned hugely at the sailing memory, and stretched out her legs so that her foot could move the arm of the tap and allow a further inch of steaming hot water to pour into the bath.

They had been good days when she had first met Rob, and they had fallen for each other almost immediately. Life then had seemed one long date. They both were successful in their chosen fields and their money allowed them to live the life they wanted. Romantic meals in bistros and wine bars in the evenings, short breaks abroad a few times a year, sailing HS when the weather was fine, or driving through the countryside in the somewhat battered open-topped sports car that she had owned back then in search of picture-book pubs to have a drink or a meal, or perhaps even stay the night. It was an idyllic existence which led very quickly to the decision to marry and move in together.

She lay back, allowing the suds to climb around her neck and clog her ears. She felt relaxed and decided to stay here a little longer, letting the warm water soothe the tension from her body. There was nothing really to be anxious about, but she could not help it whenever she was constructing a new lecture. It was difficult to arrange one's thoughts in such a way that it kept the interest of her audience. It was not an easy skill, and she was always terrified that one day it might not work out quite as she intended.

Oh well, she would take another look at it after she had made supper. She had discovered over the years that if you thought about something completely different for a couple of hours and then went back to the piece you were working on you could view it with fresh eyes and recognise immediately any shortcomings.

She sat up and lifting the large sponge, allowed water to cascade over her shoulders and down her back. She groaned with pleasure. *Oh that felt good, so good.* She did it again and closed her eyes with pleasure.

What was that?

She wiped the suds from around her ears and tilted her head to one side. She had heard a sound downstairs. The bathroom door was open, what did it matter? There was no one else there.

There it was again. What the hell? It sounded almost as if someone was crying down in the kitchen. With a frisson of alarm that seemed to send a shiver down her back, she remembered Sue's remark the other morning about hearing someone crying, and they had all dismissed it as either a fox or her drink-fuelled imagination – she remembered their laughter. But now sitting alone and vulnerable in her cooling bathtub it did not seem so funny.

"Hello!" she called out ludicrously. Nothing. The noise had stopped.

"Hello!" she called again. "Is someone there?"

Only silence answered her.

Hurriedly, she stood and stepped out of the tub onto the tiled floor. Reaching for her towelling robe she shrugged it on without bothering to dry herself and moved out on to the bare floorboards of the landing.

"I said hello." Again, she called out, more to reassure herself than to receive an answer. What should she do? What would Rob do? But that was a silly thing to think about. Rob was not there.

Feeling a mixture of annoyance and trepidation, she crept down the stairs and peered into the kitchen. Nothing. It was exactly as she had left it an hour before. The radio still played very quietly. Her laptop was still on the kitchen table, open as she had left it. Outside, she could see the shrubs and bushes of the garden as they enjoyed the last of the fitful daylight. It was all so completely normal that her heart ceased to pound, and she began to curse herself for a suspicious fool.

She moved over to the worktops near the sink and clicked on the kettle to make a coffee. What a bloody silly thing to have imagined. *Damn you Sue for putting such imaginings in my mi*nd, she mused, especially as she knew that Jane was going to be on her own for a couple of days.

She decided she would not mention this to Rob, as he would just scoff and think she was an idiot or being dramatic. But one thing she *would* do, she thought, would be to mention it to Paul. He knew something about this place, things he had not wanted to mention when they were all together. Well, too fucking bad. The next time she saw him she would insist that he tell her. Yes, she nodded, she would insist.

She wrapped the towel around her, snuggling into its enfolding comfort and squatted at the table to enjoy her drink. John Legend came on to the radio singing one of their favourite songs *Ordinary people*. She thought the words a little dramatic, but the song itself had impact and of course, Legend's voice was something else. She sipped her coffee appreciatively and wondered what Rob was doing at that moment.

****

Chapter Six

He loved the sound of rain pattering on to his anorak. It was somehow primal, the feeling of getting back to nature, being out in the weather. He had always loved to be out in the elements, close to nature. The trick was to be dressed for it. So many times, Paul had seen people on hillsides, or even on mountains in Wales or Scotland dressed in trainers and a tracksuit hoping to get to the top of a two-thousand-footer. He remembered an old saying by someone that "There is no such thing as bad weather, just inappropriate clothing." Absolutely correct. He remembered as if it were yesterday, coming down from the top of Ben Nevis one afternoon. He and his fellow climbers had left before it was light and made the summit three hours later, and to get out of the snow had sat in the plastic bothy on the top munching damp sandwiches and drinking lukewarm coffee from a thermos but feeling happy and proud of their achievement. Within two hundred yards of the car park back down near the road they had encountered a middle-aged woman in a flimsy lime-green tracksuit and leather strappy sandals with a small Jack Russell on a lead asking if it was much further to the top. They had all laughed uproariously and told her that she would not get there before dark. Paul was still not sure to this day if she had believed them. He shook his head now, grinning at the memory.

He sat nodding smugly to himself as he ruminated on his walking achievements over the years. Most of the peaks in

Snowdonia, Ben Nevis, and Ben Tee in Scotland. The five sisters of Kintail, Bonny Schiehallion too, although he'd never seen anywhere less bonny. He'd also tramped the full length of the Offa's Dyke path, all one hundred and seventy-seven miles of it. He'd seen some great views and enjoyed the immense gratification of the achievements. Someone had said once that what made life bearable were our occasional 'little victories.' He agreed. He glanced down at his waterproof walking trousers, his gaiters, and his thick thermal socks encased in heavy walking boots. The sturdy woolly hat that completed his ensemble kept his head not only warm but dry. He had been doing this as a hobby for as long as he could remember, and his tried and tested equipment never let him down. Not that you needed much of it, just basic common sense really, but he was always amazed when people did not show it in the face of the elements.

He had decided first thing that morning that he needed a walk, needed to clear his head, and had set off towards this first Tor on Dartmoor as the grey day was just beginning to lighten. He had done this many times before and knew from previous experience that it was about ten miles from the village, so by the time he arrived home later today he would have given himself a decent workout. The rain suited his mood, and he had found himself enjoying the solitude as he walked.

He looked out at the bleak vista of a damp Dartmoor crouched beneath the scudding pewter-coloured clouds. From up here next to the Tor they seemed to be just above him. The saturated stumpy grass was dark green in this light, punctuated by glistening granite rocks sprouting lichen. In the distance back where he had come from the sky looked lighter and as he watched, a break in the cloud allowed a single beam of sunlight to spear the ground and move across the land like a spotlight.

He was leaning against the base of this small rock formation, enjoying the relative comfort of a back rest. To his right a wizened and stunted tree bowed before the wind giving it the look of an old witch caught out in the rain. The view did little to lighten his mood.

Although he had not mentioned it to anyone, it was three years to the day that Marion and little Charlie had been killed. He hated the date every time it came around, but of course, remorselessly, it did. It seemed much longer than three years in many ways, but he could still picture their faces and hear their voices as if it was yesterday. Perhaps he always would, who knew. Everyone touched by tragedy coped with it in their own way. His initial reaction had been to rail and rage at God for doing this to him. He had always tried to be a good man, do the right thing, treat people well, and this was his reward. He almost turned away from his calling, so great was his anger and despair. He had drunk too much for some months and was bitter and resentful to anyone who tried to help. He was on a downward spiral to God knew where, until one day an old vicar who was close to retirement had taken him aside, sat him down in one of the dusty chairs at the bishop's residence and told him to "get a grip, son." He remembered the craggy, wise old face staring intently at him and saying, "What's happened to you is terrible, your young family snuffed out in an instant. That's as bad as it gets, but God doesn't cause car accidents, and you know it."

Paul had nodded glumly. "Don't you?" persisted the old man, his concerned and lined face under a shock of white hair close to Paul's. It was then the tears had finally come, despite his efforts to stop them. They just flooded out of him, running unchecked down his face and on to the floor. He couldn't stop. The old man had said nothing more, just stayed with him whilst he cried himself out and then handed him a glass of scotch. "Lift up your head now, Paul," he had intoned. "Face it, and bear it, and in their memory get on with your life."

Now, three years later, he found himself responsible for the spiritual wellbeing of these plain-spoken but largely decent people who made their living in this harsh landscape. It was a long way from his career aspirations as he graduated from university with a degree in theology based on his final thesis on 'World events and their effect on church doctrine.' He smiled slowly as he acknowledged the strange byways that life led us down.

A fitful gust of wind slapped rain into his face, and he looked up from his reverie to the far horizon, wresting his thoughts back to the present.

Not long after he'd arrived here, he became interested to know why Dartmoor, Bodmin Moor and Exmoor were here. Had they always been like this? These great swathes of desolation amongst an otherwise semi-verdant landscape. Had they always been like this? And he was surprised to learn that they hadn't.

In fact, he now knew that they were very early examples of manmade ecological disaster areas. The damage that little mankind can wreak when he is unchecked.

Early hunter-gatherers in the Mesolithic, or maybe earlier, had presumably followed the deer and other game into the southwest and there found a plentiful supply of not only fresh meat, but fish and shellfish and seabirds aplenty. Gradually, as the Mesolithic became the Neolithic and then the Bronze Age, and people moved from purely hunting and gathering to utilising the land, villages sprang up. The plentiful forests of oak and hazel had been remorselessly chopped down for fuel or building materials, and the soil, too thin for proper cultivation, had been used merely for the pasturing of hardy domesticated animals. The damage had been done and was exacerbated by more immigration and pasturing during the Anglo-Roman periods.

Aside from the aggressive and relentless deforestation, the early generations of peoples who had lived and died here had left little mark on the landscape, apart from the odd stone ring, crude burial chambers, flint concentrations, or wall or walkways. Thus, it was that the knowledge Paul now pondered on had only been gleaned from the sparse evidence in the soil by intrepid archaeologists wielding the latest technological advances in recent decades. He had a vague idea of writing a short book on the subject at some time in the future.

He took a last swig from his now almost cold coffee and began to pack his sandwich wrappers and detritus back into his backpack. He realised that mulling over the events that had shaped this landscape had taken his mind, albeit briefly, off Marion and Charlie, as he had intended it would.

He had pondered on the dinner party the other evening as he walked. What did he make of these 'new' people in his life? He had liked Jane immediately and also her husband Rob. They would be a welcome addition to the village and promised to be entertaining company as he got to know them. True, they were just his parishioners, and it was always advisable not to get to close to those in one's pastoral care, but they were much the same age as he and everyone liked a little company from their own generation, didn't they?

He was drawn to Jane almost as soon as he met her. Not only was she a good-looking woman but she appeared to be very friendly and intelligent, and there was an immediate empathy between them, or he had thought so anyway. He had intended when he called in yesterday morning to tell her what little he knew about the infamous 'grey lady', who he knew had supposedly appeared to any number of people over the years and more recently to the aged couple who owned the old place before Jane and Robert. The last visitation had proved to be the final straw for the couple, who had promptly announced to the world at large that they were selling up and moving away as soon as possible. But yesterday morning, catching Jane looking to him very alluring in her old-fashioned nightdress, had rather put him off his stroke, and it had slipped his mind. He must be very careful not to let his attraction to her show, that would never do in a man of the cloth. But that was just it, wasn't it? Despite his calling, he was still just a man, and a lonely one. He shoved these uncomfortable thoughts to the back of his mind.

Brian he thought was a bit of a bumptious arse, too much money, and not enough sense, but he doubted he would see much of him anyway. Sue, he had been wary of from the moment he shook hands with her. He had seen eyes like hers on women for most of his life, full sensual eyes that invited further contact. One show of interest on his part and she would be up for whatever came her way.

Hoisting his now considerably lighter backpack across his shoulders, he set off back the way he had come and decided he would call in at the local pub when he got to the village. It was as good a place as any to catch up with the local news. It was part of his job, his duties if you like, to be abreast of local concerns and current events. Also, he needed to sound a couple of the more vociferous locals out about the 'grey woman'. Any snippet of information about her had now become of great interest to him. Many locals had mentioned these sightings to him on numerous occasions since his arrival there a year ago. He had not taken much notice to be fair, not interested in old folk tales probably designed to put the wind up the new young vicar and he had dismissed them without thought. But Jane had been so adamant that she had caught a glimpse of the figure in her garden, that he had decided to find out more. The local records office in Exeter would surely furnish firm details about such a persistent visitation, so too might the county library. It was said that she was the wife of the firebrand holy man by all accounts, who had not been a nice person at all, but Paul would be very lucky indeed to discover anything concrete about his wife.

Two hours later, a little weary, and muddy, but refreshed in mind and body, he strolled into the village. It always gave him pleasure as a previous town dweller to look appreciatively around him at the triangular village green, which had a large duck-infested pool at its centre. This was the hub of the place. Dotted around the green were the small but functional general store, the greengrocers, the tiny single pump garage, and of course the pub. The houses were a hotchpotch of half-timbered dwellings mixed in with Georgian or Victorian brick cottages, some standing alone, some in groups of four, all painted a variety of white or pastel colours. It was, as many had commented, pure chocolate box, the archetypal English rural village. Considering some of the inner-city hell holes that many of his contemporaries from the theology course at uni had been sent to it was paradise. He ambled towards the half-beamed dormer windowed pub, noting that even for so early in the evening there were a few people ahead of him. Three or four large gleaming motorbikes were parked on their stands in front of the entrance porch making it a little difficult to get to the front door. One of the leather-clad bikers, enjoying a pint whilst lounging on small pub benches, seeing the problem, apologised profusely and moved his machine a few feet out of the way. Paul nodded and grinned his thanks as he swung open the old, battered, black- painted wooden door and walked in. Ron the landlord, sporting his usual check shirt, yellow waistcoat, and a dickie bow, offered his most welcoming smile.

"Afternoon, vicar. Welcome. Pint of the usual, is it?"

Paul shrugged off his backpack, which seemed to have grown considerably heavier during the last hour as he tired, and set it down against the bar.

"Yes, please Bill, thanks."

Bill chattered on as he poured the brown liquid, making professional enquiries to a regular customer, and Paul gave the usual responses to queries about his walk, the weather, and the state of his health. At the same time, he glanced around this old bar room. The floor was stoneflagged, as a genuflexion to the amount of farm workers that came in regularly with their muddy boots, although Paul knew that the small lounge just off the bar was carpeted. Small wall lights added to the ambience, the yellow light from them reflected in the many horse brasses that seemed to adorn every black ceiling beam in the place. In a corner, a group of teenage girls and boys hovering dangerously around the legal drinking age lounged on stools next to the clucking games machine. They were not talking to each other but all texting away on their mobile phones, frowns of deep concentration on their young faces. Over near the mullioned window, two older men sat nursing what was left of their pints for lack of anything else to do. Their conversation was sporadic and seemed to follow the same predictable course that it probably had for many years.

Bill's wife Audrey, a brassy blond with an open, pleasant face slashed by crimson lipstick was leaning over the counter at the far end of the bar talking conspiratorially to two friends as she told them some juicy item of gossip in a low murmur. They had all decided on a 'quick one' after returning from a shopping expedition to Exeter.

Trying to appear casual, Paul picked up his pint, took a long appreciative swig and strolled over to the two men by the window.

"Evening gents," he said genially. "Mind if I join you for a few minutes? I don't really like to drink alone."

Both men grinned up at him, good-naturedly, pleased that someone new would join their stilted conversation.

"Surely," said one of them, moving a stool out from beneath the stained wooden table. "Sit yourself down, Vicar, and welcome".

"Thanks, and I've told you before it's Paul."

They both nodded. "OK," said one of them. "No problem."

The three of them chatted inconsequentially for a few minutes discussing the weather, local gossip, and football, until finally Paul decided he could now manipulate the conversation on to the subject he had really come across to discuss.

"Oh," he began, as if it had just occurred to him. "I know what I wanted to ask you guys. What's this about this grey lady people keep telling me about?"

The men glanced conspiratorially at one another and one winked good-naturedly.

"Well now," he began. "Hers been seen in these yere parts for many a long year I can tell you, Vicar… Paul. Long afore we were born, and even afore our grandparents came into the world people has been seeing her. Yes, that they have." He nodded to emphasise his words and drained the last dregs of his pint.

Taking the hint Paul said, "Let me get you two guys another drink and you can tell me everything you know. I'm interested." He held up his hand. "Two more beers here please, Bill."

The landlord grinned and nodded. "Coming right up, sir," he chuckled. "Right up."

****

Cecily felt sore and degraded as she always did after these incidents. She moved gingerly down the steep wooden stairs to the kitchen, her arm leaning against the wall for support. She looked a bit of a sight, that she knew, but Nehemiah was not someone to be kept waiting when he was in this mood, which seemed to be increasingly often these days.

Arriving home from wherever he had been for most of the day, he stumped straight away up the stairs demanding that his young wife follow him as he had 'something to discuss.' Cecily and Margaret had exchanged knowing glances as they stood up in unison from the kitchen table where they had been talking about the meals for the next few days.

Cecily sighed resignedly and called over her shoulder as she left, "Could you ask Thomas to kill two chickens then please, Margaret. I'll leave it to you both which ones you choose."

Margaret, her face inscrutable, stared after her young mistress and shook her head slightly. "Yessum," she muttered.

It was of course what she had feared. Nehemiah had taken his young wife without subtlety or care, throwing her across the huge bed, hoisting up her skirts and grunting and swearing above her as he worked his unspent passion on her. There was no affection whatsoever, no kissing, or lovemaking, just harsh, brutal penetration as he slaked his ever-present lust. He bellowed his satisfaction as his groin butted at her. He hated that his God had visited him with worldly desires unbecoming of a man of the cloth, but God had also seen fit to place within his grasp this sensuous young woman for him to plough his furrow and offer temporary release from his fever.

She was his wife, his property, his chattel, and must do as she was bid, or she would pay the consequences. He saw no wrong in occasional chastisement to keep his woman biddable and compliant. He noted that the latest bruised eye that he had inflicted some days ago was now almost invisible. Good, she could now resume her duties in the village as the local clergyman's wife.

He reached his shuddering, grunting climax and opened his eyes just in time to catch the unguarded look of revulsion on his wife's face.

"You could at least attempt to enjoy our conjugation, ungrateful strumpet," he snarled as he levered himself up off her. "The good Lord has selected you to serve me in this way, be thankful that you offer yourself in his service."

Cecily looked up at him. He was still fully clothed, his breeches down around his knees, his pale, cadaverous face filmed with sweat, and she knew that she could not hate anyone more than she hated her husband.

"Yes, my husband," she managed. "I am here to let you have use of my body. I merely wish that sometimes you might show some affection or even love. Is that not what our union should be about? Is that not what the Lord tells us?"

"You dare to lecture me on what the Lord intends, woman?" His disdain was palpable, and not for the first time Cecily found herself wondering if he was in full possession of his wits.

Grabbing her arm, he levered her off the bed and shoved her towards the door of the room. "Fetch me some bread, cheese and wine and be quick about it. I must go out again soon to be about his work." He slumped down on to the bed, adjusting his breeches as he did so.

She walked to the door and opened it before turning to glance at him. He was lying with closed eyes, his hands steepled in prayer, sweat from his recent exertions still glinting on his brow. Hearing her footsteps halt, he opened his eyes and peered at her.

"Go."

She turned and fled down to the kitchen. She felt abused and outraged, and also acutely embarrassed and aware that

Margaret would know exactly what had transpired, what she had suffered in that awful bedroom. Surely this was not what marriage should be like? Her shoulder hurt where he had bitten her, and she winced as she realised he had wrenched her legs as he forced them apart. The outpouring of his lust was running down her inner thighs. Women of her standing wore no underwear. She felt sick and decided that as soon as he had gone out again, she would sluice herself at the water pump in the garden.

She entered the kitchen and slumped down on to one of the benches.

"The master wants some repast, Margaret," she said not looking at the older woman. "Some bread, some cheese, and some wine. Quickly, please."

"I heard him," said Margaret, the scorn barely concealed in her voice. "It's nearly ready. Shall I take it up?"

Cecily stared up at her and the natural empathy shared between women showed that Margaret knew exactly what had transpired and was angry.

"Yes," nodded Cecily. "If you please."

As Margaret disappeared, she stood and helped herself to a small pewter goblet of wine from the earthenware beaker. It tasted cool and smooth and calmed her spirit a little. Moving to the window, she leaned her hot forehead against the cool glass and tried to breathe deeply.

"Oh God," she whispered. "Dear Lord, how long must I endure this?"

A shadow fell across her, and she looked out through the glass pane into the laughing eyes of Thomas, Margaret's twenty-three-year-old son. Tall and muscular from a life in the outdoors, he had dark unruly hair which was tousled and uncombed, falling across his handsome face and his teeth seemed very white against his ruddy complexion. She found herself responding to his grin, despite her feelings of despair. He had a struggling chicken under each arm and had clearly been chasing them around the muddy yard in his efforts to catch them.

She nodded at him and leaned back from the window to take another sip of wine. With a deft and dreadfully expert movement, he twirled one over his arm neatly breaking its neck. Dropping the corpse to the ground he repeated the process with the second bird and winked at her.

"Two for the pot, mistress," he grinned.

His effrontery at speaking to her in this way took her breath away, but such was her current mood that she decided she quite liked it. After all, despite the difference in their stations, he was only three years younger than she was, and his love of life was irresistible, and anyway, it was only recently that her standing in life had been elevated following her marriage to Nehemiah.

The sound of whistling came from the muddy track beyond the yard as a farmer and his mate drove three cows down to the village green to be sold. His brindle-coloured mangy dog ranged backwards and forwards, nipping the heels of the cows to keep them moving. Spying Thomas standing in the yard and Cecily's face peering through the window behind, the farmer hefted the stick he carried and gave a cheery wave as he passed, which Thomas returned.

The kitchen door banged open as Margaret re-entered. "The master's fallen asleep," she said with a definite edge to her voice. "I've left the wine and food on the table by the bed."

She was clearly very angry and picking up the twig broom began to sweep the dusty floor vigorously. Rushes that were spread on the floor every few days. were now going mouldy and beginning to smell. It was time they were replaced.

"Why don't you sit outside at the back, mistress?" she said. "The sun is out and it's quite warm. You can recover yourself there. I'll call you if you're needed."

A long look passed between them, and nodding, Cecily stood, favouring her wrenched leg. "Yes, I will," she said. "Thank you Margaret."

As she moved down the corridor towards the back of the house, she heard Margaret shouting out of the window at her son whom she had obviously just noticed, telling him to pluck those two birds and be quick about it. Cecily knew that her servant loved her son dearly but was extremely frustrated that at his age he had not yet taken a wife and given her grandchildren. There were girls aplenty in the village who would willingly agree to such a match, but he had resisted making any dalliance official to date. He seemed a likeable young man and was always ready with a winning smile and a cheery greeting. Cecily acknowledged that he was also very good-looking.

****

Robert lay warm and content amidst the jumbled tangle of sheets in the huge hotel bed. He was smug and self-satisfied, feeling impossibly virile as well as absolutely knackered. *If I shagged this woman any more, my cock would fall off* he mused crudely. The thought brought a smirk to his stubbly face and rubbing his cheek he realised his first order of the day must be for a shave.

He grinned broadly, unable to drown the feelings of euphoria beneath whatever guilt he felt. He knew that what he was doing was wrong, but Christ, this woman was insatiable, and who knew when or even if, such an opportunity would ever come again?

He turned his head to look at the sleeping Sue lying next to him. She seemed so childlike in her slumber, and he found himself not able to reconcile this recumbent girl with the ferocious, demanding lover of the last two nights. Bloody hell, he had hardly slept at all, and his body was beginning to tell him about it. How on earth did Brian cope? Calling his best friend's name to mind wiped the smile from his face as he remembered that this woman was married to someone else, and someone who meant a great deal to him.

Her face was like a mask at that moment, and he acknowledged that she always applied far too much make up when she slept with him as she knew that it 'turned him on' as she termed it. Her deep blue eye shadow was smudged and the mascara on her lashes had run over her cheek and was evident at the corners of her eyes. Her bright vermillion lipstick had smeared from the edges of her mouth. This all gave her the look of a prostitute that had had a rough night. She insisted on wearing a choker around her neck, again knowing that he found such an item alluring, and it was still in place as she slept. Her obviously coloured blonde hair was a mess of curls around her head on the pillow.

He smiled again as he heard her voice in a moment of intimacy telling him that she had told one of her closest friends she painted her face like this as it 'kept him at it'.

Kept me at it he mouthed silently to himself and grinned again. What a tart. But she turned him on as no one else did, he could not help it.

Did he feel guilty at all? Yes, he did, but only in fleeting moments. It did not occur to him to forego his pleasures. Nothing like this had ever happened to him before and he did not intend to let the opportunity pass him by. A good-looking woman fancied him for Christ's sake, and though she was the wife of his best friend, she had made it blatantly obvious that this did not bother her, so why should it bother him? The lack of sensibility and common decency that would have been breathtaking in others was completely unacknowledged, and therefore summarily dismissed from his mind. The product of a loveless marriage, Robert, as an only child, had been doted on by both parents who saw him as a weapon to be utilised in the constant game of one upmanship between them. As such he had been denied nothing, and his every whim had been pandered to, his every wish achieved. He was not a bad man by any means, but not getting what he wanted in this life just did not register. Jane would never find out, and you only lived once, so went his catechism.

Apart from the time spent with Sue, which had been marvellous, it had been a successful two days in terms of work as well. The meeting-cum-presentation that was the main reason for his visit to London had been highly satisfactory and the company had all but awarded him the contract to design the county library in the Midlands on the spot. Only their protocols had dictated that they view his main rivals' plans before making the final decision, but privately the chairman had confided to Robert during cocktails after the event that the decision was made. It would mean a further visit to London the following week to sign contracts, but this would be a small price to pay to finally secure this highly lucrative and prestigious project. *Yes*, he ruminated smugly. *Life is good at the moment.*

Suddenly, he wondered what the time was. He had a train to catch that morning. He levered himself into a sitting position and glanced down at the watch that he always wore, even in bed. Eight-forty. *Bloody hell!* His train left Paddington at 11.15 and he dared not miss it. He leaned down and stroked Sue's cheek.

"Oy, sleepy head, rise and shine, I have to go."

Sue slowly opened bleary eyes and peered up at him. "What time is it?"

"It's late. Come on up and at them."

A slow smile curved her mouth. "No not yet lover, let's start the day with a bang." She rolled on to her side, and reaching out, stroked her fingers down his stomach, her long, painted nails digging into his flesh. In her mind she was planning a lengthy session of slow languorous lovemaking, followed by breakfast in bed, and then possibly more love-making before she finally let him go.

He looked down at her, a slow lascivious smile curving his mouth. Was this woman never satisfied? He almost acquiesced but common sense came to his rescue, and he lowered his feet to the floor. "I'd love to, you know that, but not this time. I must go. It's back to our normal lives, woman."

She opened her mouth to argue but just at that moment her mobile phone on the bedside table chirped and vibrated.

"Of fuck," she said with vehemence, and leaning over, picked it up, her full, ripe breasts emerging like two sleepy puppies from beneath the bedclothes. She lifted the phone to her ear. "Morning Bri." Her voice had become strident, wide awake, not the sleepy languorous purr that it had been moments before.

Robert could hear the chipmunk-like chatter of someone on the other end of the line.

"Yep," said Sue, nodding ridiculously. "I've been up for some time. I'm just gonna have some breakfast and I'll be catching the train a bit later. See you early afternoon probably."

Taking advantage of the situation, Robert stood and padded off to the bathroom. Sue watched his disappearing buttocks with real regret. She had hoped that these two days might be the start of something more permanent, something to pull her away from the dull monotony of life with Brian.

"Oh, Charlotte says to say hello," she continued in her breezy tones, affecting a greeting from her sister to her husband, and then ludicrously parroted his return greeting to the sister who at this moment was fifty miles to the south in Hove. They chattered on inconsequentially for a few more minutes until she ended the call with a strident "OK, see ya later", and turning off her mobile, threw it back on to the bedside table.

Her face had changed instantaneously from expectant bonhomie to sulky petulance, like a small child who cannot have the toy it wants. She wondered again, why should Jane have caught the first prize? Life was so unfair. She had been inserted into their threesome a couple of years ago by a newly besotted Robert. She, Brian and Robert had all met at university and they had all been close for a long time now. When she and Brian became an item, it had altered the dynamic between them but not terminally, and so they had continued doing many things together. Although her own physical relationship with Robert had not then started, and would not for a year hence, she had immediately felt as if her cosy little world had been invaded by an unwelcome interloper. Robert was a good lover, not brilliant, but adept and more importantly, eager to accede to her every whim. Sue did not hate her husband, she did not even dislike him, she just liked sex, and lots of it. After ten, or was it twelve years, of marriage to plump Brian his sexual demands were minimal and sporadic. She had realised two years ago, when she reached the grand old age of forty-five, that time was not forever, and she had better start enjoying herself before it was too late. Robert was there at the right time and did not seem to find her gentle advances unacceptable, and things had happened very quickly from then on. The last two days had been amazing, not only the sex, but the thrill of being with someone else in the town where she lived. In the coffee shops, and the pub, there was always the deliciously enticing threat of discovery which she found added hugely to the enjoyment.

Remembering that this very satisfying two days was at an end, she sighed hugely and levered herself out from under the wreckage of sheets.

"Cow!" she said out aloud, picturing the smug face of Jane, then standing, she made a dash for her black lace slip and knickers, which for some reason that she could not remember were draped over the TV.

****

Chapter Seven

It was one of those beautiful mornings that spring occasionally allows as a glorious foretaste of what is to come. The sunlight had a special sharpness to it, illuminating everything with a brightness that was almost but not quite painful to the eyes. The green of the hedgerows and even the weeds seemed to glow with an inner light and the berries of a bright vermillion dotted amongst the foliage glittered to greet the day.

Cecily felt tired and exceptionally jaded that morning and was struggling to find any joy in the day. She was sore in her most intimate places and weary from lack of sleep. Nehemiah had been especially vigorous and demanding throughout the interminable night, his appetites seeming more urgent than normal, even for him. Her pleas as dawn was streaking the sky that she needed to rest were met with hostility and cruel laughter.

"Be silent, woman," he had hissed. "Be grateful that a man such as I find you even moderately desirable. Did I not rescue you from spinsterhood and a life of dry, shrivelled unfulfillment?"

She had turned her head away from his panting and stared at the sky outside of the window, wishing she could just die. Was this all there was for the whole of her life? Surely not, surely God would not allow such a thing? But in her heart of hearts, she knew that he would. She was a woman and a wife, and the wife of a servant of the church no less. Surely his demands were hers to accept? Was that not what the Good Book told her?

When he did finally achieve grunting, panting satisfaction, he shouted out in triumph and withdrawing immediately from her, rolled on to his back and promptly fell into a fitful sleep. She had edged to the farthest reaches of the bed to be as far away from him as possible and enjoyed a brief oblivion in blessed sleep.

When she awoke it was full daylight and her husband had gone. She experienced a wave of relief and thankfulness and stretched out her bruised limbs, revelling in the feel of her nakedness. She pushed back the coverlet and glanced down at her body. Pale and slim, the sunlight almost made her glow. She stroked her hands over her stomach and wondered if God would ever give her the blessing of a child. Nehemiah would surely have made her pregnant by now with his almost nightly attentions. It may be that either he or she was not able – she had heard older woman discuss such a subject and paid little heed. Well, God would decide.

She dressed in her simple attire of a grey homespun gown with its small white collar, which was the only item of clothes that her husband allowed. "Do you wish to look like a strumpet?" he had sneered the day after their wedding as he was cutting up her small collection of gowns of russet, green or muted brocade. "You are the wife of a man of God and must appear so to my flock. You must be God fearing and virtuous with no hint of coquetry. I trust you will remember this."

Thinking of these very words, she donned her wooden clogs for outdoor wear and calling to Margaret who was busy in the kitchen that she was up from her bed and would be in the back yard, she stepped out into the sunlight and decided to sit in her habitual spot on the old wooden bench seat beneath the window and take stock of the day.

The chickens as usual were scrambling around in the mud and weeds looking for items of food. The two goats, thin and scruffy, were likewise chewing on sparse clumps of unappetising-looking grass as they dragged their tethering chains after them around the yard.

Despite the travails of the night and her aching body, she felt relaxed sitting here in the fitful sunlight. There were people far worse off than she was, that she knew. Not everyone would shed a tear for her. She planned to write to her father if she could beg some parchment and ink from Nehemiah soon. They had not conversed for too long now and he would be worried. She would not tell him any details of her married life – what could he do if he knew? It would only disturb him, and in any case, for all she knew her life was the norm for a married woman.

She looked up and saw that Thomas was coming across from the forest that backed on to her garden. He came past the well and seemed to be heading straight towards her.

"Good morning, mistress," he said, his winning smile drawing a similar response from her. She knew that she should not really encourage these trifling conversations with the son of one of her servants. The difference in their stations in life would dictate that he was being impertinent even for wishing her good morning.

She looked up at him as he approached and noted unconsciously his broad-shouldered sturdiness, his dark eyes and darker unkempt hair. His jerkin and knee-length breeches were of some nondescript tan colour and his battered leather footwear was muddy.

She had tried to ignore him with studied indifference but the young woman in her noted that he was so damned good-looking, and if there was no one to see, what was the harm?

He came right up to stand before her and produced a rough bouquet of wildflowers from behind his back with a flourish.

"With your permission, my lady," he said solemnly. "I've picked these for you. Pretty flowers for a pretty lady."

It was a makeshift grouping of sky-blue cornflowers, white daisies, pink primroses, and the odd cowslip and a piece of fern. Considering the small amount of time he had had to do it after he spotted her sitting there, it was a pretty and competent gesture.

She knew she should reject them and send him on his way with a cold word, but the flowers were beautiful this lovely morning, and he surely meant no harm. Looking up into his face, she noticed that above the profusion of colour in the makeshift bouquet his eyes were sparkling and full of fun.

Attempting not very successfully to maintain her dignity, she said, "Why thank you, Thomas, that is most thoughtful of you."

She took them from him and inhaled the aroma that suddenly filled the air. "Would you give them to your mother for me and ask her to find something to place them in on the kitchen windowsill?"

Handing the bouquet back she smiled up at him. Gazing down at her he noticed how when she gave that wonderful smile, the corners of her mouth lifted, and dimples appeared in her cheeks. Her amber eyes seemed to suck him down into them and he almost overbalanced. He had not realised that falling in love could be such a quick and easy thing. So natural, so elemental.

"Yessum," he said grinning, and stepping past her, entered the house. As he walked down the stoneflagged hallway towards the kitchen, he acknowledged that he would never forget that moment for the whole of his life, and even if he lived to be old, he would remember her lovely face as she smiled up at him.

****

Jane could not quite summon up the interest this morning to finish her Arnolfini lecture. After a refreshing shower to wake her up from a fitful and disturbed night's sleep (she never did sleep well when Robert was away), she breakfasted on muesli and black coffee, followed by a cream cheese bagel. Then she sat determinedly down at the kitchen table and opened her laptop.

Nothing original to say came to mind, and she found herself gazing at the last line of the lecture that she had written, wondering how to continue. She needed to mention the continued discussion, sometimes heated, between academics as to which was the greatest Northern Renaissance painting: the 'Arnolfini Marriage' by Van Eyck, or 'Girl with a pearl earring' by Vermeer. But how to explain in the short, crisp sentences required if she was to keep the attention of her audience? As a lecturer of long standing, she knew that the successful speaker must always lace an element of humour and controversy into the text to stop students losing concentration and reverting to surreptitiously studying their mobiles as she was speaking.

But it was no good, nothing would immediately come to mind this bright morning, so she decided to give it up as a bad job for the moment and go for a walk. Perhaps the fresh air would revive her spirits.

Donning her boots and anorak over her jeans, she set off through the small gate at the back of the garden and was almost immediately in the wood that backed the property. Spring was evident as she walked, the groundhugging bushes were all beginning to sprout green buds, and the occasional gorse bush was ablaze with bright yellow flowers. Above her the trees whipped and whispered in the gusty breeze and she noted that leaves, small and ill-formed, were beginning to appear.

This was better, she was feeling more awake and aware already. Reaching a small clearing she gazed up at the blue sky, pocked as it was with windblown white clouds, and tried to locate the bird that was singing so beautifully up there. Was it too early in the year for skylarks to trill their joy at the world as they hovered high up, barely visible ? She was not sure.

"If you're going to be a country girl, Jane, you'd better start learning things like this." She spoke out aloud to herself, and grinned. But it was true, as a born and bred 'townie', she had little or no idea what the trees were that creaked so attractively in the wind all around her. Were they oak, or ash, or beech, or a dozen others? She had no idea. She must get a book.

She was still a little concerned following a brief conversation last evening with Robert. She knew better than to ring him during working hours when he was away. Many times, he had gently reprimanded her for calling him when he was in the middle of a meeting, or even worse, giving a presentation. "There's nothing more infuriating," he had said, "than being in the middle of a description of the stress factors present in the structure of a high rise and the mobile in my jacket on the back of my chair goes off. If I'm lucky they think it's funny, if I'm not, they don't."

She had spoken to him around seven last night. However, it was a strange, curt, almost dismissive conversation. He did not want to be speaking to her, that much was obvious.

"Are you OK?" she had queried. "You sound a bit stressed."

He had laughed, a short almost embarrassed bark of a laugh. "I'm fine, just a bit knackered, that's all. Sorry."

They spoke for a few more minutes, but the conversation had never been better than 'stilted'. Yes, she thought, that described it perfectly, 'stilted'. It was almost as if he wanted to get off the phone. Oh well, he would be back that evening, and they could resume where they had left off. She had grinned that morning as she entered the kitchen and seen the bare bricks in the wall where he had finished battering down the old plaster. She thought it actually looked quite nice as it was, the old bricks giving a very rustic look to the room. Perhaps they could cover them with clear varnish and hang some sort of giant kitchen clock. Perhaps.

The walk was reviving her spirits and her brain, and she could already sense a burgeoning inventiveness in the phrases that were occurring to her to add to the lecture. She had walked about a mile and a half she reckoned, making sure to bear to the left whenever she was unsure of the path. In this way she knew that eventually she would end up back at the cottage, or at worst, at the lane. It was an old navigational trick invented, she thought, by some around the world sailor, or even an old pioneering flyer. You 'aimed to miss'. Robert had explained it to her once. He had read about it and as was usual when he was excited about something he had wanted to explain it to her in detail immediately. She smiled now as she remembered his enthusiasm.

"Look," he had said, his hands waving as he spoke. "Say you are flying from one island to another. The island is thirty miles away and you have the bearing, say 180 degrees or due south. After thirty miles if you cannot see the island, what do you do? The wind may have blown you off course but which way? Do you turn left or right and hope you find it before your fuel runs out?"

He had waited for her to answer but she had dutifully shaken her head. "No idea."

He had grinned. "Exactly, you don't know and if you get it wrong you could die. So, you *aim to miss.* You aim well to the left of your destination, in this instance say 160 degrees, then when your instruments tell you that you have covered thirty miles you turn right, and sooner or later you *must* hit the island." His grin was infectious, and she smiled to herself now as she remembered. "Simple, eh?"

Well, that was the theory. Whether it worked or not would become apparent shortly. She had no idea where she was and just trudged on, hoping to spot something that looked familiar soon. She was getting a little tense now, and the thought of a steaming mug of hot coffee was inviting. She had been keeping her eyes lowered to the ground to avoid tripping over tree roots or fallen branches but now as she raised her head, she was grateful to see the roof of the cottage through the trees and bushes. Fantastic, Robert's theory had worked in practice. Then she froze to immobility and stared.

Standing at the edge of the garden, just outside the fence, her back to Jane, was the woman in the voluminous grey gown again. She was staring intently at the upper windows of the cottage as if she hoped someone would look out from them, and so great was her absorption that she was unaware that Jane was only some twenty yards behind her.

Perhaps she's in one of these re-enactment groups, she thought. The woman's clothes looked very authentic with the homespun and slightly amateurishly put-together look of the times that she had seen on the occasional surviving garment that she had seen in museums. She knew there were reenactment societies around who took authenticity very seriously, and she might be a member of such a group. *Or perhaps…* and here Jane felt a shiver of apprehension, *perhaps she's just a nutter.*

Jane stood for long moments unsure of what exactly to do, then deciding that this was silly she called out, "Hello! Can I help you? My name's Jane, and I live here."

The woman gave a start and turned around to stare. Jane could see that she was young and beautiful. Her deep-set dark eyes were especially striking, and she was struck by the wing of glossy black hair that had escaped from the small white bonnet the girl wore. This young woman was very stunning in an intense way.

A pheasant that had been skulking in a hawthorn bush just behind Jane suddenly took fright, alarmed by her proximity, and with a loud clatter of wings on branches, and a raucous screeching cry took flight, frightening Jane, who called out in shocked surprise and held up her hands to her face.

As quickly as it had appeared the bird was gone, and Jane, her heart still beating madly, looked back to where the woman in grey had been standing, about to apologise for her shout. There was no one there. No one at all.

****

Chapter Eight.

Paul sat back gratefully, feeling his back muscles relax, and stretched out his long legs beneath the modern steel and wood desk, to restore the circulation. He felt a little bemused and overwhelmed with the information that he had been assimilating during the last two hours, whilst studiously making notes in the child's exercise book that he had purchased earlier. Pages and pages were now covered in his erratic script. His writing had never been easily readable – Marion had always chided him about it, but trying to write quickly and with a cheap biro as an implement had not helped.

He leaned back his head, feeling his neck bones crack and stared up at the white sectioned ceiling above his head. The shielded strip lights gave off a fantastic white illumination that was very useful when studying, but not easy on the eyes after two hours. He rubbed his forehead vigorously and massaged the corners of his eyes. He needed to take a break and get a coffee.

He shut down the computer screen he had been crouched over, closed the exercise book with a snap and stood to move away. The teenage girl who was at the next screen grinned up at him conspiratorially.

"Had enough?" she chortled. Her red hair tied in two plaits reached down to her waist and she ran her hands down one of them in what was obviously a nervous gesture, as she had finally plucked up the courage to speak to the tall, handsome man in the faded jeans and white t-shirt who had been deep in his own research when she had arrived an hour ago.

"Yeah! For the moment," smiled Paul. "Where's the café, do you know? I'm in dire need of caffeine."

She waved a hand towards a door in the far wall of the large open plan reading room in which the computers were standing in serried ranks.

"Over there through that glass door," she said, "and just down the corridor. It's called 'The owl and the pussycat café' – can you believe it?" She hiccupped a laugh which Paul echoed.

"Ok, thanks." As he moved away, he said, "I haven't finished yet. I'll probably be back." He groaned theatrically. "God save us."

She laughed again and watched him wistfully through her long false eyelashes as he moved away.

Paul had been amazed at the size of this place as he arrived earlier. He had been expecting an old, red-brick Victorian building full of small, cosy dark corners and dusty archives to be acting as the main Exeter Library and was not ready for the large two-storey purpose-built construction of glass and steel that gleamed in the sunlight. As he entered the auditorium, he had noted that the building boasted not only a café, but meeting rooms that were for hire, study rooms, a tearoom, and computer rooms, with a separate children's library and a 'teens' area.

He saw on the crammed notice boards that courses such as 'creative writing' and 'satellite science' were regularly available along with 'tea and chat' meetings, and he supposed after a cursory glance, any number of other activities. He had forgotten, of course, that it would be the 'county library' and a titular centre for all manner of county activities. Nevertheless, he was impressed.

The prettier of the pair of meticulously made up, twenty-something young women at the reception desk had studiously listened to his request for guidance and advised him as to what to look for. Feeling slightly ridiculous, he had stated that he was attempting to find whatever details he could about a small village near Dartmoor back in the mid sixteen-hundreds, and especially the resident clergymen at that time.

He thought for a moment that she was going to scoff at him and summarily dismiss him with a platitude about 'checking on their computer records', which he would find online. But surprisingly, she had not. Perhaps it was the slightly unusual request which interested her, or perhaps it was a willingness to help the good-looking, tall blond man who had leaned over her desk on an otherwise dull morning.

She had made a few notes in a meticulous hand on a number of yellow post-it sheets which she handed to him and told him to look, among other places, in the registers of wills, church deeds, church registers, parochial records, and even the Domesday Book, which would provide details about the numerous villages in the region. She had also recommended a tome called 'The visitations of Devonshire'. This, along with the records of Devonshire industries in the 17th century, had left him a little nonplussed. So, after thanking her profusely ,he had sauntered off to find a spare screen and an empty desk. That was two hours ago, and he now knew rather more than he needed to about the medieval and 17th century industries of Devon. To be fair, he had been surprised that large-scale silver, and lead mining were prevalent, as was tin mining, which he had always assumed was only endemic in Cornwall further south. But he had no idea that a large-scale pottery industry had thrived with much of the product being exported to the 'New world' from ports such as Exeter, Dartmouth, and Barnstaple, and a similar industry of wool and cloth production was once a major income earner for the county, as were the many lime kilns producing raw materials for the construction of roads and dwellings. Parts of Devon back then must have been smoke-filled and barren industrial areas. He made assiduous and copious notes but was not sure if any of this would be useful or indeed of interest to Jane. After all, he was only interested in the so called 'Grey Lady' and wanted to find out more about her, so that he might impress Jane, whom he liked a lot. He grinned as these thoughts loomed in his mind and shook his head in mock despair at his own foolishness.

His life since moving to this part of the country, largely to forget his tragedy, had settled into a rather dull monotony punctuated by periods of intense sadness, and the occasional flare of interest in subjects that took his fancy. His keenness to get to know Jane and Robert a little better had driven his actions recently and it was important for him at this moment to be able to tell Jane more about the 'Grey Lady'.

He found the café without difficulty and ordered a large latte and a Danish, which he carried to a spare table and slumped thankfully down to enjoy them. As he took his first bite of the pastry, Marion's voice spoke with the old, well-loved voice he remembered so well.

"You'll get fat eating that stuff, and I don't want to be stuck with an unfit, wheezing portly git when I'm old."

Despite the ache of sadness that surged through him as he remembered, he grinned and spoke in a low voice to himself.

"Sorry, love," he said, "but I do love them so."

He grinned foolishly at the tabletop and suppressed a rush of the tears that he always felt were just below the surface. He remembered a line from some speech in a film that he had seen. 'As you get older in life, things get taken away from you, that's part of life'. He knew now how true that was. Gently, he shook his head to dispel the ghosts, and taking a sip of coffee, opened his exercise book to scan through his notes.

He had discovered more about the 'blood and thunder' clergyman who had seemingly appeared from nowhere in the mid-1660s and caused a stir in the village and the neighbourhood for a couple of years. He smirked as he read the name again. Nehemiah Morton, he thought. You couldn't make it up could you. Where on earth did a moniker like that come from?

This chap was apparently a real piece of work, the witchfinder general type who frequented Europe in those troubled times. England, in particular, was rife with religious intolerance and almost barbaric savagery. The country was only just beginning to recover from years of civil war, and as a result, subversion and unrest were never far away.

He had always considered himself an intelligent and moderately knowledgeable sort of bloke, but he admitted to being a little shocked by what he had learnt that morning about this green and pleasant land only a little over three hundred years ago. A country in which you could be fined for swearing, or gambling, or even non-attendance at church. Where you could be placed in the stocks or the pillory and be pelted with offal, faeces, or rubbish just for drunkenness, or argumentative behaviour. Where you could be publicly whipped for adultery, or affray.

He shook his head again as he re-organised his random notes into something like order.

Hanging was the regular punishment for many crimes back then, almost one hundred of them including murder, poaching, smuggling, arson, or witchcraft. It was a time when women were a particular target for the authorities and especially the church. The law allowed a woman who was deemed to be a scold to have some sort of iron mask affair fitted to her head and left there for many days. The 'scold's bridle' as it was called was commonplace and quietly accepted by a largely docile and obedient rural population, steeped as it was in myth and superstition. God was very real, and so was the devil in all his forms. Dreams foretold disasters, and licentious women were seen as the devil's minions who tempted men from the path of righteousness.

Women who were accused of adultery could be paraded around the town or village in a cart for all to see and yell at, or in some cases throw things at. Worst of all was the so called 'ducking stool' in which a woman accused of a crime was strapped into a chair at the end of a cantilevered arm and ducked, possibly several times, into water until she 'repented of her sins'. Occasionally, this so-called punishment led to the death of the unfortunate recipient.

Yes, thought Paul, the last couple of hours had proved to be a sobering and slightly shocking experience. Of course, he had seen the dainty little line drawings in lots of children's books as he was growing up depicting many of the punishments that he was reading about that morning, but these antiseptic little illustrations did not portray the full horror of the punishments, or the fact that they were carried out within the law, and with the full compliance and acceptance of the people.

He shook his head again and took another sip of coffee. He needed to step back a little from this – it was getting to him.

A hand touched his shoulder, and he looked up to see the pretty receptionist from earlier smiling down at him. She was a petite slim blonde, her hair cut into a stylish bob, who had obviously taken care to apply her makeup sparingly before spending the day greeting members of the public.

"Sorry to bother you," she said. "I went up to the reading room to find you, but a young girl told me you had come to the café."

"He smiled back at her. "No problem," he said. "I just needed to stretch my legs and come back from the 17th century for a few minutes."

She nodded and squatted on the chair opposite him. "Yeah, I know what you mean." She laughed. "When I was studying, I used to forget the time and suddenly you realise you're tired, and hungry, and in need of a drink."

They both chuckled.

"Uni?" he queried.

"Oh yes," she nodded, "Cardiff. You need a degree to get a job as a librarian. Any degree, not necessarily in English or English lit."

He nodded sympathetically and smiled. "I hardly dare to ask."

"Sports science," she interrupted, and they both laughed again.

She had a small leather-bound book in her hands that looked old and battered, and he glanced at it with interest.

"Anyway," she said. "After you left, I suddenly remembered this little tome that many people have enjoyed since I came here. It's never allowed out of the library but it's a regular when local people are asking for a book to read in the reference section. I thought it might be of interest to you".

She pushed the shabby little book across the table to him and grinned at him.

"Make sure you give it back to me at the desk before you leave or I'm for it. OK?"

He nodded as she arose and moved off.

"That's very nice of you. Thanks. I'll make sure to get it back to you." She smiled winningly and waved away his thanks.

He could not help but watch her as she pirouetted away between the tables, her green and red gypsy-style skirt swirling around her slim legs, her high heels clacking on the floor.

Come on Paul, mate,' he said to himself. *Get a grip, she's years younger than you.* It was over two years since Marion had died, and he only felt now that he could muse on the opposite sex without dishonouring her memory. He smirked and continued to watch as she flounced through the door of the café. She was attractive, there was no doubt, and he gazed at her until with a last look and a wave in his direction, she disappeared. Then he remembered the book and his smile died as he looked down at it.

It was probably a collector's piece, he acknowledged and should really be photographed or committed to microchip before it fell apart completely. The documents had been collected and edited in 1867 by a Reverend Josiah Walton of Ashburton in the county of Devon and it was really a cataloguing of a collection of old broadsheets and early single-sheet news items that the Reverend had obviously hunted down and collected during his long tenure as a vicar.

It covered all facets of rural life during the 16th, 17th and 18th centuries in Devon, and Josiah mentioned in his introduction that he hoped at some stage to transform them into a parochial history of the county. Clearly, he had not found the time to do this, but this single copy of his collection had somehow survived and was of great interest to old academics over one hundred and fifty years later.

Paul leafed through the pages idly, realising he would have to come back to this library to study this book in far more detail, given the small amount of time he had left today. He knew he must be leaving in a short while to make sure he was on time to conduct evensong in his cosy little church. He took a note of the title, and the ISBN number and would get the name of the vivacious young librarian as he handed it back. She would remember which book this was when he asked for it again.

He was just about to close the book and begin to move when a phrase caught his eye. It was a church record for the area in which his village was.

Anno Domini 1666. In this year the Reverend Nehemiah Morton was guided by God to this county and took unto himself the spiritual guidance of the local God-fearing parish of Stanleigh Barton. Great and holy works were done by him guided as he was by the sacred word of the Lord and aided in his endeavours by his God-fearing and obedient wife Cecily Morton, who was esteemed by God and this parish to always wear only grey garments in homage, deference, and subservience to the Good Lord.

Printed at the sign of the Black Horse in Exeter, September 1675

Despite the sickening and self-righteously pompous statements that he had just read, Paul felt a surge of elation and self-congratulation. He had not wasted this morning. He had found her. He knew who the grey lady was. He could tell Jane that she had really existed, and her name had been Cecily Morton.

****

Chapter Nine

The dulcet, rich-brown, super-smooth voice of Jack Johnson was crooning from the little speakers above their heads. The mood of somnolent relaxation was palpable, and Jane once more told herself that this had been a good idea. They were sitting at a little outside café on the wide, paved promenade, enjoying the fresh air. The benign sea in the bay glittered benevolently in the morning sunlight and seemed to add an extra reflected haze to the blue sky above. The breeze was warm, and you could almost feel their stress and angst oozing away into the morning air.

She and Robert had been so busy since the move that they had lost each other a little, and yesterday it had been especially noticeable that their relationship was a little strained for the first time in their marriage.

Nothing that she could put her finger on, but he had seemed distracted and unable to concentrate on anything that she said throughout the day. Her remarks about seeing this grey woman again had completely passed him by, and she did not have the energy to explain again. Also, there was the washing machine incident. Was she reading too much into that? Possibly. But it was so unlike him. She was not aware that he even knew how to use the thing, let alone pile the entire suitcase full of the clothes that he had taken to London into it and set it on a quick wash. Her surprise had not been feigned as she descended the stairs into the kitchen yesterday morning to find the thing droning away in the corner, as Robert tapped away busily on his laptop.

"Morning, old thing," he had said breezily. "There's coffee in the percolator. I couldn't find the regular stuff, so I opened that packet of Columbian that you brought with us. I found it in the cupboard."

"Er, thank you sweetheart," she had managed, peering at him to assess his mood. "Everything OK?"

"Yep fine," he replied looking up from the screen., "Just got a fair bit to do following the meeting. I'm telling you this could really set me on my way, and the money will make a real difference to us". He rubbed his hands together with glee and self-satisfaction and she could not help but laugh, so infectious was his mood.

But, she mused, now as she sat in the sunshine outside of the promenade café in Torquay sipping her second mocha, something was not quite right, was it? Call it feminine intuition, or a wife's complete symbiosis with her life partner, but it was all rather odd.

Finally, after a day of stunted and fractured conversations verging on the awkward, she had suggested that they take the day off and spend it together. His work could wait, and her lecture notes were almost complete, so what the hell. The South Devon coast was less than an hour from the cottage, and they would be far more effective and focused if they relaxed for twenty-four hours and just enjoyed each other's company.

He had agreed, albeit a little reluctantly, but she just put this down to his boyish enthusiasm to get on, following the successful meeting in the city and the likelihood that his plans would be accepted and taken up by the property development company that he had been courting for too long.

She looked across at him now as he perched on the wooden bench opposite staring out to the far horizon. The problem was that when anyone, let alone someone you knew well, was wearing sunglasses, as Robert was, it made it almost impossible to read their thoughts.

The eyes were windows to the soul, isn't that what they said? And it was so true. She had conducted a meeting herself last summer with a university professor who was in charge of recruiting temporary lecturers at a prestigious art college, and he had insisted on meeting at his house where his wife had prepared a jug of lemonade and scones and jam in the garden. It had been a very tricky and almost one-sided conversation as he had worn dark wraparound sunglasses which gave her no indication at all as to what he was thinking.

A large seagull flew very close to her as it searched for titbits, the proximity of its flapping wings startling her, and she brought her thoughts back to the present.

"Ooh blimey!" she laughed. "That made me jump."

He grinned across at her. "Bloody things," he said. "They can be a real pain, especially in places like this. I think St Ives further south in Cornwall has a real problem with people eating outdoors." He lifted his diminutive expresso cup to his mouth and took a tiny sip.

"Are you OK?"

"Yep fine." She smiled. "Just gave me a start, that's all. What shall we do now?"

"Well, this was your idea," he said, "What's on your itinerary? I have to say though, that this is great. Well, done, old thing. We haven't sat and relaxed like this for too long. It's good to recharge the batteries".

"I thought we both needed it," she said. "You looked distinctly peaky yesterday, and you were very distracted, away with the fairies."

He shifted in his seat uncomfortably. "Really? I hadn't noticed. It's just so close now, I don't want to bugger it all up by not being prepared for anything."

She looked around at the small boats meandering gently across the bay, overtopped by the azure dome of the sky, pocked as it was with occasional little white fluffy clouds, and decided to pose a question that she had been wanting to ask since he arrived home, tired and irritable the night before last.

"What did you do during the evenings in London? I tried to call a couple of times but mostly it went straight to answerphone."

He glanced quickly up at her and removed his sunglasses to rub the bridge of his nose. "Nothing," he said. "Just had a bite to eat in the hotel dining room and then sat and watched TV in my room. Why do you ask?"

She felt a small flare of irritation despite herself. "It's called conversation, Robert," she said tartly. "You should try it sometime."

He seemed to mull over this comment and then grinned broadly. "Yep, you're right," he laughed. "Sorry, old thing. Just a bit tired, that's all."

He reached over to her, offering his hand. "Friends?"

She smiled back at him and took the offered hand. "Friends," she said. She realised that he had deftly and expertly moved the conversation on from his activities in London but decided to let it lie. Standing, she smoothed down the yellow summer dress that she was wearing despite the earliness of the season. "Come on, let's do something. I'm sick of just sitting here."

"OK," he said, standing himself. "How about we catch the ferry across the bay to Brixham? It would be nice to be on the water and it looks so welcoming. We'll have to make arrangements to get Hissing Sid down here."

"Oh God," groaned Jane. "What have I done now?"

They both laughed. *That's better,* she thought, *he's laughing, we're laughing. Much better.*

"Hey, I know what we'll do this afternoon," he said as she linked her arm in his, feeling that this was like old times back when they first met.

"What?"

"We'll drive a bit further on to Plymouth. I want to show you the old pub that that woman who painted all those fat women used to frequent."

"Who? Beryl Cook?"

"Yep, that's her. The pub's in a lot of her paintings and it's still there exactly as it was. It's near the harbour. I was reading about it in a magazine. I thought at the time, Jane would like to see that."

"OK, it's a deal." She laughed. She did not like to tell him that she had already seen it but did not want to dispel this mood of matey bonhomie and togetherness. Perhaps he just needed to relax a bit; after all, this was more like it used to be.

They ambled slowly around the inner harbour, gazing at the bobbing boats tied in serried ranks to their mooring buoys. Many of them were festooned with scrim netting to keep off the ever-present gulls who could make a mess of a trim little craft in no time at all. Some had whirling wind-driven plastic or metal arms attached to their cabin roofs, their twirling making it impossible for a bird to land. It was still not mid-morning but already the pavements were cluttered with the advertising billboards of the many ice cream parlours, trinket shops, and cafes, all eager to take money from the tourists. It was already quite busy, and Jane recognised again how desperate people were to enjoy every moment of sunny days, heralding as they did the promise of summer after the long, dark winter.

She was enjoying herself. It had been too long since they had relaxed like this. The packing up of their old place, the move itself, and Robert's job, and her job to be honest, had all conspired to rush by ever more quickly, leaving the important things in life unnoticed.

She was still not quite at peace with the world. There was definitely something odd about Robert since he'd returned from London. He was distracted, on edge but disguising it well, and two or three times he had deleted incoming text messages as soon as he had read them. That was unlike him – he had been almost furtive.

He stopped and pointed at a postcard in the newsagent's window they were passing. It was a Beryl Cook painting of a group of large middle-aged people all completely naked enjoying afternoon tea in a garden. Each of the three or four women wore some sort of hat and seemed oblivious to the incongruity of it. He laughed out loud.

"That's a coincidence," he chuckled, "I only mentioned her a few minutes ago."

He looked down at her and smiled his old winning smile.

Jane hugged his arm closer to her and nodded in agreement. She was mentally chastising herself for her mood of disquiet. Of course there was nothing wrong, they were both a little tired and stressed, that was all. What was she thinking?

"Come on," she smiled. "We'll miss the ferry."

As they increased their pace and moved toward the harbour wall where the ferry was moored, she wondered why she had not mentioned anything at all to Rob about the woman in grey she kept seeing. She thought he might scoff and chide her for letting her imagination run away with her, and she did not want that conversation. She would certainly mention it to Paul the next time that she saw him – he would understand. Not only understand but be genuinely interested. There was some mystery there, some questions to be answered and just at this moment Rob was not in the right place mentally for her to bother him with it, and neither did she want to invite his ridicule, however well-intentioned it might be.

The ferry sounded its mournful horn, a signal to those intending to catch it that they had three minutes to board. They began to run.

****

Last night had been worse than usual. Nehemiah seemed driven in his love-making. What a misguided term that was, 'love-making', thought Cecily as she levered herself into a sitting position and lowered her legs to the floorboards, feeling the ache of fresh bruises, and pulled muscles. The bedsheets were a complete wreck and would all need to be laundered, spattered as they were now with the blood from her cut lip and the bite on her breast.

She sighed deeply and gazed out of the mullioned window at the light dappled yard. The sun had not long risen, and it was going to be a fine day. A small robin appeared on the window ledge in front of her and she watched as it craned its head this way and that trying to peer through the thick green-tinted glass. He had come before, and his inquisitiveness always brightened her day. Involuntarily, she smiled and as she did so the cut on her lip opened, and she winced in pain.

What was it that made her husband such a demon in bed? Was she doing something wrong? Did she not please him?

Margaret, who slept in a little room at the back of the house most of the time, must have heard his snarling, guttural voice as he called his wife the tool of the devil, and hell's spawn as he took her roughly time and again. He cared nothing for her own feelings and had informed her again that the good Lord had placed her in his path merely to serve his licentious needs. His work among these godless people was the task given to him by the Lord, a task that would require all of his strength and dedication. Meanwhile, his bodily needs must be assuaged, and she must never moan or complain about her lot ever again. Was that clear?

She had been slow to answer, either that or in the darkness he had not seen her head nod as she lay beneath him. Because it was dark she had not seen the blow coming and done nothing to move her face away from the stinging contact. The blood running down her cheek had seemed to excite him, and he had increased his thrusting efforts with zeal, chanting a psalm as he worked his way deep inside her repulsed body. His shout of triumph as he climaxed had come as a blessed relief to her when, as she had expected, he collapsed on to his back and was asleep within minutes. She would now have an hour or so to recover and maybe even snatch a few moments of rest herself.

As she endured the final assault, the grey light of dawn was gleaming outside the window, and she knew from previous experience that when she awoke again, he would be gone. 'About the Lord's work' as he often repeated, his litany totally impervious to any request that she might make.

Now as she sat on the edge of the bed feeling bruised and battered, the tears finally came. They ran unchecked down her cheeks and on to the floor. She could not stop them. She cried like a child, heaving and gasping for air as the spasms wracked her aching body.

Surely this was not how life should be? Surely God would not let her endure this for ever? She had never felt so alone. Her father, and sisters, if they still lived, were a full five days' journey away and had probably forgotten her by now. Margaret tried to be sympathetic, but she was a virtual stranger and apart from the instinctive care of one long-suffering woman for another, she could offer no comfort.

Gathering herself, Cecily dressed and bathed her face as best she could from the water bowl besides her bed and made her way slowly down the stairs. She did not want to face her servant just yet and moved slowly past the open kitchen door. Margaret looked up from kneading flour and seeing the hopeless, bereft look on Cecily's cut face began to move towards her. Cecily held up her hand to stop her.

"I'm going to sit outside for a short while, Margaret. Please let me be."

Margaret stopped and sighing resignedly, turned back to her kneading, albeit with added vehemence. There was wickedness in her eyes.

Cecily sat achingly down on to the bench just outside the back door and took three or four deep breaths. The morning air was clear and sharp and smelt of vegetation. There was the faint whiff of salt in the air from the sea, which in Devon was never far away.

She leaned her head back against the brick and closed her eyes. She could hear the birds singing and the rustle of the breeze amongst the trees that backed the yard. She began to feel a little better.

She was suddenly aware of a figure standing next to her and looked up into the concerned eyes of Thomas. He had padded silently down the corridor and emerged out of the door to stand at her side.

He was a servant, she knew that, but just at this moment they were merely two young people with just a couple of years' difference in age, and right at this moment she felt a deep empathy with him. He was older than his years and she younger, but at this moment such considerations did not matter. She was in need of comfort and seeing her face he was outraged.

He lowered his hand to her shoulder instinctively, without thought, in an unbidden gesture of caring from one young person to another. She looked down at the ground to hide her face, then gently reached up and held his hand.

Slowly, she leaned her head against his hip and closed her eyes.

Above her Thomas's face was white-lipped with restrained anger. He was trembling with rage.

"He'll not hurt you again, mistress," he managed through gritted teeth. "I vow it."

She smiled involuntarily. However improbable the promise was, she realised she had a paladin. Someone who cared. She was not alone. For the moment, this afforded her some comfort.

They stayed like this for a long time, frozen in a tableau of caring, each loath to break the spell of this incongruous moment.

He looked down at the top of her head and had to resist the overriding temptation to stroke her hair.

"Cecily," he breathed, and releasing her hand, gently squeezed her shoulder. "Cecily."

****

Chapter Ten

The ducks were cruising gently around the large pond in the centre of the village green, looking like a naval flotilla. A couple of drakes, their iridescent green-tinted heads nodding in unison as they paddled industriously, were followed by the rather drabber females, who clustered after them, chirruping their litany to the morning. A couple of idling coots watched them pass, their white-blazed heads registering their disdain at all this effort as they bobbed lazily in the wash from the passing fleet.

It was a pleasant scene and typical of a spring morning in an English country village. The birds in the trees behind Paul chorused a greeting to the day, and to complete the pleasant background noise, a cow lowed somewhere far off.

Paul was sitting on one of the weather-worn benches that surrounded the pond and was enjoying the mild heat from the spring sunshine. 'Lounged' would be a better description this fine morning. Dressed as usual in faded jeans and a black shirt and his dog collar, he had thrown on an old leather flying-type jacket that he had owned since his early twenties and in which he always felt at ease. Some echo of his carefree youth still seemed to emanate from this treasured article of clothing, and he luxuriated in the relaxed demeanour that he always felt when wearing it.

He had idly been throwing small pieces of bread to the small rival group of ducks that hovered near the bench, aware no doubt of the bounty that this position often brought forth. Always throwing it as far away as possible from their position, he enjoyed the sudden flurry of paddling feet and anxious quacking as they scurried to hoover the scraps up. Grinning mischievously, he noted with regret that his pockets contained no more crumbs. He always made sure he had a few such offerings about his person if he was going near to the pond.

He was feeling a little morose today. The past was more prevalent of late, and he kept seeing Marion's face whenever he closed his eyes, heard her voice in moments of silence. It had happened before, and would do so again, that he knew. He just had to work his way through it.

The weekend sermons had seemed to go well, and the Sunday afternoon christening had been stupendously attended by around forty people – some locals, but mainly relatives of the young couple whose child was the object of attention. Many of them had come from many miles away and it had been nice to see the crowded pews and hear their echoing chatter beneath the lofty arches of his normally quiet little church.

But that was yesterday, and he had not slept well last night and had decided on a walk before he settled to writing the eulogy for old Mr Thomas, a local farmer who had gone to meet his maker last week at the grand old age of ninety-five. He was going to make it an upbeat oratory about a long life well spent. God grant that we could all make it to such an esteemed age. He smiled to himself and looked around him at the cluster of houses and shops that surrounded the green.

It was still quite early, and he knew that whilst the younger members of the community would have left for their places of work some time ago, the older residents would not really be up and about yet.

He acknowledged that with every passing month he was feeling stronger, and more himself now. His troubled mind was recovering and beginning to function more normally. It would soon be time to mention to the bishop that perhaps his mid-life energy and drive might find more challenging employment in a larger town or city. He remembered that he was booked to judge a cake-making contest late that afternoon as the members of the local women's guild presented their baking efforts for his scrutiny and indeed taste. *God save us all* he thought, grinning ruefully to himself. *If my friends back in the day could see me know.*

"Penny for them, Paul."

He had not heard Jane come up behind him and gave a little start.

She touched his shoulder in apology. "Sorry," she said. "I didn't mean to startle you. I could see you were miles away."

He smiled up at her and moved up the bench a little, leaving a space for her to sit. She was dressed in jeans and a red knitted rollneck jumper, and the wicker basket over her arm showed that she was on a shopping expedition.

She sat and placed the basket on the ground beside her. "I've just come down to the village to get some vegetables, but old Mrs Andrews is still setting them out at the front of the shop, so I said I'd come back in a little while, then I saw you."

He nodded companionably and smiled. "No problem. I was indeed miles away."

"If I'm intruding, don't be afraid to tell me," she said. "I've a knack of sticking my nose in where it's not wanted."

He laughed out loud this time. "No, you're not, I promise you. I'm glad I've seen you anyway, I've got some news."

"Oh?" She settled herself a little further back on the bench to listen.

Why was this woman so damned good-looking as well as being a really nice person? he thought. He was at a vulnerable time in his life, he knew that, but his God set some wicked traps for the unwary along the way.

"Well," he began conspiratorially. "I went to the main library in Exeter a few days ago to see if I could find out more about our mysterious 'grey lady'."

"You didn't!" said Jane. Hugely interested in light of the latest viewing of her, which she had yet to tell Paul about, she was also keen to ask this good-looking vicar why he had done that, and was it out of interest himself or just to please her?

Paul had stopped and was staring at her intently. It was a long time since he had felt his heart pound merely because of the reaction on a woman's face to something he had done. A woman who was sitting close to him.

"Er yes," he said, struggling to gather his wits a little. "And I know who she was. Know her name, I mean. It suddenly makes them more human, doesn't it?"

"That's bloody marvellous. I can't believe you managed to do that, how clever of you. Tell me more."

Out of the corner of her eye she noticed that on the other side of the green the little post office-cum-café had opened, and the middle-aged woman who owned and ran it was placing a little billboard which advertised its delicacies on to the pavement.

"Come on," she said, picking up her basket and standing. "I'll stand you a coffee and you can tell me all. Have you got time?"

He stood up himself glad to stretch his long legs. "Yep, that would be great," he said, "I've had enough of watching ducks for today."

They both laughed and moved off across the green, chatting amiably. So engrossed in their conversation were they that they did not notice that standing amongst the small stand of trees behind the bench they had just vacated, was an intense, dark-haired young woman in a grey ,homespun, floor-length dress who was watching them intently.

****

It was a cold late spring day, the weather seeming to emphasise people's dark moods. Lowering clouds heavy with rain hung motionless just above the top of the church spire, its cockerel weathervane almost seeming to touch them.

A lifeless drizzle persisted as it had for most of the morning, and because of the lack of any breeze at all, the very air seemed damp and dank, smelling of decay and dirty water. The village pond looked drab and bereft of life, the flat, brown water pocked with rain drops.

Most of the village were here, it seemed, aimlessly standing around, loath to depart lest their blood-and-thunder vicar should spot their absence and loudly chastise them when next he laid eyes on them.

The mostly homespun clothes that the farm workers and villagers wore steamed slightly in the dank, lifeless air, and the aprons of the women among the crowd seemed scruffy and stained with mud or food. No one wanted to be there, but they had been ordered to by the Reverend Morton. At the end of his latest haranguing sermon last Sunday, which had been especially virulent, he had told the whole village that he expected their attendance today to witness God's punishment for a sinful woman.

His demands for that morning's procedure had been authorised by the local village council. The village elders had been overawed and cowed, as they always were by Nehemiah, during their last meeting. They had heard of such events to be enacted today, of course. Who had not in this year of our Lord, 1667? But no one had ever witnessed them.

Two farmers standing at the edge of the crowd muttered to each other in undertones as they awaited the arrival of the participants.

"'Tis my belief," said William Crowther, a stolid and ageing local landowner dressed in shabby workaday clothes, his battered brown hat drooping down the sides of his bald head, "That the Reverend's a little crazed, begging his pardon. But who can say no?"

His lifelong friend and fellow village council member Ezekial Taverner nodded sagely, his straggly grey hair flapping down to his shoulders.

"Aye, that be my belief too. But I'll not say it to any man but thyself, no sir, no I will not."

They both looked around them to check that no one was listening, but they need not have bothered. The local wives were whispering to each other in low and urgent mutters, their weatherbeaten, gaunt features pinched, damp in the drizzle, whilst their men were hopping restlessly from foot to foot or scratching themselves irreverently, wishing they were not there. There was work to be done.

"Some do say," continued William, "that our good Reverend was at Naseby fight those twenty years ago and the horror and bloodshed that he witnessed in the slaughter that day drove his wits from him. That be what I've heard anyhow."

Both men nodded sagely again, and leaning forward, Ezekial spat into the mud at his feet, studying the stained and scuffed gaiters that enclosed his legs below the knee.

"I've heard summat similar," he said. "Something like that could rob a man of his sanity. They do say it were a terrible blood-soaked carnage of a day and no mistake."

Ezekial's wife, who was standing just in front of them, turned her head, the white calico bonnet that she wore making it necessary for her to look straight at them.

"This is an abomination," she said. "Surely our good Lord would not want this?"

William nodded again and lowered his voice further. "Who can tell, sister. 'Tis ordered by the Reverend and that's all we can know."

There was a murmur throughout the crowd and heads craned to see as the church door opened and a sad little cavalcade spewed out. Nehemiah led the way, a look of gloating satisfaction bringing a smirk to his face beneath his ever-present wide-brimmed black hat. He was holding his Bible in both hands as if it were to be revered. Behind him came the leading member of the Village Council, old Ebenezer Merryman, his hands folded meekly on his belt. Then two burly labourers from Ebenezer's farm edged through the door holding young Martha Pennyford between them. She was a small woman of twenty-five but flanked by these two sturdy figures she looked like a child.

They all knew it was young Martha, but they could not see her face as it was now encased in metal. Following a chance and casual remark by her husband, young Phillip Pennyford, that his wife was forever criticising and chastising him, the charge of being a 'scold' had been levelled at her by Reverend Morton. He had singlehandedly pursued the charge and insisted that the village council order the local blacksmith, Martin Bagwell, to construct what was called throughout the land a 'scold's bridle'. Everyone had heard of such a device, but no one had ever seen one. It was fitted across the offending 'scold's' face and locked at the back of the head. They were of various designs, but this one was just two wide strips of metal fastened to a rudimentary frame. One band of metal went across her forehead and another similar band went across her mouth. Cruelly, the band across the mouth had another short strip facing inwards which was designed to fit into the unfortunate wearer's mouth and lay across the tongue. preventing them from speaking.

The terrified and tearful Martha had been sentenced arbitrarily by Nehemiah to wear it for today, in the hope that it would teach the offender the error of her ways. The council had little choice but to ratify the sentence.

Her young husband had been forced to go along with this farce but was not at all sure that he liked it or agreed with it. Loud and aggressive pressure from the council and the Reverend had prevented him from taking the matter further. He now stood at the edge of the crowd looking concerned and guilty.

The object of course was public humiliation. Young Martha fitted with the 'bridle' would be paraded around the village for all to see and learn from.

There was complete silence now, as Nehemiah raised his head and addressed the crowd in his loud, harsh voice known so well to the villagers.

"Witness ye all," he began, "That it is a sin against God for a woman to continually chastise her husband whom she has sworn before the altar and in the presence of God himself to love, to honour, and to OBEY."

Here he paused and glared around at the crowd, daring it seemed anyone to disagree with him. No one moved or spoke.

"Martha Pennyford, wife of this parish, shall wear the bridle and be walked around this hamlet for all to witness her shame. Moreover, she shall wear the bridle for the remainder of today until the sun do set, and it is hoped she will think on her sins before the Lord."

From somewhere at the back of the crowd a strong man's voice shouted,

"Shame!"

Nehemiah started with disbelief and peered through the drizzle in the direction of the cry.

"Who said that?" he demanded. "Who raises his voice against the decision of the Lord?"

The burly figure of Thomas shouldered his way to the front of the throng and stared insolently at the Reverend.

"I do, Reverend. I do." It was a challenge.

"I know thee," said Nehemiah, "and I know thee to be a quarrelsome and godless wretch who shall be shamed afore his maker."

"And what would you know about God, you rancid man?" snarled Thomas, his eyes blazing with anger. "Tell me Reverend, what does your vengeful Lord think of men who would raise their hands to defenceless women? What says the good book about wife beaters?"

"You question my judgments?" screamed Nehemiah. "How dare you. Beware lest my anger and vengeance be turned on you." He raised his eyes to the sky and intoned, "Oh Lord in thy beneficence ,allow me the patience to deal with doubters and unbelievers."

"You are an abomination. Satan has indeed walked the earth and this village since you arrived." Thomas's face was taut with anger, his lips white and bloodless.

The crowd en masse were shocked into silence. It was an age when men believed implicitly in the presence of God, in which the devil was real, and stalked the earth looking for souls to confound. It was an age that believed without question in witches, warlocks, and wizards. Steeped in myth, legends, and stories of God's wrath since the cradle, people were naive and childlike in their absolute beliefs. The clergy had the ear of the Lord and though they could be ofttimes misguided and their wisdom was not always popular, yet they must be obeyed.

Many of the throng now feared for Thomas and surged around him, partially to protect him from whatever lightning the Reverend's hands might conjure and throw at him, but also to wrestle and pull him back into anonymity among them.

Nehemiah was still shouting as the crowd hurriedly began to disperse before any further unnerving encounters.

"God and the serpent have joined hands here today," he yelled. "Do you not recall that Christ saved the world by suffering?"

Today was not proceeding as he had hoped. Turning, he pointed to the two men holding the still weeping Martha. "Walk that wretch around the village so that all may witness her penance."

The men nodded and half prodding, half carrying the young woman began to follow Nehemiah's instructions, but they were unsure as to why because everyone in the village it seemed had seen all they needed to of God's justice today. The green was emptying swiftly, leaving the centre of the village to be populated only by the chickens and geese that were always in residence there.

Nehemiah took a last look around the now largely deserted green and with a hiss of anger, turned and stalked back into his church. He decided that he would tell his wife a very different version of events when he returned home. She had not been present today, forbidden to attend by him as he did not want awkward questions about the cuts and bruises on her face. But that young minion of Satan who had so publicly challenged him would be denied access to the vicarage forever on pain of his mother's employment. That would do for starters in his retribution.

He needed to pray. Needed instruction from the Lord God. He slammed the old Norman door behind him.

****

Surprisingly, the coffee was quite good. Paul and Jane had both selected a latte from the little printed card and been amazed when they were brought to the table in long glass cups, each sporting a long-handled spoon.

It was a pleasant space to sit in. The floor was made of bare, recently stripped boards which had been stained and varnished. The walls were painted a uniform pale cream whilst the tables and chairs were all a pale olive green, topped by green gingham tablecloths. The walls were festooned with tasteful little watercolours by local artists, and all of them seemed for sale. Here and there interspersed with these were prints of paintings by Gustav Klimt, their gold colours gleaming. As he looked, Paul remembered that the proprietor had briefly been to art college in Taunton back in the seventies, and she still, it appeared, had a keen eye.

"Well, well," chortled Paul gazing after the retreating figure of old Prudence the waitress, her back bent like an old tree on the moor. "That's a surprise, I have to say."

Muted and relaxing jazz from Miles Davis played from a hidden speaker in the corner. It was all most unexpected.

He lifted the cup to his mouth and took a sip, leaving a frothy smear on his upper lip as he replaced the cup on to the table. He wiped it off with a practised gesture.

"Hmm," he began. "It tastes good too. I must come here again."

Jane smiled at him and raised her own cup in salute. "Here's hoping," she said.

She took a sip and replaced the cup. "My God, you're right. Oh, sorry, no sacrilege intended."

They both laughed in unison.

"Everything OK, my dears?" Alice Pennyford had appeared at the table again.

"Excellent, thank you Alice," nodded Paul. "I'm not sure if you've met Mrs Croyland. She and her husband have moved into the old vicarage house up the lane." He looked across at Jane. "This is Alice Pennyford, the owner of this establishment." He grinned amiably. "Alice is from one of the oldest families in the village."

"Jane," said Jane, extending her hand for shaking. "Call me Jane."

Alice took her hand but held on to it as she gazed down at Jane. "Yes," she said. "There've been Pennyfords in this village for hundreds of years. Settling in, are you? The last pair that had that house, can't remember their name now, they didn't stay long and weren't that sociable anyhow, never seemed to like it there."

"Er yes, thank you. It's a lovely, friendly little place".

"Well, welcome anyway." Alice smiled. "I hope you'll be very happy here. Call in anytime, there's always a nice cup of coffee for you." Without waiting for an answer, she released Jane's hand and turned away to serve a new customer who had just arrived.

Rather nonplussed by the sudden departure, Jane shook her head slightly and returned her gaze to Paul.

"So," she said, leaning her elbow on the table. "What have you found out?"

"Well! Her name for starters. I know the name of the Grey Lady. She was real and she existed. She was called Cecily Morton, and she was married to the local vicar."

"Cecily," repeated Jane. "What a lovely, quaint old name."

"Yep, I thought so too. Life wasn't so quaint or lovely for her apparently, though. She was married to the real blood-and-thunder merchant I've mentioned before. Saw himself as the arm of the Lord, you know the type."

"Thankfully not."

"And here's the kicker," grinned Paul. "She lived in your house".

Jane went a little pale. "Oh, bloody hell. Seriously?"

"Yep, I kid you not. There's also a mystery somewhere in this, you can tell from the little I have read about her, omissions in the old bits of info I've found."

From the other side of the café, two old ladies in coats and hats waved across.

"Morning, Vicar, lovely day."

"Yes, isn't it? Morning, ladies." He raised his hand to them and grinned.

"You were saying something about a mystery?" continued Jane.

Paul took another sip of his coffee. "This really is very good. Yep, I need to go back to the library at Exeter again. One of the young receptionists was very helpful and came up with an informative tome just before I left, so I hardly had the chance to study it properly."

Jane chortled mockingly. "So is it the book or the receptionist you need to see again?"

"Behave. The book of course."

"This is all sounding very mysterious." Jane suddenly became serious. "I've seen her again," she began. "Our woman in grey. I meant to tell you."

Paul could tell that beneath the urbane attempt at levity, Jane was quietly perturbed about this woman. It was fine discussing a possible phantom whilst sitting in a picturesque coffee shop in broad daylight, but did she really want to know anymore, particularly as she was often alone in the house?

Do ghosts exist? thought Jane, a little shocked at her own casual admission that she had had another sighting. *No of course not, get a grip*, she told herself. She realised that Paul was speaking again.

"Where?" he said. "Where did you see her?"

"The other day. I couldn't settle to Jan Van Eyck and Vermeer so needed to clear my head and went for a stroll in the wood behind our place. It did the trick, it was lovely. But then as I got back to the house, she was suddenly there in front of me, standing looking over the fence at the house. I could see her as clearly as I can see you now."

Paul did not know what to say. His whole training and indeed belief screamed at him to dismiss this information as nonsense, that it was merely a projection of her own imagination, to tell this new friend of his not to be so silly, but somehow, he could not. He had spoken with too many locals who claimed to have seen the woman in grey, and as far as he could ascertain from their brief friendship, Jane was not some empty-headed housewife type who would be gullible in the face of something unexplained.

"I see," he managed. Then realised there was something he should ask. "Did she say anything?"

Jane looked wide-eyed at him and laughed. "What?" she gasped. "Of course not. What sort of a question is that?"

They both laughed and Paul shrugged at his own idiocy. "Sorry." he said meekly. "But you never know."

"I'm not sure what I believe about this anymore," Jane said after another sip of coffee. "You read magazine articles about timeslips, and other cross-dimensional events. Some people think that everything that has happened is still happening now, and occasionally the timelines overlap, or open." She shook her head, a little dismayed that they were actually having this conversation. "Oh, who the hell knows?" she said. "Three months ago, in London I would have laughed in derision and scoffed at the pair of us."

He nodded companionably and smiled. "Well, I know what you mean. Things like this go expressly against my teaching, and indeed my calling, but I do intend to find out the facts or this. The truth about who this woman was and what happened to her. Call it the latent detective in me."

"And keep me informed, will you?" She instructed him dismissively, not wishing to discuss this matter any further today. "Shall we have another coffee? Then I really must go."

Fresh coffees ordered and delivered, they chatted on for some minutes about inconsequential things as casual friends do, until finally Jane lifted her basket and stood.

"I'm sorry but I've got to go. You know how it is." She lifted her hand in the universal gesture of apostrophes. "People to see, things to do."

He laughed and stood also. "Thanks for the coffee, Jane, I've really enjoyed our chat."

"Me too," she said. "We must do it again."

"I'll pop over to Exeter tomorrow and see what more I can find out about our mysterious femme fatale. Next time we meet I can hopefully shed some more light. I'm not keen on these appearances though." His face became serious. "As a man of the cloth, I'm not sure what my stance is on things like this. By the way, I've always meant to apologise for slapping your friend down a little about the séance she wanted."

"Oh, don't worry about Sue," said Jane as they emerged out on to the green again. "She's a tough cookie. I think, well, I know she was more than a little tipsy that night, and you were quite right anyway. No way do I want a bloody séance in my new house, especially when I'm there on my own sometimes."

He touched her arm. "OK, understood. Anyway, see you soon." He turned and strode off across the green.

Jane watched him go then suddenly realised that she still had the empty wickerwork basket over her arm and had not yet purchased anything. With a tut of irritation, she ambled off down towards the greengrocers.

Chapter Eleven

Five days later and Jane was trying to spend Saturday morning for unbroken and undisturbed work on her coming lecture on the aptly named 'Northern Renaissance'. If you asked her what had kept her away from it for these last three days, she would have been hard pressed to remember. Of course, there was the day off that she and Robert had allowed themselves to spend at the coast, but that aside, what on earth had she done with the time?

She remembered fondly the coffee with Paul in the village but apart from that, nothing. She guessed that most people had times in their life when they just floundered from one day to the next but not her – well at least not until recently anyway. This morning on rising she had given herself a stern lecture and told herself that she really must go a long way to finishing the first draft of this bloody lecture by the end of today.

She had been moderately successful so far, despite the best efforts of Robert to make as much noise as possible in the kitchen as he carried on with his 'renovation' work. His cursing and shouting vied with the hammering and banging, all backed by the booming radio.

Her efforts to keep the noise and dust out of the lounge had meant closing the door fully and playing some muted Monteverdi from the laptop's sound library.

She was getting there. She had spent the last ten minutes studying the picture of Johannes Vermeer's Delft townscape and attempting to organise her thoughts about the 17th century Dutch painter. She followed the current thinking that the great man had painted such serene and calming mundanity, however deceptively constructed, as an escape from his own hectic family existence. He was known to have fathered eleven children with his wife Catharina Bolnes. In fact, some scholars put the figure at between thirteen and fourteen. "He can't have had a telly," grinned Jane as she typed. His mother-in-law, the indomitable Maria Thins, also lived with them, or perhaps it was more accurate to say they lived with her as it was in fact her house. The hen-pecked Vermeer had also been coerced into looking after the many business interests of his formidable mother-in-law.

Poor bugger, she thought. No wonder he wanted to find peace and solace in his paintings. *It is no coincidence* she typed *that most of the serene figures in his very domestic and deceptively simple paintings of the mid 1600s were pregnant women. It was what he was used to.*

She went on to elucidate two more paragraphs about his superb use of light and shade, before the lounge door banged open and a very dusty Robert grinned in at her, his teeth very white against the grime covering his face.

"Come and have a look at this, old thing." His jeans and t-shirt were clogged with dust, and she bit back a retort about the mess he had just walked into the room. She did not like to quash his evident childlike glee at whatever he had discovered.

She sighed and rolled her eyes theatrically before standing. "OK," she said. "I could do with a coffee anyway. Lead on, Macduff."

He laughed out loud, and they tramped into the ruins of what had once been her kitchen. Hammers, chisels and a large mallet rested on old newspapers that covered the kitchen table underneath a thick coating of fresh dust. The stoneflagged floor was a minefield of stone and plaster fragments ready to trip the unwary.

"Oh, bloody hell, Rob," she began. "What on earth? I hope you're going to clear this up. You might at least have opened the window."

He laughed loudly and beckoned her over to the end wall, which was now almost completely shorn of plaster, the bare brickwork showing through from one side of the room to the other.

"Of course I will, old thing," he chortled. "Don't be such a killjoy. Now look at this, I knew I was right".

He swept his hand across one end of the wall as if he were a magician introducing his female helper on to the stage.

She peered closely and could see nothing. "What?" she grimaced.

He gave a tut of irritation and pointed at a small wooden lintel still in situ amongst the brickwork at just above head height, which was all that was left of what had obviously been a small door.

"There's another room behind here," he announced gleefully. "I bloody knew it. I told you so, you, doubting Thomas." He grinned again, preening shamelessly at his vindication.

"Oh," said Jane, trying to appear enthusiastic. "How big a room?"

"Well. It will only be small, and it can't have any windows," mused Robert, scratching his head reflectively. "Didn't they used to have large pantries in those days which were always kept cold and dark to store, oh I don't know, milk, or cheese or some such, meat, beer if they had it? I'm sure I've read about it in the past. I think they sometimes called it the buttery, or the still room."

"God knows. You should know, you're the architect."

Poking through the dusty detritus on the work surface beneath the window, Jane found the kettle and filled it before plugging it into the wall.

"Let's have a coffee. So, what are you going to do now?"

Robert was a little miffed at his wife's lack of any real interest.

Hadn't he said as soon as they moved into the place that there was an inconsistency between the inside wall of this room and the outside wall? He'd spotted it right off and now he had been proved correct. The very least she could do was to say, "Oh you were right, how clever of you." But no, not Jane – what had she said?

"Let's have a coffee.". Bloody woman. What was it they said about a prophet never being appreciated in his own land?

He perched on the edge of one of the kitchen chairs and gazed lovingly at his discovery. It was obviously a door into the other room that he had uncovered. You could see that the brickwork used to cover it up was different. Different bricks, different mortar, and put on by someone who was no craftsman, that was for sure. However amateurish it was, he acknowledged that the bloody bricks had stayed in place for well over three hundred years. Well, it just went to show.

"Here you go, my hero." Jane placed a steaming mug of black coffee on to the table in front of him. "Get that down you."

"Cheers." He grinned at her, his brief mood of churlish annoyance dispelled.

Jane sat down opposite him and decided she would finish her coffee here instead of taking it back into the lounge, as she could do with a rest from the Dutch painters. She had opened the windows, so the dust was gradually dissipating.

"When is it you go to London again?"

Taken off guard, Robert started and peered at his wife to see if there was any hidden meaning to her question, but he decided not.

"Tuesday morning. Sorry old thing, I'll be away for the night as well. But if all goes to plan, I'll be back Wednesday evening."

"Will you see Brian and Sue whilst you are there?"

It was an innocent enough question, but the mention of Sue's name startled him, and it took him some moments to think of an answer.

"I shouldn't think so. Don't think I'll have time. You never know, but I doubt it. Why?"

Jane shook her head dismissively. "No reason. Just asking."

Was he being furtive? She thought he was looking distinctively shifty. Yes, that was the word, 'shifty'.

"I must give them a ring," she said. "I Haven't spoken to them since they came here. I think Sue was a bit pissed off with me that morning before they left."

"Sue? Why?"

"The only thing I could think of was my refusing to have that bloody séance that she kept pressing for."

Rob gave a derisive laugh. "Oh bloody hell, I'd forgotten that. Your mate the vicar was not keen either, was he?"

"No. Strictly against his calling. In fact, I thought he was very patient with her. She was a bit of a pain all night, and she did not hide it very well that she fancied him."

Rob looked up from his coffee. "Fancied him? The vicar?"

"Oh yeah." Jane nodded. "Take it from me. She told me as much. I think she's been a bit of a gal given the chance, our Sue."

Something suddenly occurred to her. "Has she ever tried it on with you?"

Rob guffawed. "Nah. Don't be ridiculous." He saw the serious question on Jane's face and hastened to reassure her.

"No," he said, shaking his head. "Absolutely not."

Jane shrugged and took another sip of coffee. There was almost definitely something furtive about Rob lately. The obvious answer to her puzzlement just did not occur to her. That would be too ludicrous.

She drained her mug and placed it back on the table.

"Well, I've got to crack on. I really must finish this damned lecture. You're not going to start knocking that wall through now, are you?"

Rob knew a direct command when he heard it and realised, he needed to start tidying up anyway. Thank God the conversation had moved off the subject of Sue.

"No," he said emphatically. "I'll make a start on tidying up a bit. When you've finished, how about we stroll down to the pub and have lunch there?"

"Yep," said Jane over her shoulder as he she left the room. "That will be great. I'm famished. Give me half an hour."

Rob sat staring after her, his eyes unreadable.

****

She did not know how she had lived for this long without feeling as she did at this moment. Only recently had she realised how cold, bleak, and soulless had been her existence before she found the meaning of real love.

She had been volunteered into a loveless and latterly abusive marriage by a father who believed that he was doing his best for his daughter. No blame to him, he could not have known.

The beatings, the verbal abuse, and the sexual violence had gradually increased since she and her husband had arrived at this place and in her deepest thoughts, she was not at all sure that her husband had not deliberately thrown the dear old parson down the stairs to ensure that he could step into his shoes. The old man had been weak with age and shortsighted, and it would only have taken the merest push to send him to meet his maker.

In a moment of hopeless desolation, she had found and clung on to this young man who now walked beside her, as a drowning sailor would cling on to a rock that he found in a troubled sea. His affection and now openly declared love had engulfed her emotions and she had found that gradually over the last weeks she had come to return these feelings without realising what they were. The father that she loved had long since disappeared from her young life, and she had assumed that for the rest of her life love would be only a word, something that she had heard of but never really experienced herself.

They were two young people in a world that was inhabited largely by older people thanks to the recent civil wars. She felt no guilt in their relationship such as it was. Her loathing for Nehemiah increased with every day that passed, and every day brought fresh violence or abuse. Nehemiah seemed almost to take pleasure from inflicting pain or humiliation on to his young wife.

These brief moments together were balm to her troubled soul, and she found that when she was with Thomas, every sense that she possessed seemed heightened, more aware. The spring flowers were a profusion of colour today and would be until the woodland canopy reached full bloom and blocked out the sun. Red Campion vied for space amongst the bushes with purple foxgloves, and white cow parsley. The bluebells, their brief weeks of glory now almost at an end, were fading but still added soft hues of blue to the palette of colour. Here and there a solitary gorse bush thrust its way through the undergrowth, its bottle-green spines topped with bright yellow flowers which almost seemed to glow.

Coming from the city, Cecily had not known what the calls of the birds were, but during their many moments alone Thomas had taught her to distinguish the differing calls of song thrushes, blackbirds, wrens, robins and even on one occasion the freshly arrived nightingale who was given his name, she was told, because the male birds sang their lovely song deep into the night. She found that when she was with him the world was a lovelier place – the colours brighter and more vivid, her vision clearer, the bird calls more lyrical.

They shared their wonder of these things with each other and laughed sensually as they embraced and clung together tightly, strolling through the small lesser-known deer tracks, so that they did not wander near the more frequently used pathways.

They had not yet consummated their love for each other. Their intense feelings at present were above such base longings – they were somehow spiritual and blessed. It was enough for them to be together, to share intimate moments in the touching of hands, or the chaste tender touch of one human being with another. Someday soon their feelings might well overcome the morals of the time that were ingrained in their very being, but for the moment such moments as this short together time today were a calming balm to her spirit. The knowledge that he was never far away gave her comfort. He was always in her thoughts, always there to ease her troubled spirit with tender words and a loving embrace was always with her. He was hers; he was hers forever, that is what she kept telling herself.

She would repeat his name over and over in bed at night as Nehemiah worked his grunting lust and thrustings on her. She would turn her face to the window repeating over and again in her mind, "I love you, Thomas. I love you, Thomas.".

They had walked together this morning for over an hour, and she knew she must return to the house soon, before Nehemiah came home. Margaret would never say a word, even if she guessed the truth, and providing no one saw their strolls together through the forest, where was the harm?

She was leaning into his sturdy figure as they walked, his arm about her shoulders. Her arm was around his waist. She drew comfort from the weight and strength of his arm about her, and the warmth of his strong body that she felt through the coarse stuff of his jacket calmed her troubled spirit.

She had been telling him a little about her childhood in London. He himself had never strayed further than five miles from where he had been born and secretly marvelled at the descriptions she so casually supplied about the mighty river Thames, and of the many large and austere buildings that crowded either bank of the grey and rapidly spreading capital city. She told him of the bridges across the fast-flowing water, and how experienced boatman took pride in 'shooting' the bridges as they called it, which entailed navigating perilously the swift flowing channels between the closely packed pillars on which the bridges were built.

He loved this girl with a passion that he had not thought that he possessed. She had altered the whole axis of his life and all he craved was to be near her, to speak with her, to hear her laugh. He found it a wondrous thing to watch the dimples appear in her cheeks if he made her smile. Feeling her now as she leant into him, drawing him closer to her, gave him a feeling of such tenderness and protective yearning that he felt his chest constrict with emotion.

He looked down at her and saw that her upturned face topped by the small white calico bonnet was waiting for his kiss. A kiss of farewell.

"You must leave me now, my love." She smiled. "We are getting too close to the house. It's not safe to go further."

He nodded and proffered the invited kiss. "I know it, sweetheart. I hate it every time that I must leave you. God strike Morton down, vile creature that he is."

Her face clouded and became troubled. "You must not say such things," she said. "Especially to me. In the eyes of God, he is my husband and whatever his faults they must be borne. That is my lot in life."

"It is a foul and unfair lot then. Surely it is not the Lord's plan for you to suffer such an odious man for your time on this earth?"

She held her finger up, placing it on his lips to quell his outburst.

"Hush," she said. "Hush, my sweet. For as long as I have you in my life, I can bear it. Must bear it too, for there is no other way." She tilted her chin again and kissed him long and hard.

"Never leave me," she whispered, the catch in her voice showing him that she was only barely controlling her emotions.

He grabbed both of her hands and held them up to his mouth to kiss them. "I will never leave you. Do you know how much I love you? Just to be with you, just to touch you. I know not how I would bear my life if I were ever to lose you now."

She gazed up at his earnest face, framed as it was by the swaying elm branches behind him, and knew he spoke the truth. It was the same for her. God had brought them together and whatever happened to her temporal body, she realised that their souls would always be together.

She clung to him then for long moments until lifting her face for a final kiss, she let him go, and ran off through the trees before he could move after her.

He stood there for long moments watching her disappearing figure, glimpsing the whiteness of her ankles as she skipped across tree roots, imagining her slim body beneath that cursed grey dress. He knew that she was walking back into that abominable house and knew what she would face once more. There was nothing he could do about the situation. Not a damned thing. Were they doomed to live like this until they were old, only sharing brief moments together as the years sped by? Would they still be sharing brief tender moments of love when they were both old and grey-haired, all passion spent, and the fires of youth dimmed forever?

Suddenly the trees in front of him disappeared and became blurred as his eyes filled with tears. For some minutes he cried like a little boy who has lost his favourite toy. He could not stop but wept large tears, which dripped from his face on to the forest floor, until he knuckled his eyes to make them stop. He retched a couple of times as he fought to control the feelings of grief and bitter emptiness that continued to well up inside of him despite his futile attempts to stop them. Why had God allowed him to meet this woman? The woman who was now the driving force of his life, who filled his every waking moment. Who came to him in his dreams. Who he knew could never be his. What was the Lord's plan in all of this?

He was just a simple country youth, who had grown up never very far from where he now stood. How could he have ever imagined that he could feel this way? It was magical, but also terrible.

His anger suddenly overpowered his feelings of self-pity and with a shout of rage he turned and punched the nearest tree. Blood ran freely down his hand from his skinned knuckle, and he watched it dispassionately as it dripped on to the floor. The pain calmed him a little and withdrawing a piece of old cloth from beneath his shirt he wound it around his hand.

He remembered that he must be at old Farmer Pearsall's holding a little later that afternoon to help him with the rebuilding of some of his fences. Lost in love he may be, but he still had to earn his way. His mother depended on the little money that he gave her. He hoped the work today would be arduous and long. He desperately needed the distraction, but he knew that whatever he was doing, the face of Cecily would always be under his eyelids, smiling at him in her beguiling way. Each night as he struggled to sleep, he would imagine her lying next to him, the imagined warmth of her body calming his restless mind. With an effort he pulled himself together and sighing deeply, he set off through the trees.

As he disappeared down the pathway, a robin fluttered to the forest floor and began to poke about in the crushed vegetation and small bruised flowers, looking for anything that may have been disturbed. Perched unsteadily on a small branch above him, a fat pigeon fluffed up its feathers and uttered its hooting call into the small breeze.

There was nothing at all to see, no evidence whatsoever of the recent passion that had erupted there.

Chapter Twelve

Jane was not sure what had awakened her. One moment she was enjoying a pleasant dream about strolling on a sunkissed beach somewhere warm, and the next she was wide awake and staring at the raftered ceiling above her bed.

Glancing across at the illuminated red figures on Rob's bedside table clock, she saw that it was three thirty in the morning. Having worked hard on the lecture until around ten she had decided on an early night and taken a cup of cocoa to bed with her. Robert had again left very early yesterday morning, and she had not heard from him since. Truth be told, she was glad of the peace and quiet. He would be back tomorrow evening and no doubt there would be more crashing and banging and swearing from the kitchen the whole day.

She stretched out her legs in the large bed feeling the old-fashioned nightdress that she was wearing ruck up around her hips. She was too warm and threw back the duvet to cool down. Immediately she felt the slightly chilled air caress her body and revelled in its touch. Ten seconds later she knew what had awakened her as with an electric flash, lightning illuminated the room and the whole house seemed to be shaken by a tremendous thunderclap. She became aware of the heavy rain lashing at the mullioned bedroom window and the sound of the wind.

Bloody hell, she thought. *The storm must be right overhead.*

She sat up and turned on the bedside light. She loved to hear rain at any time, had always found it soothing, but this rain was what used to be poetically called a tempest. She could hear water rushing down the guttering from the eaves and hoped that the aged roof of this place did not have any leaks. Somewhere in the distance she was sure she could hear a frightened cow lowing.

She sat for some minutes listening to the cacophony, trying to decide whether to get up and make a cup of tea. She might as well, she thought, as she was now wide awake and would find it hard to drop off again.

With a sigh she stepped out of bed and shoved her feet into Rob's old leather slippers that were much warmer than her own and by chance were on her side of the bed. She did not really want to go downstairs; it would be dark and cold but that was where the kettle was.

Don't be an ass, she chided herself. *If you're getting windy about being on your own as you get older, get a bloody cat, or a dog.* Grinning at her own foolishness, she padded down the creaking stairs and despite her annoyance at her own foolishness, she turned on every light as she went.

She was thinking about Sue's irritating obsession of a few nights ago of having a séance and mentally praised herself and Paul for resisting. It was all very well being brave when surrounded by friends and with all the lights on, but a very different thing when you were alone, in a darkened house in the middle of a thunderstorm and in the dark hours of the night. The urge to turn around and retreat back to her warm bed was strong indeed but chiding herself for a suspicious idiot, common sense prevailed, and she forced herself to keep moving downwards one step at a time.

She moved from the hallway into the kitchen and for a moment could not think where the light switch was. The tiredness of the last few days was clouding her mind a little. She must still be a little sleep befuddled she thought. Of course, this was the new place, and the switch was just to the right of the door as you entered. She clicked on the light just as another hugely bright electric flash was accompanied by another thunderous clap of sound.

She suddenly felt the blood in her veins turn to ice and she was halted in her tracks, her hand still clinging to the kitchen door jamb. Standing at the far end of the kitchen, staring at the bricked-up doorway that Rob was so proud of, was the woman in the grey dress. Not an ethereal phantom, not floating in the air, but a very real and solid looking figure. As Jane fought to remain standing and not to faint, the figure turned slowly and looked at her accusingly. She was startlingly beautiful, dark-haired and dark-eyed, but with such an air of sadness about her that it was palpable.

Jane simply could not move, or speak, such was her shock and utter disbelief. This kind of thing happened in Hollywood films, or horror books but never in real life, not to her.

Suddenly with another percussive crash, lightning flashed again and simultaneously the lights went out. Maybe it was a general power cut or perhaps the house had itself been struck. In the seconds before her control finally broke, Jane incongruously considered this trivial question. It was then that she saw the figure start to move towards her illuminated by yet another lightning flash. Jane screamed shrilly and fell to the floor in a dead faint.

She came around some moments only later and without conscious thought, merely the instinctive reaction of an animal in danger, she scurried on all fours back out of the kitchen to the stairs and clambered back up the rickety flight, panting and crying, fear and panic urging her on despite the pain in her hip from her fall on to the stoneflagged kitchen floor.

She made it to her bedroom and slamming the door behind her, jammed one of the small bedroom chairs under the handle. It was then that she recalled that as she had scuttled in terror out of the kitchen, she had noted that it had once more been empty. The grey lady had gone again. No one would follow her. Perhaps no one had been there in the first place.

She was trembling uncontrollably and hugged the duvet around her for warmth and comfort. She managed to find her mobile on the bedside table and forcing her hand not to shake, phoned Roberts number.

It rang for some time before Rob's tinny voice came on as his answerphone kicked in. *"I can't answer your call right now. Leave a message and I'll call you back."*

"Rob! Answer your fucking phone, you absolute arsehole," she yelled, her control in tatters. "I don't care what time it is; you're answering your phone. Wanker."

She pressed redial.

Two hundred miles away in a darkened hotel bedroom, a mobile phone began to play Stevie Wonder singing *Isn't she lovely* as Rob's ringtone for his wife kicked in.

Lying next to the snoring Rob, dozing in somnolent self-satisfaction, Sue gave a tut of irritation, as the insistent ringing roused her from her erotic musings. She was remembering fondly the strenuous love-making of a few hours ago and marvelling with pride at the suppleness of her body despite the onset of middle age. Peering up at a panting Rob, she had been amazed that her stockinged feet, still encased in her strappy high heels, could reach up either side of his head to rest on his shoulders. The memory had brought a lascivious grin to her face, and she was extremely annoyed at the phone's urgent and intrusive summons.

She elbowed the figure next to her. "ROB! Your phone's ringing."

There was no response, and the snoring continued. "Rob!" she repeated a little louder now. "Your phone's ringing."

Still no response, just a break in the snoring and muttered, incoherent words, before he turned on to his side.

Fully awake now and really angry, Sue reached over him and lifted the phone to her ear.

"Yes?" she barked. "Who is this?"

There was a muffled gasp and a silence at the other end of the phone. Sue suddenly realised too late what she had done and silently mouthed 'oh fuck'.

"Sue?" said Jane. "Is that you, Sue?"

Sue just did not know what to say, but just sat there holding the mobile and listening.

"Hello" came the tinny voice again. "Hello, Sue. Sue?"

Panicking, at last Sue clicked the off button on the phone and threw it across the room. As she did so the slumbering figure next to her suddenly opened his eyes.

"What's the matter?" he said sleepily. "Who was that?"

****

Paul had been awake for some time. He had been given a small, half-beamed cottage right next to the church when he arrived in the village, which served as the local vicarage, and he loved it dearly. It had come fully furnished, if that's what you could call the random collection of old Edwardian furniture and shabby Indian rugs. Two bedrooms, a lounge-cum-dining room, and a small kitchen, but it suited him at this juncture in his life. He had attempted to make the place his own by placing photographs of Marion and his son on various surfaces around the place, and his treasured dark wood writing desk given to him by Marion back when the world was young and at which he constructed his sermons resided under the front window so that he could look out at the village green and the church as he wrote.

However, at this moment he would be hard pressed to see anything out there. He loved to watch a storm. Loved the unrestrained visceral violence of it. So, he had risen from his bed when it started and was sitting fully dressed in the lounge nursing what was left of a mug of barely warm coffee with a large brandy chaser and watching the heavy rain crash against the window, his curtains thrown wide to allow him the best view.

Marion had loved a storm too, and he well remembered the pair of them crouched in a Romanesque church porch in southern Italy laughing like children as they watched the thunder and lightning crash around them, echoing from the surrounding hills as they drank from a bottle of local red wine.

He was going through one of those periods in time when she was always on his mind. He knew it would pass. Since her death he had endured on several occasions moments like this with grim fortitude. There were times, weeks sometimes when he hardly thought of her and his son at all. Perhaps God allowed him to forget, for what would the constant agony of remembrance bring but yet more anguish and anxiety?

His mobile that he had left on his desk suddenly rang, making him jump with surprise. It was four o'clock in the morning, who would be ringing him now? What on earth?

Fifteen minutes later, soaked through despite his waterproof, he was avoiding the puddles in the dark, potholed lane as he approached Jane's cottage with trepidation. He was not at all sure he should be doing this. She had sounded almost manic when he answered his phone. Jabbering about some apparition and something about Rob being a selfish wanker and she would like to kill Sue. Had it been anyone else in his parish he would have calmed them down on the telephone and told them it was pouring with rain outdoors and he would pop and see them first thing tomorrow. But he was drawn to Jane in some way, he could not deny it. She did not look anything like Marion but there was some quality about her, a calmness of spirit almost that reminded him of his late wife. Apart from that, she was a very pretty woman.

As he opened the little wicket gate and splashed down the driveway, it seemed that every light in the place suddenly came on, and he realised that the power cut had finished. Thank the lord for that, he would not need the large torch that he had shoved into the pocket of his anorak as he left his cottage.

He knocked on the door and waited. It was still raining hard, and the rumble of thunder could still be heard but the storm had moved on now and the village was no longer directly beneath it. No one answered so he knocked again, louder this time.

"Hello," a small voice came from an upstairs window. Stepping back from the door, he looked up. Jane's pale face peered down at him from an opened window.

"Oh, thank God, Paul. It's you!"

He waved up at her ridiculously, but she did not see, her head had already disappeared. He heard the thump of hurried footsteps running down the wooden stairs and the front door was thrown open.

He was about to step into the hallway but before he could move, she was in his arms. Hugging him with a desperate strength, she almost dragged him through the door. He could feel her trembling even through his soaked waterproof.

He allowed himself to be pulled into the kitchen and she pushed him backwards on to one of the kitchen chairs. She stood over him one of her hands still on his shoulder and he realised that she was seeking comfort from the touch of another human being.

"She was here," she said her voice as well as her body trembling. "Just over there." She nodded into the far corner.

"Who was?" Paul was trying to be a calming and reassuring presence, but Jane was clearly very distressed and did not seem to be making much sense. Her eyes were wide and credulous, her hair all awry.

"Her," she said. "You know. Her. The Grey Lady." She nodded again at the far corner. "Standing over there. I swear to you."

Paul gave a start and looked around. "No," he said emphatically. "Jane, you were dreaming, surely." He knew he did not sound very convincing and hesitated to be condescending. He tried to smile up at her, but he realised she was not looking at him but continued to peer fearfully into the corner. Her hand was still gripping his shoulder firmly.

What should he say? Her story went against all his beliefs, against all of his preaching. He was a man who prided himself on keeping an open mind on many subjects, including the occult and the visitation of spirits. But at the end of the day, he was a vicar and the spiritual leader of this little country community. He could not accept that there were such things as ghosts, could not acknowledge visitations. Could he?

It was true that many times when attending the death of an aged parishioner, he had felt the warm waft of air as the soul departed the body at the very moment of death, or imagined he had. He had spoken with many of his colleagues on this subject and almost all had noted the same phenomenon many times during their careers.

But ghosts appearing in someone's house? Surely that was a step too far for him to casually acquiesce to as if it was fact.

He reached up and took her hand. "Sit down," he said and standing guided her to another chair. "I'll make us a cup of tea." He knew this sounded banal as if he were soothing an old lady who'd had a fall, but it was all he could think of to say.

Jane nodded and finally let go of his shoulder. He busied himself with the kettle and with arranging two mugs. He rooted around and placed two teabags in the teapot. As he waited for the kettle to boil, he turned and looked down at her. She was a little calmer now the trembling of her body had abated a little.

"Jane," he said. No answer. "Jane." She heard him this time and looked at him "Had you just woken up when you saw this?"

"Yes."

"And had you been dreaming?"

It was some moments before she registered what he was trying to say, and the realisation made her angry.

"What? You think I'm some neurotic who had a nightmare and then imagined I saw someone in my kitchen and called the local vicar to come out in a storm to give me an aspirin?" The anger had done more to calm her down than anything else he could have said. "Paul, how dare you?"

He held up a placatory hand. "OK," he said. "OK, I'm sorry. It was an obvious question to ask, but I can see that I've offended you." He poured freshly boiled water into the pot and stirred vigorously, as he considered his next questions. He decided to accept her bald statement at this moment, he did not wish to add to her agitation. He handed her a steaming cup and sat down next to her.

"Whatever you saw, you've had a shock, so drink that and we'll talk."

She was only a little placated and he knew his next few sentences must be chosen carefully. "Did she say anything?"

She took a long sip of her tea and her glance when she looked at him was scornful. "No, of course not. I only saw her for a second, but she was here alright, standing just there. She turned to look directly at me and when she took a step towards me… well, I think I passed out for a few moments."

"Passed out? Are you OK? That's a hard floor."

"I'm fine. I banged my hip but it's nothing." She took another sip of tea, and an unwanted shiver shook her shoulders. "When I came around only a few seconds later she was gone."

Paul peered at this woman that he liked a lot. Indeed, he had to admit to himself he fancied her, and he did not want to cause further offence.

"What did you do then?"

She gave a small sigh of irritation, the first show of something other than fear or panic since his arrival, and he realised that she was recovering her composure a little.

"What do you think I did? I darted up those bloody stairs as fast as my hands and feet could take me, slammed the bedroom door shut behind me and jammed a chair under the handle."

He thought now that he could risk a small chuckle, and she returned it as she continued to sip her tea.

"When did the lights go out?"

"Just as she turned towards me. It was as if it was a stage production, or a bloody horror film, but let me tell you it's completely different when it's real. I think I screamed as well. Me! I've never screamed in fright in my life."

Paul answered her smile. "So what happened then? Is that when you called me?"

Her smile vanished as she remembered.

"Oh no, the second part of my night from hell was just about to reveal itself. I called Rob. Phoned him at four o clock, didn't care if I woke him up, just didn't care if he was annoyed or sarcastic, I needed to speak to him." She was getting angry again and Paul could see her face becoming rigid.

"And?" he said.

"He's in London, as you know." She stopped and peered into her cup.

"OK." He waited.

"And fucking Sue answered the phone. The absolute fucking cow. Can you believe it?"

Paul had to stop himself from nodding. Yes, he thought, having met Sue, albeit briefly, he could well imagine it. He had known women like her before. No conventions of behaviour or moral considerations would daunt Sue if she wanted something badly enough. Again, he blinked at her language but now was most definitely not the time for a gentle reprimand.

"Are you sure there's no logical explanation?" He was grasping at straws, trying desperately to be fair, but he knew it was a lost cause. "Was Brian there as well? Or were they all at a nightclub together? It could have another explanation than what you fear."

"I called him back and Rob answered himself this time." Jane's voice was noncommittal. She wanted to tell the whole story but did not want to think about it again until the morning when she was calmer, stronger, not so vulnerable. "He admitted it all when I challenged him. When I asked what the fuck Sue was doing in his room at four in the morning, he told me the truth. Admitted that they've been having an affair for some time. The words sheepish or contrite don't do him justice, let me tell you."

She gave a little unexpected sob, and instinctively Paul leaned over and held her hand.

"Jane, I'm so sorry" was all he could think of to say.

"We're going to…" Jane held both hands above her head, fingers raised in the universal description of apostrophes, "…have a real chat and sort it out when he gets back." She swore foully and bared her teeth. "He'll be lucky if I don't stab him."

Now that she had told it all the shock and anger were beginning to take over again and a further, louder sob escaped unbidden.

"Oh, Christ Paul, what a mess." As she stood up to run out of the room he stood and instinctively opened his arms. He could not help it, even though he knew it was the very last thing he should do in his position, but it was the instinctive reaction of a man faced with a woman in distress.

She moved forward and sank into his arms like a little girl seeking comfort from her daddy.

Wrapping his arms around her heaving shoulders, he kissed the top of her head.

Chapter Thirteen

All in all, Brian thought that had gone rather well. He had not made any obvious gaffes and the questions that had been put to him had been fielded with moderate success and what appeared to be knowledgeable insight.

Yes, that had been a moderate success. He leaned back into his expensive black leather office chair and reached for the small mug of Black Ivory coffee that had been placed at his elbow a few minutes ago by one of his young staff, together with the New York bagel topped with cream cheese this made up his traditional elevenses.

The office was very busy that morning and there was a general hubbub of telephone conversations from the twenty or so staff who all sat hunched over their glass-topped desks, peering earnestly at computer screens, paying infinite attention to the small and constant changes in the markets, as if they were staring with reverence at the Maciejowski Bible. He would be overseeing them with his usual blend of casual bonhomie and flinty reprimands this morning, were it not for the instruction from Sir Anthony to fully brief the two new university graduates who had been recently recruited; "explain to them what it is we do here," he had been instructed. It was a task that Brian hated, but he seemed today to have got away with it moderately well. His explanations of the workings of the Nasdaq Composite Index and how it differed from the Dow Jones Industrial Average and the S&P 500 Index had impressed them and they had both scribbled furiously with their newly presented company 'Cross' pens into their pristine, leather-bound company notebooks.

At least I look the part, he thought glancing down at his blue and white striped shirt, boasting as it did a pure white collar in contrast. He was pleased that the bright crimson braces that Sue had bought him for Christmas nicely enhanced the look of stylish 'city highflyer.' It was all about image, wasn't it? Some crumbs from his bagel dropped into his lap and he leaned forward, cursing, to quickly brush them on to the floor.

The view of the 'square mile' of the City of London through the huge picture windows on the fourteenth floor of this glass and steel edifice were stunning, and without conscious thought he revelled in his success at finding himself a niche in the big game.

"Brian, there's a call for you on line two." It was the young and stylish Kimberly who had called to him across two rows of screens. Her Cambridge-educated, middle England clipped voice always irritated him for some reason. Perhaps it was because it seemed to impress Sir Anthony.

"Who is it?" he called back. "I'm in the middle of something here."

"Some woman, says she absolutely *must* speak to you."

Was that sarcasm he noted in the little bitch's tone? He was annoyed that she had chosen to make this conversation public. Even in his lofty position, personal calls were frowned upon whilst the markets were open.

"Tell her to call back." "I've tried that – sorry, she's very insistent. Says her name is Jane and you will absolutely want to speak with her."

Brian put down his bagel and reaching forward, picked up the small plastic receiver on his desk. *Jane?* he thought. *What the hell did she want?*

"Jane. Hi, this is unexpected."

Jane sounded a little breathless, he thought, a bit stressed. He glanced at his Rolex and noted that it was still only ten fifty in the morning.

"Brian I'm so sorry to bother you, especially at work. I dialled the office number as I know you've mentioned in the past that your mobile must be turned off when you are at work, and this was too important to leave a message."

All of this came out in a rush, and he thought it sounded as if she had rehearsed it.

"That's OK, no worries, Jane. Nice to hear from you. What can I do you for?"

"Do you know?"

There was a silence. He waited for some moments thinking that she would continue but she did not.

"Sorry," he queried. "Know what?"

He clearly heard her take a deep breath. "Then you don't. This is going to come as a shock." Again, the deep intake of breath. *What the hell?* he thought.

"Rob and your Sue have been having an affair. It's been going on for some time apparently. I found out last night."

Brian moved the phone away from his head and frowned at it as he collected his thoughts.

"Bollocks," he said. "Sorry old girl, I don't buy that for a second. I'm not sure they even like each other that much."

"Brian, it's true. I'm sorry, but it is. Rob confessed to me last night. He's in London as we speak, did you know? I'll bet you didn't. He's coming back home this evening and wants a 'serious chat' is how he termed it." A small sob escaped. "I'm going to kill him, I swear. The absolute bastard."

"Jane." Brian struggled to keep his voice calm; people would be listening in the office around him. "You've rather knocked me for six here. I can't take it in." He was still not sure he believed it but then with an icy realisation he remembered that Sue had gone to her mates in Chiswick last night for a girls' night out as she called it and had not come home, and if Rob really was in town… "What the fuck?" he hissed. "Jane, leave it with me, will you? I need to, well I just need to think." As he finished his sentence, he made a mental note to contact Sue's sister to check if the silly cow had really been down in Brighton last week when she said she had.

Jane sounded genuinely sorry. "I know you do, Bri, and I'm sorry for both of us, but I thought you should know."

There was a click as she finished the call. No goodbye, no 'see you soon', nothing, just a click and then a hissing silence.

Brian took great care to replace the receiver on to its bed very gently then in an action so unlike him that it caused gossip and conjecture for the rest of the day amongst his colleagues, he leaned far back into his chair, looked up at the ceiling and bellowed, "Fucking hell."

****

This wasn't working – no matter how much she tried Jane just could not concentrate. Rising early that morning, she had decided to finalise the script for the forthcoming series of 'talks' – if she would ever need them now, she mused. She hoped that it would take her mind off things.

It was a crisp, clear morning following the storm of last night. A bright, watery sun illuminated the garden which looked as if it had been pressure-washed. Every bush, every tree, every blade of grass seemed to glisten with raindrops. The world had a fresh, clean appearance, and the scented smell of wet foliage was heavy on the air.

Jane was sat near to the lounge window, which overlooked the garden at the rear of the house, with its trimmed lawns, lush shrubbery and the ornamental well with its little circular stone wall as its centrepiece. She had read somewhere that at one point in the distant past it had been a real well but that was long ago, and the deep hole was now paved over.

She was raging inside and had decided that perhaps losing herself in the Northern Renaissance again might lessen the sense of betrayal and hurt that now pervaded her every thought. But try as she might, she could not escape the pictures that kept invading her mind. Robert's heaving form panting and gyrating atop a moaning Sue. The vision was so real, it physically hurt to imagine it.

Rembrandt, possibly the best known of the Northern Renaissance artists, took much of his inspiration from the Italian artist Caravaggio, who immediately preceded him, being murdered as he was, four years after Rembrandt's birth. Clearly, the Italian's dramatic experimentation with light was an influence on the Dutch masters. Although Van Eyck was somewhat earlier, Van Dyke, Rubens, and Vermeer, together with Rembrandt, were all active during the same sixty-year period and all of them experimented with the same formats.

That sounded fine, but as she started to read it back, she pictured Robert's buttocks thrusting away between Sue's spread legs. *No don't go there!* she thought. *Just don't fucking go there.*

Rembrandt is one of those artists that are known to us only by one name, like Raphael, or indeed Caravaggio. Rembrandt's full name was Rembrandt Harmenszoon van Rijn. Raphael was in fact Raphael Zanti, and Caravaggio was not named Caravaggio at all, but Michel Angelo Maresi, and only came from the village of Caravaggio but gradually he became known as The Caravaggio.

She was pleased with that paragraph, and although it was not really the subject of the lecture, students enjoyed these little academic forays down the occasional dead end.

A naked Sue, astride Robert's naked body, bouncing up and down on him as he groaned with pleasure beneath her.

It was no good. She stood up and quickly snapping the laptop shut walked purposefully into the kitchen to make a coffee. Her anger was a living thing, and it evidenced in every movement of her body, every foot-tapping, finger-rapping moment as she irritably waited for the kettle to boil. It would have to be instant this morning, she had nowhere near the patience to make proper coffee.

How fucking dare he? she thought. How could he make such a fool of her?

She turned on the little CD player that Robert kept on the shelf in there. He had been playing it constantly as he battered away at the wall he was determined to demolish.

John Legend's *Ordinary people* oozed out of the speakers, and she remembered it was one of his favourites and he had played it when Brian and Sue were in there that morning attempting to recover from hangovers before their long drive home. Suddenly it occurred to her that the affair was obviously going on then. Had they exchanged secret knowing glances during those two days? Had they surreptitiously touched each other when nobody was looking?

"You absolute wanker!" she shouted at the kettle. "You hear me?"

Tears of rage and despair flooded her eyes and were quickly wiped away with an irritable gesture.

"No!" she hissed out aloud. "No crying, you silly cow."

The coffee, instant as it was, settled her mood a little and she squatted at the table, sipping appreciatively at the rich, dark brew, feeling herself becoming calmer.

Paul's face appeared in front of her, and she remembered with some pride how last night she had resisted a course of action that part of her mind was screaming for in the early hours.

Hurt and frightened, she had clung to him with desperate need and had almost in her distressed state sought further comfort from him and indeed revenge on Robert. It would have been so easy. She knew he was vulnerable at that moment and an easy target for a determined woman.

Yes, he was a vicar and she a married woman, but he was a very good-looking vicar, and he was there in her kitchen in the middle of the night, and she was in his arms, the classic damsel in distress.

But she smiled to herself with smug self-congratulation as she took another sip from her mug. She had stopped just at the last moment and freeing herself from his arms, stepped back to thank him for coming around so promptly.

Maybe she was kidding herself, she thought, maybe he was not such a pushover as that. He had looked at her with a strange benevolent but slightly puzzled expression and said that it was perfectly OK and that's what friends were for, wasn't it?

He had made her go and wash her face and comb her hair, and when she returned to the kitchen, he had made a fresh pot of tea and waited with her as she drank it, all the while talking of mundane inconsequential things, watching as she gradually regained control of herself and became more like the Jane that he knew.

There were two subjects, she now realised, he had deliberately stayed well away from – her suspicions about Robert and the appearance of the Grey Lady. She suspected that he himself was not at all sure how to approach these matters and had decided to leave it until tomorrow.

He had escorted her to her bedroom door, told her to leave the lights on for what remained of the night, and he would lock the front door as he let himself out. It was almost dawn, and the sky would be lightening soon, he said, and he had been in every room in the house and there was no one there. She had nodded and accepted his almost brotherly advice as he briefly rested his hand on her shoulder before disappearing down the stairs, and ten minutes later she was soundly asleep.

Now in the bright sunshine of a new day, she was sure that was what he had decided on as a course of action, and she would be forever grateful for his intuition, restraint and tact. Many men of her acquaintance would have taken immediate advantage of the situation. *Just goes to show what a bunch of absolute arseholes I've known,* she thought.

She felt a little better now and glancing at her watch saw that it was already past twelve. Robert would not be back before seven and she absolutely must finish this bloody talk by then. She wanted nothing to clutter her mind when the prat finally turned up and they began what she knew would be a monster of a row. Would she let him stop? She was not sure, did not even want to think about it, not yet. Better to hide away amongst the Dutch artists for a few hours.

Refilling her mug, she walked calmly back into the lounge leaving the CD player droning on, perched as it was in front of the bare bricks of the stripped kitchen wall. John Legend's *Ordinary People* seemed to be playing on a loop. She decided to leave it.

****

Paul was hardly aware of the cheese and tomato sandwich that he was eating. His chewing was mechanical, automatic, his mind elsewhere.

He glanced up at the huge oak tree above him, revelling in the gentle, soothing, rustling sound that it made as the warm breeze oozed through its branches. The newly grown leaves seemed to reflect the fitful sunshine of the morning with an emerald glow, and he smiled in spite of his mood, as he remembered an old college mate who was always quoting some sage philosopher or other, droning on about the old native American Indian saying 'Only the rocks live forever'. Could the same apply to an aged oak tree? From the size of this thing, it must be at least four hundred years old. Well, compared to the brief stay of a human being on this earth, that was forever, wasn't it?

He gave a snort of self-derision and smiling wanly, tossed the remainder of his sandwich expertly into the nearby wastepaper bin. Reaching down to the bench on which he sat, he picked up the polystyrene cup of coffee, opened the lid and took an appreciative sip.

That was better. He looked around and noticed that it must be almost lunchtime judging by the amount of people who had mysteriously appeared whilst he had been seated there on the uncomfortable bench, lost in thought. The green sward in front of him which fronted the Exeter library was now pocked with young people, presumably students, who were lounged on spread waterproofs in homage to the heavy rain of last night. Draped in a variety of languid attitudes, they discussed a myriad of subjects with the absorbed earnestness of youth.

He had driven there earlier today, needing something to take his mind off the events of last night. He guessed that he had broken the speed limit many times on his way there in his old, battered but treasured Mini Cooper. The leafy lanes gave way to main roads as he neared the city.

Two things were troubling him deeply as he pushed the gutsy little car to its limits. What did he think of the supposed visitation last night at Jane's cottage? What was his stance on ghosts and the afterlife? He was not sure. But surely in his position he should be sure, absolutely crystal clear in his philosophy on such matters? After all, his flock looked to him for guidance about such things, did they not? His ecumenical wisdom had to comfort them in times of sadness and stress. He had to offer the teachings of the church as a balm to troubled minds. But the problem was he was a man who was not at all sure where he stood on such matters, especially since the untimely and pointless death of his wife and son. It was true that he had never seen any evidence at all of ghosts or spirits, even though in the immediate aftermath of Marion's accident he had longed for her to come to him, called for her often in anguish in the small hours of the night to show herself if she was there. But of course, she never had.

Jane was an educated, rational, and very sensible woman but she was clearly hugely distressed when he had arrived at the cottage last night. Literally shaking with fear, wide-eyed with anger and despair and terror as they were speaking in the kitchen. Even when he had calmed her down to something approaching normality, she had still repeatedly glanced at the bare kitchen wall, reassuring herself that there was no one there.

But much more than this conundrum, puzzling as it was, he was deeply concerned about his own reaction to the physical reality of having her in his arms. She had been clinging to him, as a child clings to a parent in times of distress.

He had maintained control and not responded to her obvious but subtle invitations. Why had she done that? Was it a form of revenge on her possibly erring husband? Or was she simply not thinking straight in her distress and merely wanted the comfort of the touch of another human being? Either way, he had resisted, but God forgive him, only just. What would have been the outcome had she not suddenly appeared to appreciate the situation and backed away from it? He was not sure, and the unknowing was extremely disconcerting.

He took a last sip of his coffee and despatched the cup into the already overflowing wastepaper bin with a practised throw. He had work to do, that was why he had come here after all. The hectic drive had cleared his head a little and there would be time for further reflection later.

Hoisting his old backpack across one shoulder he loped across to the crowded grass to the library entrance. Dressed as he was in shabby jeans and his old leather jacket, no one would guess that he was a vicar, which for the moment suited him fine.

The pretty blonde receptionist grinned with a flash of very white teeth and assured him that of course she remembered him and yes, she would dig out the works of old Josiah Walton again and bring it up to him, oh and by the way she said, her name was Karen.

"Thanks Karen," he grinned back. "I owe you one."

As he strode off, she nodded to herself. "Yes you do," she mouthed at his back and hurried off to retrieve the book.

Two hours later Paul sat back in his chair and heaved a sigh of regret. Once again, his shoulders and back ached from leaning forward over the desk, and once again his small notebook was covered in his hastily written, spidery script. He snapped it shut with finality and reaching behind him placed it into the inside pocket of his jacket which was draped across the back of his chair. He was disturbed and depressed. *Goddammit,* he thought expressively. *Bloody hell*.

He found that he was losing the capacity to be rational about the people he was researching. They were now too real for him, too human, and he had been unable to remain detached, to be clinical. It was the lot of every researcher, he surmised, to be drawn into the story and to feel in some way involved. He had tried to remain dispassionate, but it was hard. His very nature precluded any cold, uncaring fact-finding negating any involvement whatsoever with his discoveries. He sighed hugely and ruefully acknowledged his inherent compassion.

An old man at the next desk looked across at him over the rim of his glasses and smiled sadly.

"Not liking what you have read?"

Paul glanced at him and shook his head mournfully. "No." Then feeling that this monosyllabic answer might appear rude he added, "Not at all." He gave a slow, wan smile and closed the Reverend Walton's book.

"Doing some research?" continued the old man, twitching the collar of his old tweed jacket and for the umpteenth time pushing his spectacles back up the bridge of his nose. Paul thought he had a look of Albert Einstein about him.

He did not want to talk, depressed as he was, not really, but also did not want to appear an ignorant git in front of these well-meaning questions.

"Yep, afraid so, but what I have learnt does not make nice reading. Not what I was expecting."

"That's the problem with research, it does not always give us the answers we were looking for. Historical research, is it?"

Paul nodded. "Yeah. I suppose you're right. When you are trying to find out what happened to real people, not fictional characters, but real flesh and blood human beings who actually lived, you have to take what comes, don't you? What really occurred, I mean. You know that these people have been dead for centuries, but they matter to you as if you knew them. Strange."

The old man produced a battered old pipe from somewhere and placed it in his mouth.

"Can't smoke it of course," he said, answering the obvious surprise that showed on Paul's face. "But it helps me think just to have it there. Bit like a child's dummy really." He chuckled at his own stupidity.

"You're right." He nodded. "Those people were here before us when the world was a very different place, and what they accepted as normal we now shy away from in horror." He removed the pipe, looked at it with regret and replaced it into his jacket pocket. "But," he continued, "many things that we now accept as part of the flotsam and background of our own lives they would be appalled by. It's all a matter of context. What century are you researching?"

"The seventeenth."

"Oh." The old man nodded sagely. "The civil wars, plagues, the great fire of London, the witch trials and so on and so on. It was not a great time to be alive, but then when is?"

Paul reached behind him and retrieved his leather jacket. "I suppose I've seen too many films of hymn-singing Puritans and gay laughing roistering cavaliers, but of course thinking about, it civil wars are not really like that at all, are they?"

"Think of Rwanda or Bosnia," chimed in the old man. "Civil wars are harsh, vicious, and brutal, and they tend to infect the people living through them, imbuing them with a casual acceptance of ferocity and cruelty. They become immured to it. I read somewhere that nearly a quarter of a million people died of violence or disease in the civil war period in this country, plus you had very grizzly public executions always attended by huge crowds who came to gawp at someone dying in agony."

"No more please," smiled Paul as he stood and shrugged into his jacket. "I'm depressed enough already. I'm off for a beer – I need it. Nice to have met you." He patted the old man's shoulder as he passed.

"You too. Enjoy the rest of your day." Smiling gently, the old man looked down once more at his own book.

Karen was extremely disconcerted as Paul placed the book back in front of her on the reception desk and with just a brief smile and a thank you moved away towards the entrance.

Suddenly, he stopped and with hasty strides walked back to her desk wearing a sheepish grin, his hands raised in apology.

"Sorry," he said. "I was miles away. Something I have just read has thrown me a bit. Anyway, I wanted to thank you for your help and your courtesy, Karen. Much appreciated."

The young woman beamed up at him. "You're welcome." She smiled. "Anytime."

She flicked her blonde hair back from her face with a practised movement and he caught a glimpse of long, dangling silver earrings.

"I mean it," she said. "Anytime." Her eyes, he noticed, were a startling azure blue, her gaze intense.

He nodded to show that he understood her meaning. No! He did not want to get involved, not yet, flattered as he was.

"OK." He nodded and turning, marched quickly away and through the glass doors into the sunshine.

Karen sighed and watched his retreating back wistfully. Then she returned to stamping the pile of books in front of her with added venom.

Chapter Fourteen

She had not known it could be like this. Was it the same for everyone? This overriding feeling of self-satisfaction and somnolent, all-consuming joy. She felt replete, content, fulfilled. Overflowing with the joy of being alive and walking on the earth and wishing only goodwill to everyone. Surely this was what life should be about.

She knew it was wrong and very possibly a sin before God but just at this moment she did not care. Let the world do what it would to her, for this moment in time in her young life she was happy, really, beautifully happy. She gave a little inadvertent skip of pure joy.

The world around her seemed to glow in the fitful sunshine. All of her senses were immeasurably heightened: taste, smell, vision. She was aware of every blade of grass, every small twig, every nodding flower, everything standing out in enhanced form and colour. The red of the poppies bowing their vermillion heads to the sunlight, the lemon-yellow flowers atop the gorse bushes, the blue of the corn flowers, the pure white of the cow parsley. Here and there, almost hidden in the undergrowth, clumps of mauve columbine, their delicate heads looking like the old ladies' bonnets of their nickname, swayed in the breeze.

She felt so alive, almost believing that she could take flight if she wanted. She could hear every call from the finches, the larks, and even the lowly sparrows that inhabited the trees and bushes around her. In the distance she could hear the muted call of a cuckoo attesting that it was spring. She was so glad to be alive and was sure that every creature around her, seen or unseen, was happy to be alive at this moment in time, so attuned to her surroundings was she.

She could feel her clothing where it touched every part of her body. Her very skin seemed to tingle and vibrate with passion and lust for life.

She could not supress a broad grin spreading across her pretty face, and she bubbled with slow laughter, which burst forth from her lips like a bubble of gas from a pool.

Unconsciously, she gripped Thomas's calloused hand harder and leaned further into him as they walked gently, slowly through the dappled shadows of this secret forest path. She had removed her small leather shoes and carried them in her free hand. The moss beneath her feet felt sensuous and cool, adding to her excitement. She wanted to be free of the cloying embrace of her heavy grey dress, to cast off all of her clothing and feel the warm, redolent air against her skin but knew she could not. No matter.

It had been a long struggle with her self-restraint and indeed her conscience, but this morning she and Thomas had finally let their feelings overwhelm them and they had made love in the long grass in a small clearing deep within the forest that she thought was known only to them. Lost in the moment, she had given herself unreservedly to him, and he to her. Their cries and moans of pleasure were unheard by anyone save only for the creatures in the undergrowth.

The man she loved strolled along next to her deep in his own thoughts. They did not need to speak, the final capitulation to their feelings and the consummation of their love had left them both drained and happy, overwhelmed with the emotion of the moment, and exuberant with unspoken passion. Whatever happened now, they would always have this morning to keep locked away in their minds, to bring out in the troubled times to come, to relive, to remember, and to rejuvenate them.

She stopped abruptly and held up her free hand to stroke his face.

"I must be getting back soon, my love. Margaret will already be wondering where I am."

He nodded down at her, his gentle eyes clouded with emotion. "I know." He nodded. "How can you bear it, to be in the same house with that man? His hypocrisy and bloodless piety are sickening." This was a phrase that he did not completely understand but he had heard one of the parish councillors speak it recently and liked the sound of it.

She peered up at him, her face seeming small and vulnerable beneath the calico bonnet, her hair escaping in several places and a long tress cascading down her back, errant and not to be imprisoned.

"He's my husband, Thomas. I made my vows to him before God. It is my lot in life to bear his actions. We none of us can change the world."

She leaned her forehead against his chest, breathing in the warm, earthy aroma of the forest that pervaded his clothing.

"He believes in his own way that he is doing God's work. I know in many ways he is misguided, and yes, he is harsh, but I am beholden to support him, if I can, to be his helpmeet and the object of his lust if he wants. My body is his to do with as he will, abhorrent as it seems to you."

She felt Thomas's body start and tremble with supressed anger as she spoke these words.

"That man knows nothing of God or of love," he whispered through bared teeth. "It is my belief that he is crazed. What he did to Martha Pennyford was disgusting. Why the council let him get away with it is beyond me.

What were they thinking? She cried for days. What had she done to deserve that?"

She leaned away from him and placed a small finger upon his lips.

"Hush my love, hush. Martha survived it and is fine now. If he has done evil in this world he will answer for it, not now in this life, but before God when his time on earth is done."

He wanted to answer her, but she pressed her finger harder against his mouth.

"The council are all old men and are all afraid of him, of his rages, of his eloquence, of his silky persuasive arguments and the subtle threats that underly his every action. He thinks he is in the right, and we are all sinners. It is not an act; he really and truly believes that."

"He is wrong, and he is evil," sneered Thomas unwilling, to be mollified. He drew this woman that he now loved above all things closer to him, as if to protect her from the horrors of the world. He knew that she belonged at least under the law to another man, a despicable man, but he could not help the feelings that threatened to overwhelm him as he stood here holding his love to him. He could feel her heart beating against him, fast and urgent, like a wild rabbit's heart when it is caught in a snare. He could smell the fragrance that she used to wash her hair; he breathed it in deeply. He had never felt this way about another human being in the whole of his young life. He would die for her or kill without remorse anyone who harmed her.

Perceiving the overwhelming depth of his emotions, she released him and stepped back, afraid for him. She felt exactly the way that he did; she had never known such all-consuming passion, but she was in many ways older than he was and she could keep a tight hold of such emotions. She was not sure that he could.

"Let's not talk of this anymore." She rejuvenated her smile, and he noticed again the small dimples that appeared in her cheeks when this happened – the way her eyes crinkled when she smiled bewitched and enthralled him and without thought he returned the smile.

"And now I really must go," she chided. "Kiss me once more."

He did as she asked, and she felt the breath leave her body as he hugged her fiercely to him. Frozen in a tableau of intense feeling, they stood for many minutes lost in the moment, then finally with a return to self and with a physical effort, she drew back.

"Until the next time, my love." She stepped quickly away to halt any further attempt at an embrace.

He stood, bereft, and watched her go. She stepped lightly down the path, passing through beams of sunlight and into the shade before she finally disappeared from view around a bend in the pathway.

"Until the next time, my love," he whispered, echoing her words. His eyes were bleak with loss and his chin trembled with tearful anguish. "Until the next time." He turned and sighing deeply, trudged off through the trees.

A little way off, a flash of colour moved in the shadows against the undergrowth, unnoticed by him as he moved away deep in thought. It was an old, faded, blue homespun smock such as that worn by Tobias Treadwell, who in his old age was employed to dig the graves of the recently deceased of the parish, and also to keep the small church graveyard neat and tidy. He had been out that morning to catch a brace of rabbits for his old wife who made a delicious rabbit pie that he coveted.

He had not meant to spy or eavesdrop on the young couple, but when he stood up from wringing the neck of a lively old coney, there they were only a few yards away and he dared not make himself known lest they suspected he was spying on them. Tobias was not a gossipy man, in fact he could almost be termed taciturn, but his wife Enid would be amazed and hugely grateful for this snippet of scandal when he told her. He would swear her to secrecy, of course, as young Cecily was well liked in the village and was known to do charitable works amongst the poorer folk when time allowed. Sadly, the idea that Enid was not so trustworthy when she had an item of local news to impart to her friends did not occur to him. Not until much later when it was far too late.

****

Paul could not shake this feeling of low depression. It had stayed with him throughout the day. It was persistent and pervasive, no matter how many times he remonstrated with himself to shake it off. Thoughts of Marion and his son Charlie were strong today and had been from the moment he had opened his eyes. He knew that these thoughts were just an indicator of his general mood. Whenever he was sad or in mild despair, Marion was always under his eyes. His memories had sustained him since her death, memories of love and laughter, of shared and dear moments together, but sometimes, unbidden, there were sharper, sadder memories that heightened his sense of loss, and more than that, feelings of the pointless cruelty of life, the chaos and the senseless, hopeless striving that everyone alive, everyone who has ever lived, endures and accepts.

His startling and depressing discoveries in Exeter Library earlier had further added to these feelings of despondency and he had been in no hurry get back to the village, despite knowing he had to officiate at a funeral. He knew that his normal everyday duties as the local vicar must of course take precedence over his research concerning a different, harsher century.

It was the funeral of old Mildred Compton, spinster of this parish, who had succumbed gently to what the doctor had recorded as 'old age' as reason for her demise on the death certificate. It had been a sad little affair. She had reached the grand old age of ninety-eight, outliving most of her friends and contemporaries by almost a decade. Her middle-aged bachelor grandson and his slightly younger but even dowdier sister had been the only mourners. True, after the service a few of the locals had turned up at the graveside to watch the small coffin lowered into the ground as he intoned the usual phrases, but most of them remembered her only as an old lady who knew their parents when they were young. Still, Paul mused, at least it had not rained.

He had changed into an old t-shirt and jeans as the afternoon reached its close. The sun was low in the sky now, and the graveyard surrounding the old church was speckled with shadows from the surrounding trees that rustled and whispered gently in the evening breeze. It was a place of quiet reflection, warm and somnolent with memories of the day.

Standing on the gravel path that led from the church porch down to the lych gate and into the road, he peered around him and acknowledged that Wilfrid, the pensioner who was employed on a part-time basis to keep the place neat and tidy, did an excellent job. The grass between the gravestones, some of which were new, and some which were old and askew, was trimmed and lush, accentuating the sharp lines of the gravestones, inscribed as they were with their carved written memories of those who lay beneath. Here and there a splash of colour, reds, purples, and white, glowed in the evening light as the flowers or potted plants left by family or friends reflected the warm mellow rays of the dying day.

A murder of crows squabbled and croaked in the trees above, and he spotted a small squirrel weave its jerky way between the lopsided gravestones in search of a morsel of food.

Spotting what he was looking for, he set off towards the old and battered shed in which Wilfred kept his gardening tools. It was nestled beneath a stand of elders and rarely enjoyed unbroken sunlight but lurked in the shadows as was intended, and went largely unnoticed by most visitors.

Amidst the ordered debris inside of ancient gardening tools and a battered old lawnmower, he found what he was looking for and set off to walk the small perimeter wall surrounding the little cemetery with a rake over one shoulder and a small sickle clutched in his other hand.

He knew he must be walking over many hundreds if not thousands of bodies in a churchyard as old as this. He had watched an aged, but wise archaeologist once on TV, long shoulder-length straggly grey hair moving across his kindly bearded face in the breeze, musing over the lack of bodies in most if not all country churchyards. "There are usually four to five, maybe even six generations in any century, which means that over say five or six hundred years, if you have a population of around one thousand then there must be around thirty thousand people who have died. Your average country churchyard boasts probably about two hundred gravestones, so where they hell are they all?"

The latest thinking was that they were all still there but piled in successive layers on top of one another. Thus, the average small country churchyard probably has bodies buried beneath its well-kept lawns five and possibly ten deep.

It was a sobering thought, and Paul gave a wry smile as he considered this, and unconsciously peered at the grass beneath his feet as he walked.

"Evening all," he muttered and gave a low chuckle.

Again, he noted how neat and tidy it all was, and almost took time to sit for a moment on the old wooden bench placed against one of the low crumbling walls, put there for people to sit and meditate on life. But this evening he did not have time. He knew that he had maybe one hour of daylight left, and he had to find something.

Finally, after following a complete circuit of the wall, he came across a small patch of land set way back behind the church in an area where sunlight very rarely permeated. Unusually, it was unkempt. Creepers and ivy had over the years snaked down from the trees and bushes just the other side of the wall and snaked their way across this area. The insidious but persistent weed that some called 'bindweed' had curled its way through this vegetation and whatever lay beneath this green blanket was long since obscured.

The smooth, emerald-green carpet of Wilfrid's trimmed grass lapped against the edges of this small area like a low tide lapping against a quiet beach.

This could be something. Laying the rake carefully down, Paul hefted the sickle and began to hack at the undergrowth with a vengeance.

After ten minutes of hard chopping, followed by a period of strenuous raking and hacking, he had uncovered what he suspected might be there. He almost wished that he had not found it. He wiped his sweating brow with his arm and stood looking down with a profound sense of sadness, almost grief.

With a sigh he reached into his jeans back pocket and withdrew a battered packet of small cigars. Many years ago, he had smoked cigarillos and even larger cigars as an accompaniment to a pint when he was out with friends. It had been an affectation lending him, he had thought in his younger life, a certain gravitas and aplomb. But that was long ago, and he had not smoked anything for a very long time. Driving back from Exeter earlier today, depressed and dispirited by the discoveries during his research, he had decided on impulse that he might quite like a smoke to lift his mood.

He had forgotten until just now that he had shoved the packet into his jeans pocket, as he left his cottage after changing.

Placing the slightly bent small cigar between his lips, he foraged in his other pocket for his old and treasured zippo lighter and with a practised but long unused action lit up, enjoying the remembered flare of petrol fumes as the lighter flamed into life.

Stepping back and sitting down on to the grass that surrounded this sad little plot, he inhaled deeply and considered what he had found. It confirmed his findings. He must tell Jane; she would be very interested and probably a little upset. It went some way to solving the riddle.

Then with a frown he realised that right at this moment Jane probably had more important things on her mind. Glancing at his watch he saw that it was seven thirty. Yes, he thought, Robert would be arriving home just about now.

****

"You absolute fucking wanker!"

Jane was immediately annoyed with herself for this immediate explosion of anger and frustration. Her self-control was in tatters.

From the time she had discovered Robert's infidelity and almost worse, the discovery of with whom it was that he had cheated on her , she had rehearsed what she would say endlessly. She had been repeatedly playing out scenarios in her mind, even as she had been constructing sentences for her talk on the Northern Renaissance.

She had decided to be icily calm, cold and clinical, making him feel like a naughty small child being lectured by his mother. A little later she had decided on tears of disbelief to elicit sympathy from him and confessions of deeply felt guilt.

What she had not expected and what had surprised her as much as it clearly did him was the eruption of incandescent rage as soon as she saw his face. It was the way he had strolled into the kitchen, towing his overnight case behind him and slumped down on to one of the chairs saying breezily he needed a cup of tea. She could not believe the bland, non-committal expression on his face. He had even smiled, for Christ's sake. What the hell?

If she did but know it, he had wrestled with the same thoughts of how to play this meeting himself during the long train journey back. He knew he was in the wrong, knew he had hurt his woman deeply and for the moment was truly sorry for it. But how to get that point over without complete capitulation in front of what would obviously be anger and recrimination?

Jane was leaning against the kitchen worktops, not trusting herself to move forward lest she hit him. The almost empty coffee cup was gripped tightly in her hand, her knuckles showing whitely through her skin.

Robert, unsure of an immediate response, actually gave a sheepish smile.,

"Sorry old thing," he said. "I'm really so very sorry. Not the time for a full explanation of how it happened, but I really and genuinely am sorry. I've been a complete arsehole."

"You've got that right." Jane was holding on to her temper with a great effort. Her face was taut and white with anger, her limbs barely under control.

"Look," said Robert. "I really am whacked. Can I change and have cup of something ,then we can have a proper chat?"

"Bollocks," hissed Jane, "we'll talk now. I don't give a shit if you're tired". She was not in the mood to be magnanimous or understanding in any way. "What the fuck were you thinking? Fucking Sue for Christ's sake? *Sue!*" She turned and peered out of the window, unable to look at his smug face with its blank, flat expression right at this moment.

"It's unforgivable, unbelievable. We've only been married a short while; I can't believe it." Her voice rose in volume to just below a shriek. "But with that silly scrubber. For the love of God. What the fuck?"

She was annoyed with herself for her lack of more descriptive expletives but just at that moment it was all that came to mind, and he was lucky she was keeping her hands to herself.

"Do I not satisfy you? Is that it? Am I not good enough company? Why? At least give me a clue, why?" This last question was almost a scream.

He looked down at his hands, which were clasped together on the table and sighed. "I don't know, old thing," he breathed. "She offered and I went for it. Don't know why," he repeated unimaginatively.

This stilted almost monosyllabic conversation was not progressing as either had planned or expected during the last hours. Neither was saying what they really wanted to say. They were like two automatons enacting a pre-scripted, one-act play. Jane, for her part, was waiting for him to start wheedling, to say it was not his fault, to apologise, to promise it would never happen again, and to give a thousand reasons why he had strayed so early in their relationship. But he was saying nothing, not really. Just sitting there like a bloody fool, staring at his hands. She felt cheated, let down, as if there should be much more depth to this conversation. This was not in any of the scenarios that she had gone over in her mind. There had to be much more, oh yes, a great deal more.

Robert was desperately trying to decide how to move the conversation on. The initial explosion of anger had knocked him back on his heels mentally. For one awful moment he had actually thought that Jane was going to attack him. Thank the Lord she seemed to have controlled that impulse. He noticed that her hands were trembling as if she was only controlling their movements with an effort. Her face was like a mask, unnervingly still, no expression whatsoever, and her eyes glittered through narrowed lids. He needed a drink. Either a shot of alcohol or at the very least a cup of something hot. He had been travelling for many hours and had not slept since Jane's telephone call of last night. He needed his wits about him as never before, and a drink might restore some of his scattered control.

He stood and moved towards the lounge.

"I need a drink of something," he said over his shoulder. "I'm not being rude, truly I'm not, but give me a moment." He was not going to be drawn into a long exchange without refuelling.

"Take as many as you want." Jane's voice was clipped, sharp, dismissive. She placed her own mug into the sink and moved towards the front door.

"I'm going for a walk to clear my head. Get yourself together and as you say, we'll talk properly when I get back." She hoped she sounded uncaring, hard, the wronged woman who couldn't care less what he was doing. She heard him mutter an assent as she passed through the front door. On the whole, she was quite pleased with her behaviour during the last minutes. She had, after the initial outburst, been curt and decisive and, she thought, in control of the conversation. Was this whole mess beyond repair? She had not considered that far ahead. *Let's see what he has to say when he's had a chance to change and have a drink.* She would come back in about thirty minutes, and the fresh air would do her good. It was only as she walked down the path and into the lane that the tears came, and the despair engulfed her. Where did they go from here? "The absolute bastard," she whispered again. "You wanker." They could have enjoyed a lovely life here. Was the chance for that idyll gone for ever? She did not know. His seemingly casual and thoughtless infidelity had placed everything in jeopardy. The ground beneath her feet had turned to quicksand.

As she had prophesied, the brief walk and the fresh air rejuvenated her spirits, or rather her will to battle, and she tramped back to the house, pumping the justified anger back into her very being.

Slamming the front door behind her, largely to announce to her erring husband that she had returned with a vengeance, she stalked into the kitchen and stopped in amazement. Rob, changed into track suit bottoms and a t-shirt, was lounging with both trainer-clad feet on the table, a neutral expression on his face as he spoke into his mobile, which was nestled between his shoulder and his ear.

She had caught the words, "I think I'm over the worst, it looks like, dare I say, it all might be fine" as she entered. She realised with dismay and steeply mounting anger that her husband was actually speaking to his paramour, and worse, discussing her.

"Who the fuck is that?" she shouted, knowing full well. "Is that the scrubber?"

Rob quickly lowered his legs to the floor and held up a placating hand, which on the whole made things worse.

"Now look, old thing, there's no need for this to get hostile. Sue and I have made a mistake, we've admitted it, and hopefully we can all move on."

Jane's bellow must have been heard in the lane, which was thankfully deserted at that moment.

"Move on? Move on. That *is* what you said? I can't believe what I'm hearing." She began to move forward, and some part of her brain buried beneath her rage was amused to see him jump quickly up off the chair and move backwards, staying well out of her reach.

"The only moving on is going to be you and your tart, you utter, utter twat." She could feel tears of pure anger assembling behind her eyes once more and the knowledge made her angrier still. She irritably swiped the back of her hand across her face.

Knowing that Sue could hear every word that was being said, she pumped strength into her voice. "If you thought, either of you, that you would slink back in here like the slime you are and put everything right with a little erudite contrition and wheedling, you're wrong, so wrong." She raised her voice further. "Do you hear me, Sue? You can have him, slag, he's all yours. I wouldn't touch him with a bargepole, not after he's been anywhere near you. I would be frightened of catching something."

"Now come on, old thing, that's not fair." Robert once again held up a placating hand. "Sue and Brian have had an almighty row and she's off down to her sisters in Brighton for a few days until Bri calms down. God knows how Bri found out, but she thought to phone us and apologise to you and try to explain. Thought it was the least she could do."

Incredulous, Jane could not believe what she was hearing. She simply could not reconcile this wheedling moron in front of her with the man she had married just a few years ago.

"Brighton?" she snarled. "Well, you can fucking well join her down there then, can't you?" she sneered, showing a row of white teeth like an enraged dog. The intense anger had left her feeling drained and almost incapable of reasoned thought. "And I'll tell you how Brian knew, I phoned and told him. What the fuck did you think I would do?"

Robert looked genuinely shocked, as if this was something that had not occurred to him. "You did what?"

"You and I have nothing more to say to each other, just get out," said Jane, her voice sounding resigned and weary. She held her hand to her head, which was drumming with the beginnings of an almighty headache.

Rob was startled and immobile with shock. This was not how he had envisaged this difficult conversation progressing during his long hours of deliberation on the way down here. He wanted to point out that there was no way Jane could stay here without his financial input but realised that this was probably not the best time to mention this.

"I can't just up and run out," he began and was about to elaborate that he would need to pack at least a few toiletries, and an underwear change if he was to leave her to herself for a few days, but he did not get the chance.

Suddenly it was all too much – Rob's attitude, Sue on the other end of the phone listening to this, her pounding head. Jane looked around and picking up the nearest thing to her on the kitchen side, which happened to be a stoneware milk jug, and she hurled it with all of her strength at Rob's head. Luckily, it missed him by inches and crashed with stunning force into the newly exposed brick wall behind him. Stoneware shards and splinters of old brick cascaded onto the floor, showering Rob's shoulders with dust and debris.

Far too late, Rob had realised the depth of feeling that was facing him and quickly decided on a tactful retreat. They could talk again when this jug-hurling harridan had calmed down. Hurriedly whispering "I'll call you back" into the phone, he severed the connection, picked up the small travelling case that was still near the kitchen table where he had left it and glaring at Jane, edged past her and out through the front door, slamming it with unnecessary force. It was indicative of his defeat that he forgot to take his jacket with him, which was draped across the back of one of the chairs.

Jane heard him start up the car on the drive and the scrunching of tyres on gravel announced that he was backing out and driving away up the lane. She slumped down, all passion spent and putting her head in her hands, burst into tears.

****

In fact, Robert had not driven far at all. Sitting in his small lounge, Paul was surprised to see Robert and Jane's sports coupe pull up sharply in the lane just outside his window.

He had enjoyed a salad supper augmented with a nice Italian Dolcelatte cheese and some crusty bread, and was feeling slightly more positive than he had all day. He was playing Laura Marling on the CD deck and her gutsy voice delivering her homespun but basically sound philosophy of life was reviving his spirit, aided by the delicious Italian cheese.

His research today had added to his low mood, but he had sternly told himself that it was all a long time ago, it had happened and there was not a thing he could do about it, and frankly, what did it matter to him? He was only involved at all because his 'new' friend Jane was troubled about her so-called ghost sightings. *Let it all go until tomorrow,* he decided. For tonight, he would let the music and the food transform his mood. He relaxed in the single armchair he possessed and put his feet on the matching footstool that had come with it. As he slowly began to feel more himself, he saw Robert pull up outside, jump out of the car and ring his doorbell.

With a sigh, he levered himself up and crossed to the hallway and opened his front door.

"Robert, Hi! This is a surprise."

"Paul, sorry to bother you, but I need a quick chat." Robert looked flustered and breathless.

"Of course, mate, come on in." Paul led the way and stood before his small fireplace. "Would you like a coffee, or tea, or something stronger?"

Robert looked puzzled as if Paul had brought up a completely unknown subject.

"What?" he said. "Er no, no thank you, I… Look, I need to tell you a few things. Well, to ask for your advice really. Do you have a few minutes?"

Paul inwardly groaned; he knew what this would be about. How should he play this? Should he confess to Robert that he knew all about his infidelity, that Jane had told him? That might make things worse and send the agitated man in front of him off on a tangent imagining all sorts of nonsense.

"OK," he said, smiling, and put his hands into his pockets to show that he was both receptive and relaxed. "Fire away, I have all the time in the world."

"Where do I start?" said Robert. He peered out of the window, seeking inspiration and then decided just to blurt it out.

"I've been a complete arsehole and have cheated on Jane with the wife of one of my oldest friends. Well, you've met her of course, Sue. It's been going on for some months and now Jane has found out about it and thrown me out."

Well, you had to give the guy his due thought Paul, *no messing about, just straight out with it*. He blew out his cheeks and gave a snort of surprise.

"Blimey, mate," he said, "So the shit has hit the fan, so to speak."

"Yep, big time." Robert nodded and looking around, plonked himself down in the recently vacated armchair.

"Are you surprised?"

Rob just shook his head, looking exhausted.

Reaching around to the CD player, Paul pressed stop and Laura ceased to sing. "And why are you telling me this, Robert?"

Robert sighed and rubbed his hand across his eyes. "I don't know, mate, and that's the truth. I'm swanning off somewhere for a couple of days until the dust settles. Hopefully, we can sort this out but who knows?" He shook his head ruefully. "Who knows?" he repeated almost to himself, then looking up at Paul he continued, "Anyway, you have become a friend to us both in the short time we have been here, and I thought to fill you in before I left. Maybe you can have a word with Jane. Smooth things over, calm her down maybe. I don't know. Isn't that what you guys are good at?"

Paul looked down at rather pathetic figure sitting in his chair and knew he could definitely not say what he dearly wanted to say. That this chap had behaved like a complete moron and thrown everything away by being led through life by his cock. Instead, he chose his words carefully and settled on a trite phrase.

"Robert, I can't get involved. Whatever has happened is between you and your wife. True, you have very recently become friends of mine, but this is something in which I can't meddle, you must know that."

Robert stood and striding across the room, stood by the hall door looking at Paul. "Of course you can," he said. "You know you want to. I've seen it in your eyes."

Paul realised this was a desperate man trying to apportion and transfer blame for his own actions on to someone else.

"That's not worthy of you, mate," he said. "This is nothing to do with me." Robert moved to the front door, as Paul continued, "You want my advice? Go back home, and sort this out. You and Jane had the perfect life here, and you have put it all in jeopardy. Don't make matters worse by running away. If there is something to salvage from this mess, you have to work for it."

Robert looked back at his vicar, tall and fit, standing there in his t-shirt and jeans, so self-possessed, so confident, so in control of everything, and he felt a surge of jealousy. Jane liked this guy, he knew that. Since their marriage, he had been so attuned to his wife's moods and feelings that he had discerned instinctively her attraction to him, never realising that the problems were all of his own making and nothing to do with Paul. His anger welled up inside him as mistakenly he transferred most of the blame for his current troubles on to the innocent man in front of him.

"Fuck off," he said with vehemence, and flinging open the front door strode to his car, and with a squeal of tyres roared away up the lane.

Paul was stunned and shocked by this outburst. He moved to close the front door and returning to the lounge, poured himself a large scotch from the bottle he kept for troubled parishioners when they called for tea and sympathy.

"Well, that's the end to a perfect day," he said out aloud. He downed the drink with a single swallow and placed his empty glass on to the mantel shelf. "Fantastic," he said ruefully. "Bloody fantastic."

Chapter Fifteen

It was just after midday when they came for her. Cecily had risen early as she always did and arrived at the church in good time for the Sunday service. The church was busy as usual; in this year of our Lord, 1667 in England, one could be prosecuted for not attending regular worship.

The pews were crowded as farmers chatted loudly about the weather and crops, and what ailed their livestock. Wives gossiped and children laughed and cried, occasionally breaking free from parents to run up and down the aisles until chastised by their mothers and slinking back sulking to their seats.

Many people had smiled and bid Cecily a cheery good morning, as she sat in her customary place in the front pew as her position as the wife of the Reverend demanded. She had been a distant but well-liked figure in the village since her arrival and many had noted with reservations that occasionally, some said too often, she was not seen for some days due, as her husband said, to indisposition. Her diminutive figure, clad as usual in the homespun grey dress with the white collar and matching calico bonnet, sat demurely awaiting her husband, hands clasped around the small Bible clutched in her lap, her dark eyes looking forward to the altar, backed as it was by the stained-glass windows depicting scenes from the crucifixion.

As usual the mood changed abruptly as Reverend Morton arrived and stalked up to his customary position on the raised pulpit at the front of the church to the left of the altar. The pulpit itself was of his own design and constructed by the local carpenter. It was, as Nehemiah said, important that his flock could see and hear him perfectly in order that his catechism was clearly understood and obeyed. The good Lord demanded it.

His sermon today was delivered with even more vehemence and thunderous ranting than normal, warning every one of the dangers of fornication and licentious behaviour. Eyes glittering feverishly, he had boomed on and on for almost half an hour with dire warnings of retribution and the vengeance of the almighty for transgressors.

Once or twice, he had pointedly glared down at a somewhat mystified Cecily, who smiled back at him benevolently despite the sharp pain in her shoulders from the bites in her flesh following his strenuous taking of her last night.

She had strolled back from the church and asked Margaret if she could help in any way whilst the older woman was busy preparing lunch. It was a magnanimous offer from the mistress of the house to a servant and Margaret had shyly asked her if she could possibly feed the chickens as her son Thomas was not in evidence that morning. "Lord knows where he is, mistress," she had apologised. "I sometimes despair of that boy." Cecily turned away with a secret knowing smile curving her lips. She knew what was wrong with him, knew she would see him soon. A frisson of excitement passed through her as she thought of it.

It was a blustery morning with a watery sun appearing sporadically between racing pewter-coloured clouds. Occasionally, a few drops of rain carried by the wind pattered on to her clothes as she stood in the yard scattering seed and watching the chickens as they darted here and there on rangy legs to scrabble amongst the dusty earth and weeds.

Looking up, she was startled to see a soldier suddenly appear around the corner of the house. He carried a large and cumbersome musket held casually across his chest like a baby, and the wooden powder containers strung from the leather belt across his shoulder rattled as he moved. Each small wooden flask held a powder charge and a musket ball and because there were always twelve of them, they were nicknamed apostles.

The homespun coat that he wore might once have been red but was now so faded and threadbare that it was a nondescript colour. His knee-length breeches were patched and worn and ended at the knee above battered leather boots that folded over on themselves to hang down almost to mid-calf.

"Good morning to you, mistress," he said, his smile exposing blackened teeth. "Be you the minister's wife, Mistress Morton?"

Cecily, completely nonplussed at this unexpected arrival, nodded slightly. "I am," she said. "May I help you?"

The trooper had the good grace to look embarrassed at his task that morning.

"I must ask you to come with me, Mistress." He moved forward to stand in front of her. As he came near, Cecily caught a waft of warm leather, gun oil, and gunpowder overlaying the usual aroma of male sweat. At the same moment, sensing movement behind her, she turned to see three more troopers, similarly dressed, emerge from around the other corner of the house.

Margaret appeared at the back door, flour covering her arms up to the elbow, her face stern. She had caught a glimpse of the troopers from her kitchen window as they moved up the sides of the house.

"What's all this nonsense?" she demanded, her voice strident with fear and panic. "Why are you bothering my mistress on the sabbath?"

The troopers nearest her stopped and smirked, unsure of themselves. One looked to the man in front of Cecily in a silent plea for him to speak.

"We've orders to take this lady to the church, old dame."

"Orders from whom?" Margaret moved forward from the back door, clearly apprehensive but driven forward by her outrage.

"Orders from the Reverend Morton," answered the trooper. "That be his name, isn't it?"

He looked towards the other three, who all nodded.

"And since when does the Reverend Morton give orders to soldiers?" sneered Margaret. "He's not a military man as far as anyone does know."

"Since my officer gave me the order." The man was clearly unhappy with his task that morning and was trying to maintain some authority in the face of the angry, formidable-looking woman who had emerged unexpectedly from the house, and the stunningly beautiful younger woman who appeared completely nonplussed and bewildered.

The soldiers were part of the temporary garrison at nearby Oakhampton and their help had been requested by the local Reverend to avoid a possible civil disturbance, their Captain had said, during a public punishment. Their officer, glad to be given a task to occupy at least four of his shabby, indolent troop, had willingly agreed to the request. The soldiers had arrived the evening before and been billeted in a barn just outside the village. They were a little annoyed to be told by the Reverend, a rum-looking cove if ever they had seen one, that their task was to arrest his own wife, and escort her to the church. The Reverend had told them that there might be trouble from the locals whilst sentence was being carried out. What he had failed to tell them was that the victim was both young and beautiful.

"What sort of a sentence, Vicar?" they had demanded. They wanted no part in anything illegal and in fact would actively prevent such an act. Hurriedly, the Reverend had assured them that this was nothing untoward and was wholly within the law of the land agreed to by the local village council and more importantly was the will of the most just God. He had assured their officer on this point and that he expected them to carry out their duties as instructed. He would hate to pass an unfavourable report back to the garrison commander.

The threat was crude and transparent and had Nehemiah uttered it to these aged soldiers twenty years ago during the civil war, they would have given him a knife blade to chew on, but those times were gone and now they were just elderly men who wanted to stay in their regiment until they were put out to grass with hopefully a financial reward for their long service.

"So," said the trooper anxious to be away from this house and the stern old harridan in front of him, "Shall we go mistress?" He moved towards Cecily, forcing her to turn and move away, flanked by the other soldiers who towered above her, their battered floppy hats giving them extra height.

Margaret stood and watched them go, anger and disbelief twisting her face into a grimace, as they disappeared into the lane.

"God damn you to all eternity, Morton" she said savagely. "If any harm should befall that girl, I'll kill you so long there is breath in my body. God witness my oath."

She turned and stormed back into the house, slamming the old wooden door with such force that it shook the wall. She would follow on when she had changed her footwear.

****

Thomas was happy that morning and could not keep a broad grin from his suntanned face. He would see his love later and maybe they would have a few moments alone together, the Reverend being busy with his church duties for most of the Sabbath day.

He had walked the three miles to the farmstead of Bartholomew Baynton to help with the moving of his cattle from grazing on the moor down to the muddy paddock near the old man's farmstead. He had left at three that morning and they had all but completed the task an hour ago. The farmer had been hugely relieved and pleased at how well it had all gone and slipped an extra few coins into the hand of young Thomas in grateful thanks.

Thomas would be very late for church, but he had a good excuse, and he was sure that the Reverend would be able to find little fault in his explanation. *Hateful man*, he thought, *little do I care for his rebuke. I have kept my hands from his throat and for that he should be thankful.*

He stopped for breath as the church spire came into view no more than half a mile away. The sun appeared from behind a cloud, and he gazed upwards, squinting as he sought to find the black speck of a skylark as it hovered on the air, its shrill call clearly heard on the breeze. He spotted it and shielding his eyes, watched it avidly for some moments before he moved on towards the village.

As he approached the first houses, he was puzzled. It appeared that most of the villagers were gathered around the green near to the village pond. Was there no work to be done today, why had they not all disappeared to their homes? The Sunday service must be over by now.

As he came closer, he could hear the animal growl of a crowd in turmoil. Women's voices were raised in protest, and men shouted. *What on earth?* he thought as he hurried forward. A few people at the edge of the crowd turned and seeing who was approaching, looked troubled. Two of the men who counted themselves as friends of young Thomas stepped forward, hands raised, to halt his progress.

"Thomas, do not go forward. If you value your hide, there is nothing you can do".

****

Mute with fear and foreboding, Cecily had walked calmly with the soldiers down the lane to the village. She had not thought to ask them more, aware that they were just obeying orders. The senior of them had attempted to make some sort of conversation but was met with silence from this beautiful young woman so had given up the attempt.

As they entered the village, Cecily was stunned to see that the whole village appeared to be still on the green talking in hushed voices and glancing nervously towards her as she approached with her escort.

"Make way there!" shouted one of the soldiers. "Make way for officers of the crown."

Sullenly and almost reluctantly, the crowd parted before the little group as they moved forward. There were sporadic shouts of "Shame", and "God with you, Cecily" from women in the crowd, but such calls were hushed by their neighbours.

Nehemiah was standing near the village pond with three of four of the village council standing behind him looking distinctly uncomfortable.

"Nehemiah," began Cecily. "What is all this? Explain yourself."

"Be silent woman," shouted the Minister. His eyes were disdainful, furious, his face pale beneath his large black hat.

"Sergeant, why is the prisoner not bound?"

The sergeant stood beside the diminutive figure of Cecily and clearly did not like what he was involved in.

"There was no need, sir. Your wife" – he emphasised the word wife clearly so that all might hear his disdain – "offered no resistance whatsoever but came with us willingly." One of his men uttered an oath under his breath and he looked around, the expression on his face telling the man to keep silent whatever his thoughts.

Nehemiah stepped forward, towering over Cecily, who gazed calmly up at him, looking composed and this morning quite lovely.

"What do you have to say to us, whore of Babylon?"

For the first time Cecily realised what was amiss. Someone must have seen Thomas and her, and now the whole village knew. She was afraid.

Keeping her voice steady with an effort she said, "What do you wish me to explain, Nehemiah? Is there need for the presence of soldiers? I will keep nothing from you. You are my husband; you deserve the truth."

"Wretched woman!" screamed Nehemiah, his spittle flying into her face. "You admit your sin before God and this community. Do you dare deny that you have lain in sin with another of this village?" He did not pause for her to reply but took another step forward, his voice rising another octave. "The law and our Lord Almighty God demand penance and retribution for such an abomination. Here at this time and in this place, you shall pay for your crime."

He turned his back on his wife and stalked to the edge of the pool, where he turned and gazed at the crowd.

"All must witness the punishment and learn that though it be my own wife, fornication and adultery must not dwell in this land. Retribution must be swift and without pity, our Good Lord demands it."

He nodded to the troopers who, moving forwards almost gently, took hold of Cecily's arms.

"Bring forth the instrument of penance," shouted Nehemiah imperiously. He was almost gleeful, his near insanity clearly visible for the first time.

From behind the council members, Martin the blacksmith and a hulking farm worker employed for just this task pushed forward a wooden platform hastily constructed on instructions from the Reverend yesterday. It was not something Martin was proud of, but Nehemiah was backed, however unwillingly, by at least half of the council, and he had done what he was bidden.

The platform was on four small wooden wheels and atop it was what looked like a large seesaw. But the arms were not equal. One arm was far longer than the other and attached to the end of it was an iron chair.

Cecily, having spent all of her young life in London, realised finally what this was and with a small cry of fear began to step backwards. The soldiers tightening the grip on her arms, stopped her and moved her towards the chair.

"Bind the transgressor!" bellowed Nehemiah so that even those at the back of the crowd could hear. "She must suffer the ignominy and penance of the ducking stool, so that all may see and acknowledge her guilt."

From somewhere deep within the crowd, Margaret's voice was raised in rage. "Morton, you foul abomination, let her go."

There was a brief scuffle, and her voice was silenced by her own neighbours who feared for her safety and their own.

Nehemiah had turned to watch the disturbance but now looked back towards his wife and incredibly, smiled.

"Proceed with the ducking," he intoned self-importantly. One of the soldiers, aided by the hulking blacksmith's helper, pushed the contraption to the edge of the pond so that Cecily, now securely bound into the iron chair by leather twine, was suspended over the water. With a last look at the minister for approval, they received his nod and raised their end of the beam so that Cecily, with a last cry of despair, disappeared into the brown, murky waters, a stream of bubbles marking her position.

Kneeling, Nehemiah began to pray loudly for repentance from the prisoner and forgiveness from the Lord God on high. His hands, clasped together in front of him, were holding his Bible aloft.

From deep within the hushed crowd, Margaret's voice could be heard screaming with helpless rage and despair. Even the council members who had agreed to this display were now looking uncomfortable and embarrassed. They wanted this over before events got out of hand.

Finally, Nehemiah stood up, the knees of his breeches muddy and discoloured. He nodded again to the men on the beam and with a downward heave on the beam, Cecily appeared back out of the pond. Brown and turgid water streamed from her clothes and hair. Her mouth was open and screaming and choking, green fronds of weed festooned across her shoulders.

"Whore, have you asked the good Lord for forgiveness?" screeched Nehemiah. "Do you prostrate yourself before the almighty and before me your husband and do penance?"

Cecily was coughing and retching hugely, water streaming from her terrified eyes. It was doubtful that she had even heard her husbands' words.

Receiving no answer that satisfied him, Nehemiah nodded again to the soldier. "Once more shall she face God's wrath. Lower again."

There was a concerted growl of anger and discontent amongst the crowd as the still coughing and gasping Cecily was lowered once more beneath the surface of the water. The general consensus seemed to be that if they must witness this charade, then once was enough.

"Morton, you whoreson I'm going to kill you." The voice of Thomas was huge and cracked with emotion, terrible in its rage. He was ploughing his way through the crowd, who parted before him like the bow wave from a ship. Two of the council attempted to stop him with hands raised in caution but one was felled with a blow that would have stunned an ox. After a lifetime working out of doors, Thomas was very strong, and just at that moment beyond reason, wild with pure hatred.

Turning, Nehemiah took in the scene in an instant.

"Bar that man" he shouted, anxiety and fear lending urgency to his instruction. "Bar him, I say".

One of the troopers tried to grab hold of Thomas's sleeve but was physically picked up and himself thrown into the pond with a cry.

Still Thomas came on, head down, hands working themselves into fists, teeth grinding, white face drawn back into a terrible mask of pure wrath.

Another soldier appeared behind Thomas and almost gently tapped him behind the ear with the heavy wooden stock of his musket. Thomas went down like a puppet that has had its strings cut and lay very still in a crumpled heap, almost at the feet of Nehemiah.

Turning, the shaken Reverend gestured to the men on the ducking stool.

"Raise her up once more. We consider that she has been adequately punished for her misguided and sinful actions. Raise her up, I say."

Once more, the saturated figure of Cecily emerged from the muddy water which streamed again in rivulets from her clothes and hair. Her head was lolled forward on her long neck and moved from side to side with the swaying of the stool. From her mouth there came no sound, her eyes wide open and unseeing.

Quickly, the soldiers cut the leather thongs that bound her and laid her body onto the grass. Old Ezekial Lynom, the nearest thing the village had to an apothecary, limped forward and lowered his aged old body down to kneel next to Cecily. The anxious, silent crowd watched breathlessly as he turned her over on to her stomach and pulled her shoulders backwards, pounding her back before turning her over on to her back and appearing to breathe into her mouth.

Two of the women at the front of the crowd knelt, heedless of the staining on their long skirts and put their hands together in prayer.

Nehemiah had his back to the scene as he issued instructions to the soldiers, his voice lowered so that none might hear. He was giving orders that Thomas should be bound hand and foot and taken to his house, there to be left until he had time to deal with him. Grateful to be rid of this place and this man, the soldiers picked up the still prone Thomas and tramped their way through the crowd, disappearing up the lane.

It was only then that Nehemiah realised that something was amiss.

"Has she spoken yet, Ezekial?" he queried, his voice loud in its pomposity.

The old man's head was still lowered, his grey wispy hair all awry around his shoulders. Those close by thought they heard him whisper. "Poor maid. Poor little maid."

Climbing slowly to his feet, his arthritic old legs trembling with the effort, Ezekial turned and gazed at Nehemiah, and his look was not friendly.

"No, sir," he croaked. "She will never speak again. Young Cecily is dead. And may the Lord God himself damn you for all eternity for what you have done this day."

Without saying anything further, he trudged off through the crowd. Many as he passed patted the old man's shoulders in sympathy and support.

Nehemiah was completely shaken. This what not what he had intended at all. He had thought to discipline his erring wife and at the same time enforce his standing within this small and gullible community, ensuring their obedience to his word in the future.

He realised that Jonas Moore, the head of the parochial council, was standing in front of him backed by three others of the village elders.

"Reverend Morton," began Moore, "You will leave this place forthwith, sir. Leave it and never return. If you do, I cannot guarantee your safety, as God is my witness."

Nehemiah was stunned. This nobody was threatening him. Ordering him to leave this godforsaken little place. He, Nehemiah Morton. It was unbelievable, intolerable. Puffing out his chest, he attempted to outstare the smaller man, but Jonas was outraged at the judicial murder that he had just witnessed and would not back down. Instead, he took another step forward, forcing Nehemiah to move backwards.

"I and all the council agreed to this ecumenical farce, but this was not what we intended, God pity us. But now we are all agreed, and you will go, and today. Our own consciences will punish us in the years to come. But at least we can be rid of you, a religious zealot who has just committed murder in the name of a God you have never known."

The crowd behind him cheered as one, and male oaths were raised, threatening violence on his person if he stayed.

Nehemiah cringed in the face of this concerted anger. He looked from face to face, seeking at least one ally, anyone to offer aid, but there was no one, just a sea of hard faces and barely concealed hatred. His shoulders sagged as he realised that there was indeed no help and that he must go.

"Very well, you wretches," he hissed. "May the good Lord aid me in my endeavours and punish you all for this…"

He got no further. Jonas once again stepped forward and screamed directly into his face.

"GO, you disgraceful cleric. GO!"

Many in the crowd echoed his words. It looked as if they were preparing to seize him. From the corner of his eye, he could see several of the villagers gently, almost reverentially, picking up the still dripping body of Cecily and carrying her to the church.

"Having stood by and let this happen, we can at least give your poor wife a decent Christian burial, you odious man," snarled Jonas. "It is the very least we can do. God see us, we are a sorry bunch."

He turned his back on Nehemiah to watch the sad little group walk past in the direction of the church porch. It signalled his summary dismissal of their erstwhile vicar. They wanted an end of him.

Without a further word, Reverend Nehemiah Morton settled his hat on to his head and stalked off up the lane to his house, with as much dignity as he could muster. He would go, he would find somewhere else to eke out his living and do God's work. His unfaithful wife had been taught a lesson, and a small loss was she. Yes, it was time to move on. But first there was that oaf Thomas to be dealt with. The beguiler of his innocent wife, the despoiler of her virtue, the adulterer. The root of all this trouble. He lengthened his stride.

****

Paul loved this sort of pub. Ceiling beams covered in horse brasses, white painted walls festooned with old paintings and black and white photographs, presumably of old and valued customers who had long since shuffled off this mortal coil. Small wall-mounted lamps emitted a low, yellow comforting glow through patterned half lampshades, many scorched from a too powerful bulb .

If you could see the floor, it would be covered in an ancient, patterned carpet, the colours almost obliterated by the thousands of customers who had stood on it during the last God knows how many years. Yes, he felt relaxed here.

He was perched on a tall stool against a shelf which served as a resting place for the glasses of drinkers who surrounded him, all talking and laughing as they enjoyed an early Friday evening drink on their way home.

Adele was crooning in the background and could just be heard above the chatter and laughter of the gathered throng. Every so often an old ship's bell would ring from the bar signalling that one of the staff had been bought a drink. By tradition this always brought forth a muted cheer.

Paul had needed to complete his research about Cecily Morton at Exeter Library for the final time and had been helped a great deal once more by the effervescent and willing Karen. There was no doubt she was a good-looking young woman, he thought as he watched her pirouette through the crowd towards him, and he could not help but admire her innate dress sense – reserved as befitted her position in the library but with a certain flair and panache that could not be taught. Her slimfit black jeans and a bright green top enhanced her figure, and it was no accident, he thought, that her eye shadow and nail varnish mimicked the colour of the top.

"Sorry about that," she said breathlessly as she scrambled up on to the stool that he had been guarding. "I've drunk too much coffee today, and it always means a few trips to the ladies." She laughed infectiously and he found himself returning it.

"No worries," he said. "This is a nice place. Good crowd, and the beer's OK."

She nodded as she took a sip of her vodka and tonic.

"Yep," she said, "I come here a lot. It's very handy being so near the library. I thought you might appreciate it."

She was one of those people, he noted, whose eyes can laugh as well as their mouth. She was very pretty, and again he had to remind himself that she was only in her mid-twenties, and it was only because she had been so useful and helpful to him with his research that afternoon that he had agreed to accompany her for a quick 'voddy' as she termed it before he headed home. This way lay danger and he was very aware to steer the conversation to areas that he felt were harmless.

"Thanks again for your help today," he said, "I'd have floundered a bit without you."

She smiled broadly, pleased with the compliment, and that he had agreed to come to the pub with her.

"It's a knack," she replied. "You need to know your way around these old tomes. The guys who wrote them were what we now call that awful term 'academics'. Many of them were country parsons looking for something to fill their days with in between services. I've had a lot of dealings with our friend Reverend Walton over the last two years. A lot of our old boys like to come in and read what he collated. It's quite interesting really, and most of them are really nice old chaps."

He took a long swig of his beer and wiped his mouth with the back of his hand. "Well, I'd have been lost without you Karen, so a big thanks to you." He raised his glass to her and took another drink.

Clearly pleased with the compliment, she smiled hugely back at him and nodded her head in acquiescence.

"You're welcome, kind sir," she beamed. "Can I ask what is the interest in this Cecily and what happened to her? This is third time you've been in and looked for info about her. Was she a relative or something?"

A young man in a baggy jumper and jeans ambled past a little the worse for drink, his face flushed, his clothes dishevelled. Incongruously, in this hot weather, he was wearing a purple anorak over his jumper and the colour clashed horribly with his mop of unruly red hair

"Kazza," he said. "How the devil are you, girl?"

His eyes travelled over Paul insolently, clearly puzzled as to why the prettiest girl on the library staff was spending time with this old geezer. Paul stared calmly back.

Karen's face had immediately lost its sparkle as he turned up and with a hard look, she dismissed him disdainfully.

"I'm fine, Nigel, thank you. I'm not being rude, but we're having a confidential chat here. Do you mind?"

Nigel took the hint immediately and holding up his hands to placate the obviously miffed woman in front of him, he disappeared into the crowd.

"Sorry about that," grinned Karen. "He's the village idiot. Don't know why on earth the library employed him."

Paul grinned and nodded. "OK."

"Anyway, what was I saying? Oh yes, do you think this Cecily was a relative of yours or what?"

Paul shook his head. "No, nothing Like that. Some friends of mine in the village live in the house she used to live in, and it sparked my interest. I already knew a little about her husband, the infamous Nehemiah Morton, but absolutely nothing until now about his young wife. Bit boring really."

"You seemed really interested in this other chap; the one suspected of being the recipient of her affections. They suspect he was her paramour then?"

Paul laughed out aloud. "Paramour? What sort of a word is that for someone of your age to be using?"

Karen took another sip from her glass and looked a little sheepish. "Well, it's what they called them in those days, wasn't it? It's a nice word anyway, paramour." She chuckled as she said it, and he realised again how pretty she was, especially when she laughed.

"Anyway," she continued, "I'm twenty-seven soon." It was information she wanted him to know, not only her age but that it would soon be her birthday.

Paul nodded sagely, unwilling to take the subject of age further.

"Yep, this chap Thomas seems to be the main suspect in that regard." Paul had grown a little serious. "Our friend Walton only mentions him twice, and he is not even sure if that was his actual name. I was confused by the time we found that snippet and confess to being guided largely by you by then."

Karen took another sip and topped up her glass with what was left of her tonic. "Yeah," she said. "Thomas. Our Reverend was not even sure what his surname was despite all of his searching. He must be one of those people who just pop in and out of a story, then are gone. Strange how he just disappears though, don't you think?"

Paul was peering into his almost empty pint pot as he listened to her. "Yeah," he murmured. "Very strange. Isn't it odd how we become involved with these people and actually begin to be concerned about them, even though they have been dead and gone for many a long year?"

Karen gazed at him and wished they were discussing something else, like would he take her to dinner, or could they go back to his place. She really liked this good-looking bloke who had turned up at the library. Who knew when you were going to meet someone? Yes, he was older than her but who cared about things like that in this day and age? There was something about him, though, that she could not quite put her finger on. His smile was infectious, but he always seemed to hold something back, and there was a melancholy air about him that she could not penetrate.

"It was a long time ago," she offered softly. "Over three hundred years."

Seeming to rouse himself, Paul looked up at her and smiled again. "Yep, you're right," he said. "Let's not get too down about it. How about another drink, then I really must be going?"

She nodded and grinned. "That would be great, thanks." She watched him as he shouldered his way through the crowd. He had not offered anything else, just another drink and then he had to go.

Oh well' just enjoy it while it lasts, Karen, she said to herself. But she hummed to herself as she imagined the future.

****

Chapter Sixteen

The West Pier on Brighton seafront was a major tourist attraction for over one hundred years, jutting as it did 340 metres out into the sea, allowing Victorian, Edwardian, pre- and post-war sightseers the thrill of looking back at the shingle beach from their lofty position above the restless waves, some considerable distance from the shore.

Built by Eugenius Birch in 1866, it performed its task as a tourist attraction for the town until its closure in 1975. From then on it gradually fell into disrepair, with parts of it partially collapsing. In the violent storms of 2002 major sections of it fell into the hungry sea beneath and the old edifice was finally finished off by two successive fires the following year, widely suspected but never proven to be arson.

Parts of the metal structure still remain, stubbornly resisting the elements and resembling rotting teeth in an aged and ravaged mouth. The waters froth and boil around these steel remnants and are a constant source of irritation to do-gooders who ceaselessly demand action to rid the town of this eyesore.

Sue and Robert sat on a bench on the promenade and idly gazed at the white water as it frothed around the truncated steel legs as they idly consumed their ice cream cones. Each was busy within their own thoughts.

It was a beautiful early summer morning which promised to be very hot as the morning wore on. The sea was a benevolent blue, reflecting the cloudless sky, and small wavelets benignly lapped at the beach which hissed as the shingle was moved. Out at sea, small white yachts appeared in the blue haze as they headed out into the English Channel on adventures of their own.

The crowds of later in the day had not yet materialised, but there were still couples strolling, old people sitting on benches, and harassed parents cajoling noisy children as they passed by. There were even a few hardy souls braving the somnolent but chilly sea with an early morning dip, in the hope, no doubt, that it was doing them good. A few families had already set up camp on the beach and were busy attempting to erect a canvas wall of windbreaks to protect them against the breeze. Husbands and fathers stripped to swimming trunks lustily wielded mallets with gusto as their wives, already seated on towels, were busy coating themselves and their children with suncream.

Sue was content. The turmoil of the previous week seemed to be calming down a little, and she had even had what passed for a civilised telephone conversation with Brian last night. He seemed to be calming down a little but still steadfastly refused to speak to Robert, issuing prophecies that he would never speak to his erstwhile best friend ever again. Truth be told, Sue was not sure what she wanted to happen next. Did she really want to leave Brian for good and spend the rest of her life with the man who sat next to her, or did she want to try again with Brian, and file this episode under the heading of an adventure and opportunity that she would be glad to remember fondly in her dotage? She was not at all sure, but for the moment she was content to sit in the early morning sunshine and eat her ice cream.

Robert was quite certain what he wanted to do. He had wrestled with his conscience during the last few days. Arriving in Brighton fresh from his unedifying and hasty departure from the village, he had checked into a small B&B just off the promenade and decided to spend a few days taking stock. Sue was staying at her sister's house and was adamant that he absolutely must not turn up there as she was already taking serious grief from her sibling about her actions. "What the hell have you done to poor old Brian?" was a sentence repeated often during the frequent lectures. It was clear where her sister's sympathies lay, and who was to blame.

Sue had sneaked out for a few hours each day and spent the time with Rob, in his bed, or in a bar, or just walking the prom. But somehow now that he had left Jane, and Brian knew what was happening, the thrill had somehow gone, and what had been deliciously naughty and daring was all much more mundane and a little shabby.

Rob had decided, after much soul searching, that whatever the consequences he would go back to the village and try to set right somehow the turmoil he had caused and resume his life with the woman that he loved despite it all. But he had to tell Sue of his decision, and he was not looking forward to that at all.

This ice cream was good, he had always liked salted caramel and when paired in a double cone with pistachio, it was to him the perfect blend. Sue had selected raspberry ripple and chocolate chip and was repeatedly having to wipe her chin with her tissue as it melted in the sun.

She looked good this morning, he had to admit. Her white full-length split hem summer dress billowed around her legs like the petals of a huge orchid. Her tanned legs emerging from its folds ended in strappy sandals studded with fake diamonds which flashed provocatively in the morning sunlight every time she moved. He had noticed several harassed dads chivvying children along the seafront leer at her with envy as they passed.

He loved the attention she was getting, which he felt reflected on him as her companion. He smirked with pleasure as he noticed the envious looks of the men as they glared at him wondering what he had that he should be with a beauty like that.

He waited until she had finished her ice cream and thrown the last crumbs of the cone on to the floor to be squabbled over by a pair of juvenile seagulls.

"I need to speak to you," he said.

Sue turned to look at him, the sunglasses perched on the top of her head flashing in the sun.

"You're going to go back and try to make it up with Jane. Am I right?"

He smiled self-consciously and nodded gently. "Yep," he said. "Correct."

Sue was secretly relieved. She had more or less decided on much the same course of action following last night's conversation with Brian. She was not sure what the outcome would be on meeting with her severely miffed husband, but he had seemed receptive to a chat, and she thought it was worth at least talking.

"It's not the same, is it?" she stated. She meant of course that since their illicit affair had come out into the open, the gorgeous sense of danger, subterfuge and secrecy had all disappeared, and it now seemed almost seedy.

He knew what she meant immediately and smiled again.

"No," he said. "It's funny, isn't it? Somehow all the magic has gone. I feel somehow like a naughty schoolboy who's been found smoking behind the bike sheds."

She laughed low and throatily and reaching out, laid her hand on his leg.

"Were you ever caught smoking then? I didn't know."

"Nah, I was much too well behaved for that. The most I got was a couple of detentions for failing to get homework in on time."

Retrieving her hand, Sue brushed a few cone crumbs from her dress.

"Will Jane take you back, do you think?"

Robert peered out to sea and shook his head. "I don't know. But I can't just walk away like this and leave her to it." He turned his head again to look at her. "Anyway, I've got to find out if she had anything going on with that fucking vicar."

Sue was shocked and her face showed it. "Who? Paul? What on earth makes you think that?"

Robert shook his head ruefully. "Maybe it's just me, but I don't trust that bloke, and I know Jane. I could see she was attracted to him from the get-go. Oh, don't get me wrong, I don't imagine she would ever have done anything, her family tradition of loyalty is too ingrained in her, but she likes him, take my word for it".

"And what about him? He's a good-looking bloke and no mistake, many women wouldn't hesitate with him, but he's a vicar for Christ's sake". She suddenly realised that she was probably blaspheming and chuckled, her white teeth flashing against her tan.

"So that's us finished then, is it?" she sounded suddenly combative.

Robert knew he had to be very careful here. True, there had never been any real deep feelings between them, only lust and a shared attraction to being naughty and seizing life's opportunities, but he did not want to offend this woman, he had known her too long, liked her a lot, and recognised that she had risked a great deal herself during their little interlude.

He took a deep breath as he collected his thoughts. "What do you want to do?"

Sue peered at him and made her decision almost on the instant. "I think it's run its course, Rob. It's been lovely, you're lovely, and I've enjoyed every moment of it but it's time to get back to real life, isn't it? I think Bri will get over it, certainly with me, but I fear, old mate, that you have shot your bolt forever with him".

Rob nodded "Yeah, I know, and I'm genuinely sorry about that. We go back a long way, a lot of memories. All my fault, of course. Well, ours, yours and mine."

She nodded resignedly, accepting the statement. Then reaching out, she took his hand. "I'm going now, lover." She smiled. "Take care, and if you can, try to let me know how you get on."

On an impulse she withdrew her hand and seemed to be fumbling under her dress before leaning forward to touch her ankles. He wondered what she was doing.

"Here," she said, standing up and thrusting something warm into his hand. "A keepsake, something to remember me by."

Looking down, he realised she had given him the knickers that she had just removed.

He laughed aloud and opened them out to look. They were small and white and on the front in mauve was a print of a small Mr Man figure over which was printed 'Little Miss Chatterbox'.

"Bugger off, will you," he chortled, "before I change my mind." His eyes ran over her from head to toe. "You are still such a sexy cow."

He waved her away and she laughed herself, a light, carefree laugh as if a great weight had been lifted from her shoulders. Leaning forward, she lightly kissed his cheek and ruffled his hair, before turning and striding away down the promenade, drawing envious glances from two old traffic wardens as she flounced past them.

He watched her retreating figure for many minutes as she gradually disappeared from his sight, and from his life, then with a sigh he stood up and went to check out of his digs and go to try and save his marriage.

****

Thomas was not quite sure where he was. He had faded in and out of consciousness for some minutes, but his vision would not completely clear, things were still a little blurry and refused to focus. His mind felt heavy and slow, and he was trying to remember how he came to be lying on this stoneflagged floor.

He could not seem to move his arms, or his legs, and his head hurt with a sharp, stabbing pain every time he tried to raise it off the floor.

He decided to lie quiet for a few moments and wait for things to feel more normal. He looked up at the raftered ceiling and realised that he was on the floor of the kitchen in the Reverend's house. Why was he there?

He groaned as a spasm of cramp seized his left leg and he rolled over on to his back to ease the weight on it. That was a little better but not much.

Where was Cecily or his mother? Why were they not here in this place where his mother especially spent much of her life?

He lay his head back on to the cold stones and tried to take stock, to recall what had brought him here. With an effort he took a few deep breaths and attempted to calm his mind.

Suddenly he knew. The memories of the hateful scene at the village pond in front of the church came back, and he realised that one of the soldiers (why were there soldiers on the village green?) must have hit him on the back of the head with his musket. He could feel a growing lump already the size of an egg on the back of his head and he groaned again. It hurt.

He was battering his way through the crowd to get to Morton, he recalled it all now. His rage had been all-consuming when he had seen what was happening to Cecily, his love. He had felled one of his old friends, that he knew, and he seemed to remember throwing a soldier into the pond.

Cecily! Where was Cecily? Why was she not here? If that God-cursed Vicar had harmed her, he would pay, God on the Cross he would pay. He snarled at the ceiling, his face a mask of hatred.

It was then that he heard the front door open, and footsteps moving through the hall. Lifting his head he watched Nehemiah stalk into the kitchen, his eyes never leaving the face of Thomas, like a lizard watching its prey as it crept up to it.

"So," Nehemiah sneered, "I see our good troopers obeyed my last instructions and trussed you up tightly so you cannot do further harm to anyone."

He paused and looked down at Thomas before lashing out with a vicious kick that hit the prone, defenceless Thomas in the ribs. He hissed with pain, but would not cry out, refusing to give this hated cleric the satisfaction.

"How brave of you, Morton," snarled Thomas through gritted teeth. "And how typical of your kind to kick a bound man who cannot defend himself. Are you sure you feel safe enough?"

Nehemiah smiled and walked over to the window. "It will be dark soon, oaf, and soon I shall be gone from this place forever. But first I have some things to settle".

He bowed down the better to look into the face of the bound man. "You have vexed me greatly, country bumpkin, and that is not a wise thing to do."

He kicked Thomas again, before removing his hat and placing it on the table, as if preparing for a task.

"Where is Cecily?" said Thomas. "What have you done with her, whoreson? Tell me."

Nehemiah laughed, a low, ugly sound, disdainful, and full of malice. "I have done nothing with *my wife*." He sneered, emphasising the word 'wife'. "She is sleeping soundly and no doubt very glad to be rid of your inappropriate attentions." He spread his hands, a look of condescension on his pale face which belied the glittering of his eyes. "Sadly, you will not be able to speak with her again. Not able to tempt her to infidelity with your coarse homespun blatherings. She will not hear you any further. How sad, how very annoying that must be for you."

He grinned with sheer vindictive pleasure. He was enjoying this, and though it would be his last act as vicar of this parish, he had a plan in mind to punish this malefactor, this oaf, this wife stealer. Oh yes, he had formulated a course of action as he had tramped back from the disagreeable scene near the pond.

"Go," they had said to him. "Go" to him, Nehemiah Morton. Instructions from a group of semi-literate yokels to him, their obvious superior and servant of God. Well, very well, he would go, but before he did so he would have his vengeance.

"You have not answered my question, Morton," spat Thomas from the floor, his eyes liquid with hate and pain. "What has become of Cecily?"

"Cecily?" said Nehemiah as if he were trying to recall a name that he only vaguely knew. "Oh, Cecily is dead, I'm afraid. She did not survive the second ducking." He actually smiled and if Thomas could have escaped his bonds for even a second, he would have surely killed the older man on the spot. Wiped him from the face of the earth with no more thought than treading on a fly. Sent him off to meet his God in the sure and certain knowledge that God would reject him.

"It was plain to all that she was guilty of the charges of adultery and fornication laid against her, and our good Lord saw fit to take her unto him, no doubt to rescue her immortal soul from further temptation, and to offer divine instruction for her redemption."

Thomas groaned with rage and a sadness so intense that he could not formulate his thoughts for some moment. He pictured Cecily's face smiling up at him, felt the warmth of her body pressed up against his as they kissed. Now she was dead and cold, gone from his life forever. He wanted to kill this man so badly, if only the good Lord would grant him the strength to break these accursed leather bonds.

"You foul, murdering bastard," he snarled, spittle flying from his lips as a testament to his rage. "That's you for hell then, you charlatan, you diseased cleric. Your God burns murderers, does he not? You will suffer the torments of the flames for all eternity…" He would have said more but his anger overtook him, and he finished on a cry of pure anguish. "Cecily," he screamed. "Cecily, my love." He lay back on to the cold floor and sobbed quietly to himself.

Nehemiah gazed down at him, wondering what it was like to feel such emotion, to love someone so much that it inspired such outpourings. He realised that he would probably never know. He turned and strode out of the kitchen. He needed to check that he had the necessary instruments and materials to follow through with his plan to finish this little mummer play before he departed this wretched place forever.

Chapter Seventeen

Paul had a christening later today, and his presence had been requested by the local women's guild group just after lunch, so he had decided to don his black shirt and dog collar for the day when he dressed that morning. There was little sense in lounging around in jeans and a t-shirt, then having to change later. He was, after all, he reminded himself, a vicar. People expected him to look the part if they called on him unexpectedly for advice, or comfort, or the million other reasons they announced when they rang his doorbell.

He was sitting in his parlour nursing his second coffee of the day. It was one of those 'morose' days that he experienced periodically, along with everyone else he expected, and for no apparent reason. He had slept badly last night and had a recurrence of the dream that he had experienced several times in the last few years. He was walking up a steep, grass-covered hill, Marion some way in front holding the hand of their son and try as he might, he could not catch up with them. She appeared not to hear his shouts for her to slow down and wait for him, but moved ever further away, clutching the hand of the little boy tightly, refusing to look backwards. His shouts became more strident, more insistent and always in the end he awoke at that moment, sweating and anxious. It was disconcerting and always left him rebellious and angry, railing at the uncaring and vengeful world that had done this to him.

He heard now, as he often did, the worldly-wise old vicar in the retreat giving him another talking-to during the terrible weeks after the accident.

"Has your wife come to visit you, my son?"

Paul had morosely shaken his head. "No."

"Well, no matter, sometimes they do and sometimes they don't. We are not meant to know why."

Paul gave him a flat look. "Sometimes I struggle to remember what she looked like."

The kindly old man smiled gently. "Don't try too hard. Put her face in context, in a specific memory."

Paul nodded glumly and looked at the floor. Gently, the old man reached across and laid his hand on his shoulder.

"And you keep those memories tight, hold them fast, never let them go because they are something that the darkness can't take away from you."

The memory of this conversation brought a slow smile to Paul's face and shaking himself, he peered out of the window.

It was sunny outside, a clear blue sky heralding a warm day, but even that did not lift his spirits much this morning, and he decided to go for a brisk walk around the parish to meet and greet his flock and reassure them that he was ever-present in their lives. Yes, that was what he would do, but first, well, he would have another coffee. Who was there to stop him? He prided himself on never being dilatory, always finding something worthwhile to fill his daylight hours, but every now and then he awoke to this fatigued lack of drive. Well, everyone did, didn't they?

The door chimes came as a welcome break to his thoughts, and he ambled to the door with something like enthusiasm.

It was Karen from the library, looking beautiful that morning, her blonde bob glowing in the bright sunlight. She was dressed in skintight white jeans, and a yellow strappy top. Silver earrings falling in a straight drop of chain reaching from her lobes to mid-neck completed her ensemble. Her slightly tanned skin seemed to glow.

She was smiling self-consciously and chuckled infectiously as she saw his look of complete surprise.

"Hi," she grinned. "I hope you don't mind, but I have something to show you and wanted to surprise you."

Despite himself, Paul had to grin in reply. "You have indeed done that. How on earth did you find where I live?"

"You mentioned this village in passing and I knew a few enquiries among the locals would soon find you out." Her smile looked a little uncertain now as she suddenly realised, he might not want to see her again.

"But what did surprise me," she carried on, "Is that you're a vicar. Bloody hell, a vicar." She covered her mouth with her hand to suppress another expletive.

He could not be angry; it was not a secret after all but merely something that he did not broadcast outside of the village. Her smile and effervescent good humour were very welcome this fine morning, just what was required.

"Sorry," he said stepping backwards. "Where are my manners? Come on in." She followed him inside and looked around her with interest.

"You live alone then I see," she said tartly.

"Is it that obvious?" He had moved into the kitchen. "Coffee?"

"Yes please, black."

"How's this?" He called over the clink of cups. "No work today?"

"Nope, I get a day off in the week as I have to work Saturdays." She did a slow circuit of the room, peering with interest at the picture of Marion and a small child. She was humming to herself; the first few minutes of this meeting had gone better than she expected.

He came back into the room and handed her a mug. "Here you go, only instant, I'm afraid. Sit down."

Taking the coffee, Karen perched on the end of the sofa and removed her shoulder-strapped handbag and laid it next to her.

They chatted amiably about nothing for a few moments. She was obviously very nervous, and he was wondering why she had sought him out, pleasant as it was to be tracked down by a pretty young woman.

"Look," she said finally, laying her cup down on the coffee table in front of her. "I had no way of knowing if you would ever come back to the library again, and I discovered something yesterday that I just had to show you."

"I'm glad you did track me down," he said, mimicking her phrase. "I realised how rude I had been the other day, just disappearing off into the sunset like that. I enjoyed myself in that pub."

She felt a frisson of excitement pass through her as he said this. It had been worth it then; he was glad to see her. He was a really nice man, even though he was a vicar. She did not want to just leave things as they were. Girls like her in their late twenties tended to realise that there was not that much out there in the way of eligible males. A good looking blond-haired, broad-shouldered albeit older man was not something to let pass by.

"I'm glad," she smiled, "so did I."

She leaned down and extracted what looked like some photographs from her bag.

"I remembered yesterday that we boast a large collection of old photographs of the county, so I spent an idle hour yesterday afternoon going through them. Thankfully, someone many years ago had the foresight to write on the backs where they were taken, or where they guessed they were taken. Some of them go back to the mid 1800s. I thought you might like to see them."

His interest was piqued immediately. "Yes, indeed I would," he said. "Bring them over to the table, the light's better there."

They stood very close together as she laid out half a dozen sepia toned black and white photographs. She was inches smaller than he was, her head was level with his shoulder but this close he was very aware of the scent that she was wearing.

"There," she said, finishing her arrangement. "Have a look."

One faded old photo was of the village pub and from the look of it, back around 1910. There were hanging baskets full of flowers on the front wall either side of the windows, which he knew were not there now, and the porch had been drastically enlarged over the years. A large farm wagon of some sort was near the front door, a patient carthorse standing stoically between its shafts. Arranged behind it were three or four serious looking gents self-consciously posing. They all had large moustaches which was the fashion of the time, and each wore a collarless shirt and waistcoat. One sported a bowler hat.

"I bet you if I took these down to the pub there would be someone there who recognised an old grandad or some other relative here," said Paul. He leant down and peered at another picture which showed a group of women all in bonnets and long aprons posed in front of the church, each holding a wicker basket full of vegetables or flowers. Turning it over he read 'Village fete 1913'.

He shook his head and looked down at Karen, who was grinning up at him, taking pleasure in his absorption. This had been a good idea.

"Thanks for doing this, Karen." He smiled down at her. "I owe you one."

He leaned his hand on to her shoulder.

She laughed. "I know you do. But it's this one that I think you will find of interest; I know I felt cold when I came across it." She tapped her long, painted fingernail against another photograph.

Paul leaned his arms against the table and peered more closely. It was a photograph of an open-sided, thatch-roofed shack. In the darkness within could just be made out the glowing embers of a forge of some sort. Huge bellows stood at the side of it. Standing at the front of the building was a burly figure in a full-length leather apron. He was holding a large sledgehammer over his shoulder, his other hand resting proprietarily on the head of a young boy who was obviously his son. Both were smiling shyly at the camera.

The handwritten legend on the back when Paul turned it over said, 'Village blacksmiths forge, circa 1919'.

He was puzzled. "That's not here," he said. "This village has no blacksmiths forge. It must be somewhere else."

Karen rested her hand on his arm and said, "Oh yes, it is. I did some checking. You're correct there, is no blacksmiths here now but there was, and it was here for many years, possibly hundreds. It became your local garage back in the thirties. It seems that little boy in the picture did not want to follow in the family tradition and be a blacksmith so when his old dad died, he turned it into a garage, petrol stations being a growth industry back then."

Paul stood up and smiled broadly. "Bloody hell, you're right. The building's not thatched anymore, and it's not much more than a big shed now. A little shop at the front, and just two pumps mainly used by the local farmers, I think. Well done you."

Karen drew his attention back to the picture by tapping it again. "Look closer," she said conspiratorially. "There's something else in the picture that you might find interesting."

Intrigued Paul leaned forward once more. The age of the photo meant that the closer you looked the more you could see the graining in the old monochrome.

"Look to the left of the forge," said Karen. "What's leaning against the wall almost obscured by the weeds and an old cartwheel?"

Paul did as he was told, and his mouth dropped open in amazement. At the same time, he felt his blood run cold.

"My God," he breathed. "Karen, my God."

Turning, Karen walked back to the sofa and sat down feeling smug. His reaction was all that she had hoped. He was still standing at the table, stupefied.

Lifting her mug, she finished her coffee with a gulp. "Shall we have a stroll around there and have a look?"

It was only a three-minute stroll from the tiny vicarage, past the church and the two or three tithe cottages, roses climbing their walls in profusion, and there it was. As Paul had said, the two modern fuel pumps set in a tarmacked front sweep looked completely out of place in this setting. But in the modern world they were a necessity of life. Behind them, fronting the old wooden building, was a small shop which sold the usual collection of sweets, soft drinks, and prepackaged small engine parts, spark plugs, and air fresheners.

Now that he knew what it had been Paul could discern the shape of the original old forge incorporated in the later wooden structure.

Fronting the faded green painted and chipped wooden front was an old wooden sign painted in yellow BILL DAVIES. MOTOR REPAIRS.

They strolled slowly across the forecourt towards the shop. It was very quiet that morning. The tarmac beneath his shoes was warm in the bright sunlight. Bees buzzed loudly amongst the buddleia that grew up the side wall, and just in front of the shop an old labrador lay deep in snoring slumber, its back leg twitching as it chased across a field in its dream.

Bills son, Ron, a late middle-aged and balding bachelor, came out to greet them, glad of a break in the monotony.

"Morning, Vicar, how can I help you today?" As he spoke, he was staring with obvious appreciation at the pretty young woman who was with Paul that fine day. "Morning, love," he said.

Karen nodded back and smiled.

"Morning, Ron," began Paul. "Strange reason for our visit today, so bear with me if you will."

Ron looked a little wary at this strange opening but maintained his smile. "OK."

Paul produced the photograph from inside his jacket and proffered it for Ron to look at.

"Have a glance at this old photo my friend Karen here has come across."

Karen looked sideways at Paul and smiled at this sentence.

Ron took the picture and peered at it for some moments, squinting as he did so. "My God," he said ,"it's my great-grandad Walter, and my grandad Harry. Where on earth did you get this?"

"It was in our archives at the county library," explained Karen. "I work there."

"Blimey," chuckled Ron. "Who'd have thought? Can I have a copy of this?"

"Not that one," answered Karen, "but I can get you a facsimile, sure. I'll give it to Paul; he can get it to you."

This was all going so well; she now had another excuse to see Paul again. Moving up to stand at the side of Ron, Paul pointed at the photo. "This is what I'm interested in,

Ron. Can you see leaning on the wall of the old forge there? Is it still here somewhere?"

Ron studied the picture intently. "Blimey," he said again, unimaginatively. "If it is, it will be in the old lock-up shed at the back, that hasn't been opened in donkey's years – it's derelict really. I was just a little nipper when Dad and Grandad were piling stuff in there to store. We can have a look if you want?"

"Yes please," said Paul and Karen in unison and smiled at each other.

Having fetched an old, rusting bunch of keys from somewhere in the bowels of the shop, Ron tried three of them in the huge and aged padlock that kept the rotting swing doors on the storage shed at the back of the garage tightly closed. The structure was so rickety that it was clearly only still standing because it leaned like a drunkard against the back wall of the newer building. The roof sagged like an old worn-out horse's back, and it looked as if the whole structure could collapse at any time.

Finally, the last key turned the tumblers, and the padlock opened with a click. Pushing his hands into the central gap in the doors Ron gave a heave but the door only moved a couple of inches.

"Give me a hand if you don't mind, Vicar." He grunted, and stepping forward, Paul stood next to him and taking hold higher up the door, added his strength to the heaving. Its base complained and scraped on the ground, the old door gradually groaned open, and a couple of disturbed pigeons flew out into the sunlight.

Paul, Ron, and Karen all stood peering into the gloom trying to make out the shapes in the darkness.

"Now then," said Ron stepping into the dim interior. "It's quite large by the look of it in the photo, so it will probably be against this side wall."

He began moving old cartwheels, several worn and ripped tyres, and a pile of old and rotting cardboard boxes. An old bird's nest fell to the floor in a flutter of feathers. Somewhere towards the back there was a skittering as a disturbed rat disappeared.

Ron waved a hand in front of his face to dispel the dust.

"Bloody hell," he said in disgust, and then finally after a few more pieces of detritus were removed. "Ah, there you go." His voice was triumphant. "That's what you're looking for, isn't it?"

Paul had gone pale; he felt cold and for no reason other than comfort he took hold of Karen's hand. She squeezed it reassuringly and peered herself at what his eyes were looking at so fixedly.

Nestled in the darkness, covered in bird droppings and old straw was the unmistakable, woodworm-riddled but still discernible rotting remains of the three hundred-and-fifty-year-old ducking stool.

****

He had been tramping these godforsaken pathways for more than a day now and was not even sure that he was going in the right direction. He thought it prudent to stay off the main roadways, even though they were little more than glorified tracks, sometimes lined with gravel or stones, most times not, just mere rutted earth solid after the sun of previous days. He had stumbled often, and his black clothes were now dusty and stained, his shoes scuffed and filthy.

It was intolerable. He was a man of God, why had the good Lord forsaken him? That he, Nehemiah Morton should be ejected from this almost comfortable living amongst these God-fearing and simple folk by a pompous, ageing and self-righteous tinpot village council. It did not occur to him that their action had most probably saved his life as the whole village population were baying for his blood.

He stopped to recover his breath after struggling up this steep incline and removed his hat. The sparse hair beneath was slicked down to his head by sweat and he wiped grimy fingers through it to massage his scalp.

"Oh Lord, help me in my hour of tribulation," he shouted at the lowering sky. It was so unfair. So unjust.

He grinned to himself as he recalled how he had at least served one of them out. That oaf Thomas who had ruined everything for him had paid for his sins, and no mistake. He nodded to himself and chuckled wickedly. Oh yes. There had been some justice to herald his departure.

"Oh Lord God redeemer thy vengeance is profound, and the transgressors have paid for their sins." He ended this rant with a harsh laugh.

He realised he was hungry. He had found an old barn to sleep in last night and the Lord had offered up his bounty by allowing him to milk the old cow that munched the straw in the corner. There had also been a box of freshly picked apples there, and three of these had, along with the milk, allowed him some degree of satiation. But it was now well past noon, he judged by the position of the sun, and he needed fresh sustenance.

He would sit and rest for a while, he decided. The trackway was just entering a wood, and he decided to enjoy the shade of one of the trees as he decided on his next course of action. His stomach rumbled, but he almost welcomed it, seeing himself almost as the good Lord Jesus doomed to wander in the wilderness for forty days.

He slumped down, revelling in the cool of the shade and the comforting feel of the ankle-deep, lush grass beneath him. Yes, he would rest awhile and when he was rejuvenated be on about the Lord's work once more. He closed his eyes and recited the Lord's Prayer; it always made him feel much better.

He suddenly realised he was not alone – a shadow fell across him and alarmed he looked up and behind him. He could see a head and a hat silhouetted against the sun which was glaring through the branches of the tree. It was then that a mighty blow struck the side of his head just above the ear. His vision starred and he felt the grass rise up and hit him in the face. There was the metallic taste of blood in his mouth, and he tried to call out through the pain, but he could not. His eyes were open, but his vision was fading, and cartwheels of bright light were coalescing in front of his eyes. As he lay there, another blow struck the back of his head and his vision faded completely, and there was only darkness.

He was still aware of what was happening, and he found that he could still hear.

"Is he dead?" he heard a woman say.

"No not quite". The voice of a man this time. He thought he vaguely recognised the voice but could not place it.

"He'll last for a few hours more, God rot him, but he's a goner right enough, I've seen enough of head wounds to know it for a certainty."

"I hope he thinks on his sins," said the woman. "Thinks on them and is afraid".

The man uttered an ugly laugh, an all-knowing laugh. "Oh, he will think on them, have no fear. The devil will turn his ravaged face way from the flames of hell and welcome the Reverend Nehemiah Morton into his kingdom, be assured of that."

Nehemiah felt a blow to his ribs as either the man or the woman kicked him.

"Come," said the man's voice. "Let's depart this place and leave him to his final hours. May his soul rot in hell for all eternity." Footsteps moved away.

With his last strength, Nehemiah managed to roll over on to his back. He tried to call out for help, but his voice was little more than a whisper. But it would not have made any difference. There was no one there to hear him.

****

Karen thought he looked slightly better now, more like the man she had met just a couple of weeks ago. Some colour had returned to his cheeks, and the drained, hopeless look in his eyes had disappeared.

Noting his distress and anxiety after they had discovered that awful contraption, she had taken control of the situation, and thanking Ron for his help had steered Paul to the village pub for, as she called it, 'a stiff one'.

The large scotch had burned its way down into his body and revived him a little. He took her hand as they sat in the little window seat enjoying the fitful sunlight that streamed through the mullioned windows.

"Thanks, Karen." He smiled. "That was a bit of a shock, I wasn't expecting that it would look so intact. Suddenly the past, and what for me had been just a research exercise to help a friend came up and slapped me right in the face".

She smiled back at him and nodded. "I thought you were going to faint for a moment there. Your mate Ron looked really concerned".

Paul withdrew his hand and smoothed it through his hair. "He's not a mate, or anywhere near a mate, but he's a decent chap".

"It's all got to you a bit this whole thing, hasn't it?"

He nodded ruefully "Yep. They were real people who actually existed and lived their lives such as they were in this village. Sometimes when you find things like that atrocity of a device back there it all becomes very real".

She nodded and sipped her own drink. "I take it that this has all got something to do with this woman you're interested in, what was her name, Cecily?"

He drained the last drops from his whiskey glass and made to stand. He looked down at her and smiling held out his hand.

"Yes," he said. "Cecily. If you've finished, I should show you something".

She looked a little surprised but dutifully drained her own glass and standing followed him out into the sunshine.

She held Paul's arm enjoying the sensation, as he led them the few yards up the lane past the cottages and to the church. They entered the graveyard through the lych gate and walked across the manicured lawns to a far corner, which even on a sunny day like this was in the shadow of the overhanging trees. She noted that an area had recently been cleared and guessed that it was he who had done it as the implements he had used were still leaning against a nearby tree, something that any part-time gardener would never have done.

Together they moved into the shade and placing his arm on her back he gently moved her forward and pointed down.

"Look," he said. "This is what I've found. I searched for it thanks to you and your latest findings from the depths of the library archives.

There was an old, weathered gravestone lying flat and nestled in the grass. It was evident that earth and foliage had recently been scraped off it, but even after just a short time, leaves were beginning to gather on top of it once again.

She leant forward to read what had been carved into it over three hundred and fifty years ago.

Here lyeth the mortal remains of
Cecily Morton
Wife of the Reverend Nehemiah Morton.

Taken unto God in the twenty third year of her life
22nd July. In this year of our Lord 1667 anno domini
God knoweth how.
May God have mercy on her soul.
"Media vita in morte summus."

She stood up straight again and took hold of Paul's hand. "What does the Latin phrase mean?"

"'In the midst of life, we are in death'."

"I feel suddenly sad," she said in a small voice. "She was so young."

He smiled and nodded. "Yes, there was little she was spared. Such a waste. Her story has got to me somehow. I know what you mean about the sadness. I'll tell you what I would tell no one else, when I found this the other day I just sat here and had a little weep myself. Funny, isn't it? I never knew her, and until recently knew nothing about her. Why would I do that?"

His eyes looked as if he might be moved to tears again.

Karen moved closer to him and peered into his face.

"I don't think you were crying just for Cecily, Paul. I think you were crying for Marion, and your Charlie, and for all the useless waste of young life in this world. We all need a good cry now and again".

It was an insightful thing for such a relatively young woman to say and he loved her for it. He put his arm around her and kissed the top of her head.

"You're probably right," he said, "and bless you for saying it".

With an effort he roused himself smiled down at her again. "Come on, I'll make you some lunch – you must be starving".

She laughed and nodded. "Yes" she said, "I'd like that".

Together they moved off talking in low tones, and the leaves began to gather again in the fitful breeze and settle on the gravestone.

Chapter Eighteen

There was no doubt about it, this was a hellish drive. Robert felt like a wet dishcloth, weary and dishevelled after over four hours at the wheel, his mind a little befuddled and soggy. He just wanted to get home and have a coffee or even a cup of tea would do, he mused ruefully.

He had not in fact left Brighton yesterday after all. If he was honest with himself the last meeting with Sue had upset and disconcerted him more than he would acknowledge. Yes, the decisions they had reached were the right ones, but he had not expected her to be so matter of fact, so breezily philosophical as she clinically terminated their relationship, which he had to admit had been important to him.

Arriving back at his 'digs' after they parted, he had packed his few belongings into his gym bag and then hesitated. It was a nice day, he had paid until tomorrow anyway, so why not just lounge away the remainder of today with a couple of nice drinks and face that hellish drive tomorrow? A long journey with who knew what reception at the end of it. Tomorrow would do.

It had worked out well. A brisk walk along the breezy seafront had restored his spirits a little, and he had whiled away the afternoon in a small bar overlooking the sea, casually sipping a succession of large gin and tonics as he reviewed his life and people-watched.

He had chosen to use the motorways rather than the slog along the busy A roads of the south coast through

Portsmouth, Southampton, and Yeovil. Instead, he headed north for the M23, then on to the slow-moving car park that was the M25, then miles and miles of the westbound M4 before turning south at Bristol for the last leg on the M5. He had only a few CDs in the car so had cruised along, entertained in quick succession by U2, Eric Clapton, and latterly Adele. Finally, weary and in need of sustenance, mind fatigued by the engine noise and the music, he stumbled into Sedgemoor services which seemed swollen and over full of summer tourists. Caravans and overloaded cars clogged the car park, and for one awful moment he thought he might have to move on to the next services at Taunton, but a departing caravanette offered a reprieve and he nosed into the space gratefully.

He grabbed a quick burger with his coffee and having consumed these, squeezed into a plastic seat in the crowded eating area noisy with screaming children, laughing adults, and crying babies, retreated to the sanctuary of his car and fell into a fitful doze for thirty minutes. The impromptu nap revitalised him a little and he set off on the final leg with renewed optimism.

Now as he traversed the winding lane that led to the village, he hoped that Jane would not be too combative on his arrival and realising that he was extremely tired allow him at least to have a shower and a drink before hitting him. This thought brought a grim smile to his face.

They had only been in this village for a short while, but he already considered it home. It meant peace and quiet and a bolthole from the stress and strife of the modern world, and he knew that Jane loved it. Would she still love him? That was the question, wasn't it? The million-dollar decision on which the rest of his life probably depended.

Down the hill now the high hedgerows heavy with vegetation seemed to hem in the lane, bathing it in a cool green haze. Past the little lopsided wicket gate that led into his garden and then turn right through the open five-barred gate that opened on to the gravelled sweep at the side of the house.

He switched off the engine, revelling in the sudden silence and sat for some moments listening to the ticking of the cooling engine, and the birdsong that oozed in through the open windows. He was home, back to whatever awaited him.

Perched at the kitchen table, Jane was poring over her laptop, putting the finishing touches to the 'Northern Renaissance' talk script. She had to admit to being pleased with it. She considered it to be both entertaining and informative, if not groundbreaking, and hoped that it would hold the attention of a young student audience, and even impress the smattering of university lecturers that would inevitably be present.

She had set the music processor on to 'random' and as she finished her editing and sat back in her chair, arching her back and stretching out her arms to get rid of the cramps, it started to play *Ordinary People* by an anguished sounding John Legend again. She had always loved this singer and indeed this song, but she acknowledged that in her current predicament the words were more than usually pertinent. She lifted her mug to her lips to finish the last dregs of her by now stone-cold coffee and it was then that she heard the crunch of gravel as a car pulled on to the drive.

He came into the kitchen somewhat sheepishly, uncertain of what would happen next. Jane had turned slightly to face the door and was leaning with one arm over the back of the chair.

"Hello," he said, "Can I come in?"

She nodded noncommittally. "It's your house as much as mine."

He gave a crooked, embarrassed smile. "I suppose it is, yes, but even so…" His voice faded to a stop.

"You look all in," she said standing up. "Where have you driven from?"

He did not answer.

"Brighton?" she continued. "Have you driven all the way from there without a stop?"

"Not exactly. I had a coffee at Sedgemoor services."

She shook her head slightly at his failure to be safe. "Sit down. I'll make us a drink." He was a bloody fool who had wandered off after the beckoning finger of another woman and in doing so had thrown her whole life into turmoil, but she still loved him, God help her. She moved to fill the kettle as he slumped down gratefully into one of the other chairs.

"Thanks," was all he could think of to say.

"Where did you stop?" She could not bring herself to turn around but busied herself with the kettle.

"A B&B," he answered. "Not exactly the Ritz but it was OK."

"You and Sue?"

It was the first time she had forced herself to mention her name to him.

He looked up sharply. "No. Just me."

She nodded to herself. "Sue's sister was having none of it, eh?"

Robert nodded and then realising that she had not turned around and would not see, said, "No. The subject never came up."

The conversation continued on this almost monosyllabic lofty plane for some minutes whilst she made them both a cup of tea and bringing them to the table, sat down and placed his in front of him.

"So," she said, staring him straight in the face. "Where do we go from here?"

It seemed to her that they were like two wrestlers circling the ring, watching for an opening, wary of an attack.

She was icy cold, clinical almost; he had not expected that. He suddenly realised that she was far more mature than him, more analytical, more in control of her emotions. It unnerved him a little.

He took his time, taking a few long sips of his tea. It was strong and very hot, the way he liked it, and he could feel it rejuvenating him, adding strength to his voice. He placed his mug carefully down on to the tabletop and looked straight at her, taking a deep breath as if he was about to plunge into a pool.

"Jane, I'm so sorry. I've been a complete idiot. I know that now. I don't know if it was an early mid-life crisis, or a rush of blood to the head or what, but I can't believe what has happened and now I'm thinking straight, I can't believe what I've done."

He stopped, waiting for her to answer him, but she did not. She just sat calmly sipping her own tea and waiting for him to continue.

He had rehearsed this speech many times during the drive, and each time the conversation followed a different course dependent on his wife's answers but what he had not planned on was no answers at all.

"You've finished with the slag, I take it?"

Her voice was cold and matter-of-fact, as if they were discussing a matter of little consequence, almost as if she were listening to the problems of a stranger.

He nodded contritely. "Yes, oh yes. I doubt we'll ever see either her or Bri again."

Janes voice was bitter and derisory. "Oh, I think you can say that again. I've never heard Brian so angry; he was, what's that word? Incandescent." She did not feel the need to enlighten him further about the lengthy character assassination that she and Brian had conducted when he had called her back the evening of her bombshell to him. It served little point now, and she would only be parroting his words, which she had felt at the time with delicious compliance were absolutely correct.

He looked down at the table and nodded. "I can believe that."

"Is Sue going back to him?"

"Don't know. I think so." He coughed to give him time to consider. "I think so."

"Who finished it, you or her?"

"It was a joint decision. Well not a decision really, we'd just both arrived at the same conclusion."

Jane gave a snort of contempt. "I'll bet. Once your little liaison was out in the open, it became seedy and sordid, didn't it? Well, it would in her eyes."

He took a last sip of his tea and leaned back in the chair. His back was aching, and his eyes felt heavy.

"Look Jane, I can't keep saying I'm sorry but believe me I am." He paused to construct his next sentence.

"Can I at least stop here tonight, and we'll talk in the morning when we're both fresh and thinking straight?"

He was genuine about this; she knew him well enough to be able to tell. He could have the spare bed in the back room for this evening, and he was right, he was tired from the journey, and she was jaded and fatigued from the uncertainty of the last few days. The decisions they had to make were momentous for their futures, for their marriage, for their lives. She found herself nodding.

"OK," she said, sounding less than enthusiastic. "There's another cup in the pot, pour yourself one and I'll go up make up the spare bed." She noted with wry and savage amusement the surprise in his eyes at this immediate acquiescence. But also, at the modification to his plan which he had obviously not considered.

"You didn't think for one moment that you would be sharing my bed, did you?"

"Erm… No, no of course not."

She wrinkled her nose as she strode past him towards the door. "You might also consider a shower."

He nodded morosely; he knew that. Allowing him to stay the night was more than he deserved. He grunted a thank you and moved to the kitchen side, hearing as he did so Jane disappearing quickly up the stairs.

He gazed out of the window at the front garden, such as it was. The term 'garden' did not really apply, it was just the large, open, grassy space that completely surrounded the cottage. The sloping lawn leading up to the small dry wall with its wrought iron gate that led into the lane needed trimming. He would take care of it tomorrow, whatever happened between them. It seemed ages since he had been bothered about such irrelevancies.

It was then that Jane screamed upstairs. It was a high-pitched terrified scream, not the inconsequential cry of someone who has stubbed their toe.

He sprinted up the stairs two steps at a time and hurried into their bedroom. As he walked in, he saw Jane on their large bed against the far wall. She was scrabbling against the headboard as if she wanted almost to climb behind it. Her eyes were wide and panicked, peering into the corner to the left of the door through which he had just entered. He was with her in three strides, her hand reaching out to grab his with amazing strength. Still, she did not take her terrified gaze from the corner of the room. Her eyes were huge.

Robert turned to look and the blood in his veins turned to ice. The hairs on the back of his neck stood up and he gave an involuntary cry himself.

Standing in the corner looking straight at them was a dark-haired woman dressed in a long grey dress. The small white collar and the white muslin cap that she wore gleamed in the fitful light in that darkened corner.

"Holy shit!" he heard himself shout. "Holy fucking shit."

When he had heard about ghosts in the past, indeed when Jane had mentioned this woman to him, he had imagined some ethereal figure floating in the air, transparent, insubstantial. This figure was anything but. She seemed all too real. He could see the weave of her clothes, see the strands of black glossy hair that had escaped from her bonnet, he saw the small, muddied leather shoes that peeked from beneath the hem of her dress. The dark penetrating, almost pleading eyes looking directly at him. He could see her, for Christ's sake. Could see her standing there, looking as real as Jane or himself. *Fucking hell* he thought. *Holy fucking hell'.*

Jane was attempting to crawl behind him, to get away, to go anywhere so long as it was further from the figure in the corner. She was still gripping his hand so tightly that it was hurting him, her nails digging into his flesh, and she was whimpering with pure terror.

His breath was coming in gasps, and he could not seem to draw enough air into his lungs at any one time. He could hear himself swearing continuously, trying to regain some control. His heart thumped painfully in his chest, and he wondered for an instant if he might have a cardiac arrest.

Suddenly the woman began to move and walking slowly from the corner, she disappeared unhurriedly through the door, turning towards the top of the stairs as she passed through and out of the line of their vison.

Recovering himself a little Robert stood up slowly on wobbly legs and hauled the still incoherent Jane to her feet.

"It's OK," he heard himself say. "She's gone now."

Jane clung to him like a small child, her control only gradually returning.

Together they walked timidly towards the door, Jane clinging to his arm tightly. They peered around the door jamb fearful in case the figure was still there but there was nothing, no one at all. Once again, the woman had gone.

Jane was trembling hugely, he could feel it, and he was only a little more controlled himself.

"I'm sorry," he muttered.

"What for?" It was a whisper, but at least she could talk now, and had stopped whimpering.

"I thought you had imagined her, you know, the ghost. I thought, well I don't know what I really thought. I'd convinced myself she was just a projection of your thoughts. But you were right, and I was wrong."

She merely nodded and rested her forehead against his chest.

"I need a drink," he said. "Come on old thing, let's get at the scotch bottle, that's if my hands can stop shaking enough to open the bloody thing."

Clutching each other for morale and physical support, they stumbled slowly down the stairs and made for the kitchen. Yes, a drink was what was needed.

As they entered, Jane gave another shrill cry of alarm. Looking up Robert saw that the figure was back, and standing against the far wall, the bare, newly uncovered bricks stark behind her.

"Oh, fuck me, not again," shouted Robert. "For Christ's sake." His voice was loud and strident, fear and shock lending it a shrill timbre.

She was looking at them, her back to the wall, and it occurred to him through the mists of his barely controlled panic that she seemed to be pleading, trying to tell them something. Jane was shaking uncontrollably; Robert could clearly feel her heart pounding in her chest against his arm.

What to do now? He had no idea.

The loud rap on the front door made them both start, and Jane cried out in fear again. Together they turned and grateful for the excuse, stumbled across the hall to open it. Paul was standing there. He was wearing jeans and his leather flying jacket, and he looked anxious, agitated, his eyes alight.

"I've just seen your woman," he said to Jane, his voice raised and excited. "Just now as I was walking down towards your front door. I just glanced through the kitchen window and she's there right now. I could see her clearly."

"Oh, we know that," scoffed Robert, his voice still loud for reassurance. "Yes, we know that alright."

Paul eased himself between them and moving to the kitchen door peered inside. His shoulders slumped with disappointment.

"She's gone," he said, and he sounded sad.

"Thank Christ for that," said Jane, at last recovering the power of speech, feeling safer perhaps because there were three of them now. She slammed the front door shut and moved to stand beside Paul to scan the kitchen warily.

"Thank Christ," she repeated unimaginatively.

"I could not believe it when I saw her." Paul's voice was awed, hoarse with disbelief. "I mean, you know, a real ghost for goodness' sake. I'm a vicar, I'm not supposed to see things like that."

He turned to look at them both. "You saw her too then?"

Robert gave a shrill half-laugh, the tension slowly dissipating now they were all talking.

"Oh, yes, we saw her. My God, did we see her. In the bedroom upstairs first, and then down here in front of that wall."

They all moved slowly into the kitchen, Jane scanning each wall in turn with care, reassuring herself that no one was there.

Robert moved to one of the kitchen cupboards and removing a bottle, placed it on the table before reaching down three tumblers.

"Let's sit down," he said. "I think we all need a drink."

They did as they were told and all three just sat silently for a few minutes, sipping the amber coloured liquid and reflecting on what had happened.

Paul again was calmed by the burn of the liquid as it seeped into his chest, warming and reassuring. He noted that Robert had recovered a little and some colour was returning to his face. Jane had stopped shaking and was looking more like her old self but still very pale.

Robert picked up the bottle and without asking refilled each of their glasses, taking a large sip from his own as he plonked the bottle back down on to the table. He slumped back into his chair and looked from Jane to Paul and back to Jane.

"Well, you can't say nothing ever happens here, can you?"

It was an attempt at humour to ease his own fear and tension, but Jane and Paul just gazed back at him as if they had not heard.

It was only now dawning on Paul that he had probably barged into a very delicate situation. He had not expected Robert to be there, and only realised it at the last moment as he moved towards the front door and noticed Robert's car in the drive. Had he not seen the figure in the kitchen, he would probably have turned around and left them to it.

He had decided to call around to both check that Jane was OK, but also to fill her in on the latest developments, his latest findings thanks to Karen, and the discovery of the ducking stool behind the local garage.

"Look, you two," he began, swigging back his scotch with one swallow. "I'm going to leave you to it. You obviously have things to discuss, and my barging in is an unwarranted intrusion. I apologise."

He stood up.

"No wait, Paul," said Robert standing himself. "First off, I owe you an apology. My behaviour when we last met was well out of order, and I'm sorry."

He held out his hand, unsure what Paul's reaction would be but willing to risk it.

Paul merely nodded and briefly shook the proffered hand.

"No worries," he said. "I've got broader shoulders than that. I know you were both under a lot of pressure. Plus, I'm a big boy now. Just forget it."

He looked at them both. "But as I have just said, I'm in the way here, I'll leave you to it." He suddenly stopped as his eyes noted something on the stripped wall. Moving over to almost the same spot where the grey lady had been standing, he poked his finger into a hole that he had just noticed in the brickwork at about head height. He could just get his finger inside it, but it appeared to go right through to the other side, where he could feel colder air .

"What's this?"

Jane looked hugely embarrassed. "Well," she said choosing her words slowly. "During our last few words before Rob left, I threw something at him. It missed, thank God, but hit the wall there."

Robert moved over and peered at the aperture as Paul had.

"This goes straight through," he said. "I told you, old thing, there's another room behind this." Forgetting his present troubles for the moment, he looked triumphant. "I knew it, I bloody knew it."

"How very clever of you." Jane's tone was sarcastic, scathing, reminding him of the situation that the events of the last few minutes had interrupted.

Paul held up both hands in a placatory gesture.

"As I said, I'm intruding. I'll leave you to it. It's not my place to interfere. But can I just say, donning my spiritual guide to the community hat, that you two are a lovely couple who obviously care a great deal for each other. Yes, one of you has behaved badly…" His eyes passed over Robert, who looked down at the floor, contrite.

"And the other party must be feeling hurt and betrayed. But you have a lot to throw away. Don't make any decisions, either of you, without a lot of thought, and discussion." He rested his hand briefly on Jane's shoulder as he passed her on his way out.

"My advice, such as it is, is sleep on it and talk in the morning. Robert thanks for the scotch, and both of you, if you need me, you have my number."

The front door slammed behind him, and his footsteps could be heard moving away up to the lane.

There was silence in the kitchen as each of them absorbed what he had said. The large kitchen clock could be heard ticking loudly in the silence.

"Rob," said Jane, "This does not mean anything, but you can sleep in my bed with me tonight. There's no way I'm sleeping alone in that room ever again."

Robert moved over to sit beside her and refill their glasses, the ghost of a smile lifting the corners of his mouth.

"Okey dokey, old thing," he said. But despite his attempt at nonchalance, his voice still trembled.

****

He was not sure how long he had lain here. He was aware in his delirium that a night had passed. Occasionally, when he had awoken from his pain-wracked blackouts, he knew that it was dark, and that it was not just his failed eyesight that was the reason for the complete darkness.

His body, those parts that he could still feel, felt cold and wet, and he knew it was the dew on the grass beneath him. His head, especially at the base of his skull, hurt and throbbed with a recurring agony that did not seem ever to dissipate.

He had dreamed or hallucinated about the past during the last interminable hours. He knew that but he could not remember any specifics. It was a long, never-ending nightmare that he was trapped inside.

"Oh God, why hast thou forsaken me?" he cried out once, but nobody answered, there was no one there, only the sigh of the wind in the branches above him, and the occasional bark of a fox. Once he was sure something had crawled over his legs, but try as he might, he could not move them but whimpered to himself with fear and loathing. Eventually, whatever it was moved away.

He had always tried to be a good man, hadn't he? Had done the Lord's work, as he saw it, without reward or favour. Surely that did not condemn him to such an end as this?

Perhaps for the first time in his life he confronted his actions, and they screamed back at him with a banshee's call that he had done evil in his life.

He groaned and spoke aloud for the last time. "If I have done evil, oh Lord, it was in your holy name and to maintain my path of righteousness. Surely, I can be forgiven for that."

Such was his delirium that he imagined he could see the gentle face of God smiling down at him. "Come, true knight," it said. "You have laboured long in my service. Come take your rest."

These words calmed him and with a last sigh he died. The face of Nehemiah Morton looked composed and content.

It was two months later that his badly mutilated corpse was found by farm workers who were collecting fallen branches as they were copsing this area of the woodland. His body had decomposed, and small animals and birds had feasted many times on what remained, so he was unrecognisable. He had tramped over twenty miles from the village, the scene of his crimes, so had he not been so transformed it was unlikely anyway that anyone would have known who he was.

He was buried in a quickly dug grave just within the confines of a small local village churchyard. No gravestone marked his resting place, merely a crude wooden cross on which had been scrawled, 'Known unto God'.

Chapter Nineteen

It was eleven o'clock in the morning and the library entrance hall was as busy as it would get. There were two school parties in and despite teachers circling the groups of excitable children like watchful, careworn sheepdogs, the general hubbub of excited young voices only seemed to increase. One party were all sporting navy blue jumpers or cardigans, the other group from an obviously different school were resplendent in red. It was a scene to make one smile as one remembered one's own school trips with affection –the excitement of being with one's friends and somewhere new in schooltime. Karen was reminiscing on exactly that, a broad smile creasing her pretty face. Life for her at this moment was good. She had always enjoyed her job, and the sunshine streaming in through the plate glass windows only enhanced her general mood of ''joie de vivre' on this lovely morning.

As the chattering, laughing youngsters were ushered and shepherded through various doors to their respective study areas, a feeling of quiet and calm once more descended on to the atrium. There were several elderly people chattering in small groups across the welcoming sun-blasted open space, mimicking with their animated enthusiasm the recently departed children who were sixty years behind them. She knew most of them by sight. and was aware that these meetings of people of a similar age and experience were an important part of their weekly routine. They exchanged news and gossip with the wisdom of long lives and viewed most current news stories with quiet and wry amusement.

Karen gave a little wave to attract the attention of her colleague, who was answering a query from an old couple who were looking for books on ornithology.

"I'm just going to fetch a coffee from the café – do you want one?"

Her friend just smiled and shook her head. Walking down the corridor to the coffee shop, Karen reached into the small shoulder bag she had picked up from under her chair and withdrew her mobile phone. She stopped just before the door of the café and leaning casually against the wall, dialled the number she now knew by heart.

It rang three times before the rich, dark voice of Paul answered.

"Hi Karen, this is a nice surprise."

"Hiya you," she replied, and she could hear his slow chuckle.

"Are you at work?" he queried.

"Yep, afraid so, but I like my job so it's not the end of the world." She could picture his smile as she mimicked one of his phrases.

"That's great. A chap I used to admire a great deal, an old archaeologist actually who was always on the TV at one point, used to say to his students 'Find something you really want to do as a job, and you'll never work a day in your life'. I think there's a lot of truth in that."

She chuckled back. "You are funny, some of the things you say."

He laughed cheerfully, glad to hear her voice.

"So, what are you doing today?" she chirruped.

"Hmm, well it's a little bit tricky actually. You remember I told you briefly about these two friends of mine who've had a serious spat following the husband's straying, well he came back, the evening before last, half an hour before by coincidence I turned up. I took my leave as soon as I could and left them completely alone yesterday, as they needed time and space to themselves if they were to salvage something from the wreckage, but I felt I might pop up to their place in a little while. I am the local vicar and spiritual leader after all, as well as their friend."

"And nosy" she chortled.

"Excuse me?" He feigned outrage but could not maintain it, and relapsed into a laugh, "and yep, you're right, I'm nosy." His voice became serious. "But also, on a more serious note they are friends of mine and I want to check they are OK."

"Look," she said knowing that she only had a few minutes, and she wanted desperately to get to the point of her call. "I finish at five tonight, after that can I come over. I thought we could have a drink or something?"

There was a silence, and she held her breath as she waited for his response. When it came, she almost jumped for joy.

"That would be lovely, but can we do it tomorrow evening? I have no idea when I'll be finished today, and," he said, his voice suddenly increasing in intensity, "There's been a major development on the subject of our Cecily, which I can't wait to tell you about."

"Oh?" It had taken Karen a few moments to realise who the hell Cecily was.

"Oh yes indeed. It will be worth the wait, I promise you. I tell you what, I'll cook us supper, and when we have eaten, we can go down the local pub for a drink. Yes?"

She could have shouted out loud that yes that would be absolutely and deliciously great, but restrained herself and answered solemnly,

"OK. Fine I'll see you then. Ciao."

Clicking off the phone and walking into the café, she chided herself bitterly. Ciao? Why on earth had she said that? It was something she never, ever said. Oh well, what the hell, she was seeing him again, that was brilliant. As she moved to take her place at the rear of the small queue, she gave an inadvertent little skip to show her pleasure.

****

Paul was not at all sure that he should be intruding. Maybe negotiations were at a delicate stage, and the old adage about never interfering in someone else's marriage was very true, as he had discovered on a few occasions in the course of his parochial church council duties.

He finally decided that he would merely telephone and apologise for not calling yesterday as he had promised. He personally hated people who did not do as they had said they would or were habitually late for meetings. These were small matters, he knew, but the human being is an idiosyncratic creature, and many different things elicit different reactions as we navigate our way through this life.

It was Robert who answered the house phone. He had decided not to call either of their mobile numbers as it might be construed as taking sides.

"Paul, morning to you." Robert sounded genial, and full of the joys of spring.

"Hi Rob, sorry to bother you, nothing important really. I just wanted to apologise for not popping in yesterday as I said I would I...er well the truth is I thought you could do with some time to yourselves."

Robert chuckled lightly. "Yeah, and we did. I think we have sorted out a few things and Jane is allowing me to stay." There was a pause as if he was choosing his next sentence carefully. "But I'm very much on probation. I don't blame her at all, I was a complete idiot, long and short of it is there's no excuse, and I hurt her badly, rocked her trust in me. Let's hope I can earn back my stripes, and I was even a moron to you. Did I apologise the other night? I can't remember, I was a bit out of it."

Paul smiled and gave a small affirmative grunt. "Yep, you did. No need, as I said at the time I'm a big boy now, and I have broad shoulders."

"Look," said Robert, speaking rather quickly to hide his embarrassment. "I'm glad you called; I had half a mind to ring you. I'm going to pull down the bricks that were obviously put in place to block up that doorway in the kitchen, God knows how long ago. Oh! Sorry for the blasphemy." He laughed and Paul joined in.

"None taken," he chortled.

"And I wondered if you wanted to come and help, or at least watch me. You're as involved in this as anyone, and that particular spot seems to be of interest to our ghost."

"I'd love to, and I'll bring a hammer and chisel to give you a hand. Give me half an hour."

"Roger dodge."

Paul clicked off the connection and went to find his tools and change his clothes. It seemed that they had somehow negotiated a truce, and Robert had been given another chance. He was not at all sure if in similar circumstances Marion would have been so obliging, but then people were very different, and to be fair Jane was extremely vulnerable at this moment following recent shocks. It might be that for the time being she was prepared to go along with events until things settled down, merely to ensure that she was not alone in that house. Oh well, all would be as it would be. It was, after all, none of his business.

An hour later and they were all chatting amicably. Paul, changed into old jeans and a t-shirt, had arrived to discover that Jane had made a pot of tea with toasted muffins and jam, all laid out on the old kitchen table and his place set and waiting.

It had been a pleasant little interlude as they all discussed inconsequential things, obeying a mutual desire to stay away from more complex and personal matters whilst consuming the food and the tea. Jane seemed relaxed and less fraught than she had been for some time, the dark patches beneath her eyes were fading, and she smiled more. As Paul was finishing his second cup of tea poured from the voluminous stone teapot, and whilst Robert fetched his own tools from the shed at the back of the cottage, Jane had told him that they had reached some sort of understanding. He agreed that he had been a complete wanker, she said. Paul had blinked at this language from Jane but had to acknowledge that she had been born and brought up in the big city and not in this rural little backwater.

Robert knew that he was on a 'final warning' as Jane called it, and she was prepared, at least for the moment, to give him the benefit of the doubt. Of course, they would never be seeing Brian or Sue again, that was her paramount condition, and Robert, meek with contrition, had readily agreed. Whether they would ever return to the loving relationship that had previously existed remained to be seen, but it appeared that for the moment the new arrangement would have to do.

Paul had decided to accept without comment anything and everything that they told him, although he could discern that the recriminations were not over by a long way. Jane, for the moment, it appeared was accepting the situation and seeing what developed. She had been deeply hurt, and he guessed that for a woman like her the wound would take some healing. Without thought of the consequences, Robert had thrown a large spanner into the smooth-running engine of this fledgling marriage and the repercussions were an unknown quantity for the future. He was supremely contrite now, deferring to Jane on almost every topic that came up. Paul had to give him credit for more tact that he had thought.

In a way the appearances of the 'grey lady' had poured a soothing balm for the moment over the rupture and open wound of their relationship. Their joint fear and shock during the latest manifestation had thrown them together both mentally and physically. Each had described in some detail how they had clung to the other in terror during the sighting of the apparition. This, above any other consideration, had for the moment allowed them to temporarily at least, heal the rift and enable them to attain some sort of jerry-built truce. He supressed a slow smile as he realised that a tragedy from the past may have averted a tragedy of the present. What was the old saying? 'God works in mysterious ways.'

He realised that Jane was speaking and forced himself away from his own musings.

"So," she said, "Let's see how we go from here"

Paul nodded and sipped his tea, feeling that this was the time to draw a line under this little one-act play, and anything further he could say would just be frippery. It was up to the two of them what they made of this cessation of hostilities.

He suddenly remembered that he had not told Jane about his discovery at the garage. He did not want to repeat himself, so waited until Robert emerged once more into the kitchen.

"I need to bring you both up to date with some further info that I've found, or should I say my friend at the library unearthed for me."

"What friend?" said Jane, her interest piqued.

So, Paul explained about Karen and what a great help she had been to him. Privately Jane thought *I'll bet she was*, but such thoughts were uncharitable, and now that Robert was being so apologetic and humble, she was once more, for the moment at least, a happily married woman, so kept her observations to herself.

It was when Paul mentioned his, or rather their discovery of the old and rotting ducking stool behind the village garage that she leaned forward with a lightning bolt of interest.

"You're joking, really?"

"No, I'm not. I couldn't believe my eyes. Karen, that's my friend's name, had spotted it on an old photo from the early 1900s when, believe it or not, the garage was the old forge. There it was, leaning against the side of the building, rickety and falling apart even then, but of course back then it would still have been around 250 years old. I'm amazed its survived at all. Two wheels are missing, and it's riddled with woodworm."

Jane and Robert looked like two of the small schoolchildren did when he occasionally was called in to read a religious story at the small local village school. Their eyes shone with interest, their mouths slightly open with awe. He burst out laughing and had to tell them the reason for his amusement. They both laughed with him.

"There's more," continued Paul, after finishing his tea with a final flourish. "The reason for her ducking."

He told them about a couple of brief mentions in the old local new sheets, such as they were, usually just a single amateurishly printed page knocked out at the local hostelry, of a shadowy figure named Thomas, no surname, who it was rumoured had enjoyed a relationship with the Reverend's wife Cecily and, unfortunately for her, the fire-and-brimstone husband had found out.

It appeared that she had died unexpectedly during the ducking. It was rare but not unknown in those times. The locals had taken a dim view of this and hounded the rabid Morton from the village. Of both Nehemiah and Thomas there was no more information. They just disappeared, never to be seen or heard of again.

Jane leaned back in her chair and quite unexpectedly her eyes filled with tears.

"Such sadness," she said. "Suddenly they've become more real to me. You know, real people, not just two-dimensional figures in a story from long ago. They had feelings, they loved and hated. That poor girl, she didn't have much of a life, did she? But then I suppose a lot of people had very hard and short lives in those times."

The two men looked at each other and with the unspoken camaraderie of the male of the species decided that action would divert any further tears.

"Well let's get to it," said Robert, standing up again. He nodded towards the wall and Paul, taking his cue, picked up his tools and moved over to the corner.

Robert pointed up at the strip of wood still just about showing through the brickwork a little above head height and almost obscured by the ageing and flaking plaster.

"This was the lintel, you can see it, and if you look more closely you can see that the bricks if that's what they are, from just below the lintel down to the floor do not quite match the rest of the wall, they are slightly smaller and longer and have been laid very shoddily, as if someone was in a hurry."

"It's exactly what I said to Jane when I first took the plaster off." He turned to grin at Jane. "That right isn't it, old thing?"

Jane smiled and nodded. "Yes," was all she said.

Both men started tapping at the mortar and ancient bricks. Their hammers and chisels tapped in unison, dust rising immediately. Jane stood and moving to the windows threw them wide in a vain effort to avoid them all breathing in the enveloping cloud.

"Shouldn't we be wearing masks or something?" she queried.

Both men stopped and looked at her. Realising the good sense of her remark, Robert disappeared into the hall and came back with two old scarves from the coat hooks on the wall, which they proceeded to wrap around their lower faces.

"You stand out in the hall old thing," ordered Robert, and Jane obeyed, at the same time smiling at his reassumption of giving fatherly advice to his wife

After little more than thirty minutes, most of the bricks were down and in a heap at their feet. The air was thick with acrid dust despite the windows being open.

"Let's give it a minute in the hall," said Paul his voice muffled through the tartan scarf that he had been given. "The dust will settle quite quickly and have you any torches anywhere, Rob? We can use the lights on our mobiles, but a proper torch would be better."

Rob disappeared out into the garden again, all boyish enthusiasm and haste.

Paul looked at Jane who had been silent for the last half an hour, merely watching them at their work.

"Are you OK?" said Paul.

Jane nodded; her eyes still looked a little watery.

"Yes," she said. "I'm OK. Can we leave it for the moment, Paul? I'm giving him another chance and we'll see what he does with it. It's up to him now. Everything else is just flotsam but it's all been a bit much and I'm feeling a little teary – bloody hormones."

He nodded and touched her shoulder. "OK," he smiled, "All the luck in the world to you both."

Jane nodded at the wall wanting to change the subject and her eyes began to fill up again. "It's all so sad," she said thickly. "Your mentioning finding the ducking stool. You're right, it suddenly becomes very real. Should we burn it, do you think?"

It was some moments before Paul realised that she meant the stool. "Absolutely not. It's a very rare discovery," he answered. "Ron was ringing the museum in Exeter as we left, and I imagine they'll rip his hand off for it. A lot of restoration needed, but it's a real find."

"It's horrible." Jane found a tissue from somewhere and dabbed her eyes, "That poor girl, and it all happened here, much of it probably in this house. I'm not sure I want to live here anymore."

Paul laid a hand briefly on her shoulder again. "It was all a long time ago," he smiled, "and it may just be that we've all fallen for the stories and imagined seeing this woman."

Jane looked up at him. "You don't believe that and neither do I."

Robert returned to the hallway from the back door carrying two torches and caught the last few words of their conversation.

"Paul," he began, "I've never really asked you. You are a vicar after all. Where do you stand on ghosts and the like? Surely in your profession it's a no-no."

Paul smiled and shook his head slightly. "Do you know, mate, this whole thing has unnerved me a little, especially when I saw our friend myself the other night in your kitchen."

He took one of the torches off Robert and busied himself checking that it worked as he formulated a reply.

"The Catholic Church believed that there are such things as spirits who have not yet for whatever reason been sent to heaven or hell, but with the Reformation, the Protestant Church found such beliefs to be undesirable and to this day refuses to acknowledge any such thing. As you know, Protestantism rejects purgatory."

"Does it?" Robert looked a little nonplussed, so much so that Paul laughed out loud.

"Anyway," he said, "These are philosophical and ecumenical questions that have puzzled mankind for centuries. Shall we just get on and see what's behind this blessed wall now we have knocked a large section of it down?"

"Yep, righto."

They all moved into the kitchen, which was now almost dust free, and across to the mound of rubble in front of the gaping black hole in the wall. Robert made to step through, but Paul held his shoulder.

"Hang on, Rob, always check your footing first, right. It might be that you stepped into a cellar and found out the hard way that the floor level is way down."

Rob nodded appreciatively. "You're right. Let's have a look."

He and Paul were now standing on the rubble at the lip of the doorway. They both shone their torches at the floor, and both gave a start.

"Bloody hell!" Robert's voice was loud as he took an involuntary step back.

At their feet, lying on the stoneflagged floor that had not seen daylight for over three hundred years, was a skeleton. Both men were more startled than they liked to admit, and it was some moments before each, taking their cue from the other, squatted down for a better look. Behind them, Jane's voice sounded querulous.

"What is it?" She moved forward and leaning one hand on each of their shoulders peered into the gloom.

Neither man spoke. The bones still had the tattered remnants of some sort of clothing wrapped around them, the jerkin looked as if it had been of leather as the material that remained was much thicker, and coarser than the cloth of the breeches. The mouth, still with most of its teeth intact, was forced open by a large, knotted piece of cloth forced into it as a gag. It took both shocked men some moments to notice that the arms were behind the body and lengths of leather twine could still be discerned tying the wrists together. Similar twine was wrapped around the bones of the feet.

No one spoke. Jane stood back and bringing her hands to her mouth let out a small cry.

Paul looked down at the bones, sadness and regret working in his face. It was what he had suspected for a few days now, but the certainty of the discovery still came as a profound shock.

"Hello Thomas," he said, his voice low and brittle with emotion, little more than a whisper. "It is Thomas, isn't it? Bricked you up, did he?"

"You know who this is?" queried Robert, his voice a little shaky.

Jane was weeping softly.

Paul nodded. "I can guess," he mouthed. "This I'm almost sure, is the shadowy Thomas, mentioned briefly in the old records and blamed for the fall from grace of our Cecily. He and the Reverend Morton both disappeared forever immediately after the ducking death, leading to 'much talking and whispering' according to the local broadsheet. Well, now we know why."

He stood up brushing dust from his jeans.

"Thinking last evening about this doorway that you had uncovered, and putting two and two together, I had an idea that we would possibly find something like this." He shook his head.

"What an arsehole that Morton must have been. Totally deranged," exclaimed Robert, his face shocked.

He pointed his torch down at the remains at his feet.

"There were probably quite a few bastards like him around in those troubled times, as there are today."

Feeling a little self-conscious in the presence of his friends but knowing nevertheless that he had to do it, Paul slowly knelt amongst the rubble and dust, and clasping his hands together, recited a prayer for the soul of the dead young man on the floor in front of them, who had lain there alone and cold for over three hundred years.

****

He did not know how long he had been lying here in the dark. It could have been hours, but he suspected that it was days. His head was swimming not only from the concussion received when the trooper knocked him out but also now from lack of food or water, and he was disorientated. His mind was swimming with dreams of the past, interrupted as he became fully conscious sporadically.

He groaned, despite the cloth gag that was wedged across his mouth. His chest hurt, jarring him with a sharp nagging pain and he knew that that whoreson Morton had cracked two of his ribs with the last vicious kick he had received. He knew that a shard of bone had probably penetrated something in his body, and he could feel that he was bleeding inside. He was getting weaker, much weaker, he knew that. Every so often, despite the gag, his mouth filled with blood, and he had to spit it out as best he could.

All feeling had gone from his arms and legs, and he had given up on the effort of trying to move some time ago, or was it days ago? He was not sure.

Lying there in the pitch darkness and riding waves of pain, he was aware that he was dying and that it was only a matter of time. It did not matter; his only regret was the not knowing what had happened to his love. He had dreamed that he was walking through sunny meadows with Cecily, she was smiling up at him, clutching his hand in hers, and they were happy. He had cried out her name and awoken back to his pain but with the reassuring calmness that the dream had left with him, like the fine white froth when a wave withdraws from the beach back into the sea.

He had cried a little at the injustice and callous cruelty of this world, but he was beyond tears now, his body had no more liquid to give up. He knew that if what the scriptures promised was true, he would see Cecily again someday, he had to believe that. Christ and his angels, he hoped it would be so.

He breathed her name over and over as best he could during his last moments. The memory of her giving him solace. "Cecily." He whispered as if it were a prayer. "Cecily."

He closed his eyes for the last time.

****

Cecily Morton was buried with all the ceremony that the sorrowing and remorseful little village could muster. Why they had allowed evil to stalk this place for so long they could not comprehend and avoided discussing. The members of the village council had been shown the error of their ways with many a harsh word, and two members had been replaced by more compassionate village elders. There had been two actual bodily attacks on council members that were deemed most to blame, but these had been quickly stopped before real harm could be perpetrated. Nevertheless, it was a chastened population that moved forward into an uncertain future.

Of the Reverend Morton or of Thomas there was no word or sighting from that day forward. Margaret wept and railed at the disappearance of her son but consoled herself that he would one day return. That was what she told herself until her dying day twenty years later. She never went near the old vicarage again.

The upstart Oliver Cromwell had been dead for nine years now and King Charles, the second of that name, had assumed his father's throne only seven years past. England was still a country of volatile reactionaries, out-of-work soldiers, and a traumatised population so the gallows throughout the land were seldom empty. For a small village on the edge of Dartmoor deep in rural Devon, it was best to maintain a communal silence about what had happened there.

Time passed. For many years no one would go near, let alone enter the erstwhile vicarage, set as it was a little apart from the centre of the village with its church, and is central green, and its pond.

Nature began to reclaim the old building, the surrounding land became overgrown, rife with brambles and nettles. Part of the roof collapsed, and many of the windows were broken by generations of children throwing stones for a dare.

A little over one hundred years later a local landowner from some miles away who had thrived following lucrative business dealings, decided to acquire the old run-down house and to repair and rejuvenate it as a family home for his eldest daughter who had recently married. During his initial somewhat hazardous inspection of the jumbled interior, he noticed that one of the bare brick kitchen walls seemed to have been repaired. The repair was slipshod, and unsightly, and had obviously been done in haste by someone who did not have any skill with the laying of bricks, so he instructed the workman as a matter of urgency to plaster the entire wall to render it less unsightly.

He had enquired of the locals as to why the place had remained empty and uncared for so long, as it could be a comely property with a little time and money spent on it. No one knew, although there were rumours passed down from generation to generation. No one was inclined to inform the wealthy incomer of these legends and the very few who suspected they knew the real truth, told to them by ancient grandparents, kept it to themselves. It was all a long time ago, they reckoned, and best left in the past.

Chapter Twenty.

Epilogue

The two little boys were crouched across the pathway that led from the lych gate to the church porch, their intense concentration rendering them totally oblivious to their surroundings. One was clutching a small electronic screen on which cartoon characters fought ferociously over bags of gold as they traversed some sort of rainbow bridge. The other boy was leaning into him to get a good view of the screen and offering advice and encouragement to his mate.

Karen was very late, due to unexpected roadworks a mile from the village, and a lengthy impatient wait in the queue at the temporary traffic lights set up to control the traffic. She hated to be late for anything, feeling that it showed rudeness and a lack of adequate planning, and she was flustered and embarrassed.

Hurrying from her car that she had only managed after some searching to park just up the lane, she almost tripped over the small boys as she hurriedly entered through the gate.

Her shout of surprise and annoyance elicited a rapid retreat by the little boys who, recovering from their shock, jogged off giggling between the gravestones to find a safer place to resume their game. Their parents, decked out in their Sunday best, were inside the church, with almost everyone else in the village so they knew they would not be bothered for some time.

Despite the unusual circumstances, this was a funeral after all so Karen had chosen a dark grey knee-length pleated skirt with matching high heeled shoes and a dark blue blouse. She hoped the effect made her look attractive but also respectful, and a little older than she actually was. She was aware that she would probably be meeting Paul's friends and parishioners and wanted to make a favourable impression. The breeze was from the northwest this morning so she could taste salt in the air, reminding her that the sea was not far away. Gripping her small black leather clutch bag, she moved towards the church door, but never got there.

As she approached the ancient oak door it opened, and the funeral procession exited bringing with them the booming sombre sounds of the organ from within. It was clear that the service was over and the whole congregation were moving to the gravesite.

She shook her head and held her arms wide in the universal gesture of apology, but Paul, looking magnificent in his full clerical robes, white over black, leading the assembled throng through the doors only smiled and nodded silently telling her that it was OK, and her apology was accepted.

He was wearing his full regalia today, his black floor-length cassock, overtopped by his equally long white surplice, its voluminous full sleeves hanging down to knee length. Around his neck and hanging down in front of him was the decorated scarf known as a Tippet.

The small procession was headed by a diminutive choir boy self-importantly serious-faced and carrying the gold-coloured crucifix out in front of him.

Behind him was Paul, and behind them both came the modern-looking coffin of light-coloured wood, carried by four sturdy men of the village. Robert was among them, looking very serious in his dark grey pinstripe suit and black tie. Jane followed immediately behind, also dressed sombrely in a slate-coloured trouser suit, made to look stylish by the high heels she had selected for today. Her dark hair was pulled back into a bun, her hymn book still clutched in both hands. Walking behind her was old Alice Pennyworth with her husband Bert, and behind them Ron Davies, wearing an old suit that had probably not seen the light of day for more than twenty years. The trainers that completed his ensemble did not quite fit the occasion, but no one seemed to mind.

Behind this group, all walking quietly and slowly in procession came most of the village, decked out in their Sunday finery. For most of the younger members of the group, it was probably the first time in a many a long year, if ever, that they had set foot in the little old Norman church.

Word had spread like wildfire amongst the little community of the rather gruesome discovery during building work at the old vicarage now owned by the city folk. Paul had done his best to negate many of the more fantastic stories that had begun to circulate, especially after the police cars and coroner's vehicle had spent time in the lane near the place, and in the end had to issue a statement pinned to the church notice board advising everyone of exactly who the remains were, and what had been the probable connection of the deceased to the village. The 'grey lady' they felt was one of their own, one of them, and it was only fitting that her ill-fated lover should be laid to his rest with their blessing.

Karen joined the end of the procession and noted as she walked very slowly, being careful not to step on to the heels of the old ladies in front of her, that they seemed to be heading for the small, secluded area where Paul had shown her the gravestone of young Cecily.

The assembled throng slowed and ballooned out to surround the small reopened grave of red earth, nestled as it was beneath the gently swaying trees.

Karen nodded to herself and smiled sadly as she realised that it was indeed the grave of Cecily. The small carved gravestone had been laid reverentially to one side on the grass to be replaced after the service.

She suddenly realised what was happening. They were going to put Thomas in the same grave as his love, ensuring that the tragic pair would be reunited in death and together for all eternity. It was fitting and lovely and she felt tears gathering in her eyes. It was a beautiful thing to do.

Irritably, she withdrew a tissue from her handbag and dabbed gently at her eyes, as she did not want mascara staining her face. She must not think of the ill-crossed pair, it was a long time ago, and they had both been dead and gone for centuries. Yes, that was the way to look at it. That was the way to control your emotions. But it was lovely, truly lovely. She wondered if it was Paul that had thought of it. She shook her head to keep at bay the tears and forced herself to listen to what Paul was intoning at the head of the grave.

Pitching his voice quite loud to be heard above the rustle of the leaves as the trees above them swayed in the slight breeze, he told the brief story of the two young people. He kept it free of conjecture or folklore about ghosts, merely stating the facts as he had discovered them during the last weeks. He told them that all of this had happened during a time of anguish and uproar in England that they could not comprehend today, especially living deep in this sleepy corner of the county.

Finally, he told them that he thought it was time to put things right, as far as they were able.

"Amen to that, Vicar." It was the voice of Alice Pennyford calling from the crowd. There was a general murmur of assent.

Paul moved smoothly on to recite the traditional prayers for the deceased, and as had been obviously planned, the whole congregation sang the hymn *Abide with me*, as the coffin was lowered into the ground to join the far older one that had been uncovered.

Karen was off again, tears rolling down her cheeks to be angrily brushed away. She was rooting around in her bag for another tissue so failed to notice that most of the congregation had slowly begun to drift away, as the brief ceremony finished. Lifting her head she saw Paul standing talking with the couple she assumed were his friends Jane and Robert, so she walked over to them.

"Jane, Rob," said Paul as she arrived. "This is Karen. Karen, these are my friends Rob and Jane."

They all grinned at each other and exchanged a brief word of greeting.

"I was just saying," said Paul, "Give me a minute to get out of this clobber and we can all go for a drink to wish Cecily and Thomas on their way. What do you think?"

Karen nodded and smiled. "That would be really nice." She liked the look of Robert, who had twinkly, good-natured eyes, and Jane, although a little reserved at this moment, seemed to be a nice woman and could be stunning if she wanted to.

Paul stopped as he fancied he saw her liquid eyes.

"Have you been weeping?"

She gave an embarrassed smile and nodded. "This was just such a lovely thing to do. I know it was you who thought of it. Those poor young people, all they did wrong was to love each other, and look at the price they paid. Maybe this will enable them to rest in peace." She looked around at the three of them and was gratified to see an answering nod from Jane, who leaned forward and squeezed her arm.

"Yes, it was a beautiful idea, wasn't it? It could only have been Paul who thought of it."

Paul thought this was becoming maudlin so spreading his arms, he ushered them all towards the church porch. "Come on then my children, let us away, a nice beer and convivial company await us." They all laughed and moved off. Karen sidled up beside him and took his arm.

Paul could not suppress a broad grin. A strange feeling had invaded his psyche recently for the first time in too long. It had taken him some time to realise what it was, and when he did it was with a sense of disbelief. He was happy. It seemed that life beckoned him forward, onwards to fresh adventures, and with a vivacious young woman at his side, he intended to obey the invitation. He would never forget Marion, never, ever of course, or his young son, for as long as he lived. That was a given, but he was still here, still alive on the earth, and God willing, would have many more years ahead of him. It was in their memory and so as not to let them down that he must move forward. Marion would not want him to mope his life away, that he knew. She had been a very practical no-nonsense sort of person. It was the lot of everyone who had ever lived to encounter difficulties and the casual cruelties of life, and to find in themselves the strength to overcome them and carry on.

Of one thing he was moderately certain, there would be no more appearances of the 'grey lady' about the village as there had been for the last three hundred years. Hopefully, her spirit could now be at rest.

He looked down at Karen and smiled. Together he and she and Jane had done their best to right the wrongs perpetrated on two ill-fated young lovers all those years ago. He hoped it was enough. But for now, he had his own life to move on with. Karen squeezed his hand and laughter bubbled out of her from the sheer joy of living, of being alive and present on the earth at this moment. He squeezed her hand in reply.

Jane, walking with Robert, slipped her arm through his and thought that life was full of pitfalls. She had decided after much soul searching to give her erring husband a second chance and what he made of this partial reinstatement was up to him. She hoped it would work; she loved him still and his obvious contrition and willingness to please her was touching and gratifying. She had kept singing that song he loved so much in her head recently. *Ordinary people* – that after all was what they all were, just ordinary people trying to get through life as best as they knew how. It was the same way back then for Cecily and Thomas, just ordinary people tossed around by life and the fates. A small smile curved her lips as she peered forward into the future.

Behind them in the shadows thrown by the tall guarding trees, the gravestone lay flat in the emerald grass waiting to be placed back over the open grave once old Wilfred had filled it in once more. The inscription had been added too and now read:

Here Lyeth the mortal remains of
Cecily Morton
Wife of the Reverend Nehemiah Morton
Taken unto God in the twenty third year of her life
22nd July in the year of our Lord 1667 Anno Domini
God knoweth how
May God have mercy on her soul
Media Vita In Morte Summus
Here also lies the body of Thomas
Taken unto God 1667   Anno Domini
Beloved of Cecily
Together once again forever.

The End

Printed by Libri Plureos GmbH in Hamburg,
Germany